Summer
Flings

BEST
Gay
LOVE
STORIES

Summer
Flings

BEST
Gay
LOVE
STORIES

edited by

BRAD NICHOLS

alyson books
NEW YORK

© 2007 by Alyson Books.
Authors retain the rights to their individual pieces of work.

Manufactured in the United States of America

This trade paperback original is published by Alyson Books
245 West 17th Street, New York, NY 10011
Distribution in the United Kingdom by
Turnaround Publisher Services Ltd.
Unit 3, Olympia Trading Estate, Coburg Road, Wood Green
London N22 6TZ England

ISBN-13: 978-0-7394-9302-1

Cover design by Victor Mingovits

CONTENTS

INTRODUCTION

OF ALL THE SEASONS, there is something about the allure of summer. Maybe it's because the world slows down, and people tend to go about their lives in a more leisurely fashion. Everyone just seems more...relaxed (not to mention all tan and buff from the beach).

Heck, maybe that's because everyone has just fallen in love.

Wouldn't that be a nice idea? Falling in love...and in the summer? I can't imagine a more perfect mix of intoxicating feelings, the heat of the day, the cool breeze of the night, and a lovely companion at your side. I can almost feel the electricity pass between us as our hands touch while we sneak beneath the boardwalk and begin to kiss, the scrape of his stubbled face against my lips...

Wait, that's my fantasy, my own love (or at the very least, lust) story waiting to happen. And until that magical time occurs, let the twenty writers in this year's edition of *Best Gay Love Stories* take you into their steamy, seductive world.

Whether these are true summer "flings" or the start of lasting relationships, there is no denying the heat that sizzles between these men. So, no matter the season you find yourself reading this book in, it will no doubt spark memories of your past summers—and hopefully, future summers filled with love.

Enjoy.

—Brad Nichols

IRENE'S CABIN

RYAN FIELD

THAT SUMMER you could say he was a young man who had just begun to blossom, or maybe he'd always been blooming and didn't know it; maybe all he needed was someone else to point this out. His lean, muscular limbs were connected by perfectly proportioned knobs of bone; his straight, solid jaw was as well hinged as a Greek statue. But when Noah entered a room he secretly assumed people were staring at him because they didn't like what they saw; he'd lower his brown eyes, crease his brows and hunch over a bit as though pretending not to be tall could actually make him invisible. Mostly, though, the people who stared were only trying to imagine what it would be like to get into his pants.

Noah felt chiefly self-conscious when he walked into the air-conditioned biology lab in early June and asked a young man, "Is this stool taken?" A brown metal stool, the only empty one at the end of a long gunmetal gray lab table near the entrance of the large biology lab. They could have held a football game there; at least thirty identical lab tables in the same color, but only about fifteen students all bunched up front that day because it was a summer course. Noah was actually an English major with no aptitude for the sciences and the advisor at his *real* university had suggested he take his biology credits over the summer as a guest student, "in a smaller community college where it's cheaper and you can get it over with faster," he'd said, and then added, "and if you fail you can take it again here and it won't go onto your transcript." So Noah registered for a course at a community college near his parents' summer home in the hills of northwest New Jersey.

"Ah, no, it's empty," the guy said, shuffling his papers. His deep voice sounded wrecked and his movements were sudden and awkward, more like a guy late for an important appointment than someone who was about to sit through a three-hour biology lecture.

Noah reluctantly claimed the stool; a moment later the Professor handed out the course objectives and began to lecture. But Noah couldn't help cautiously glancing toward the anxious guy sitting on the next stool. Dark, sandy blond hair cut short and parted on the side, florist-wire-thin silver reading glasses that rested on a small straight nose; hands so wide and strong with thick sausage-like fingers. He wore a plain white T-shirt and knee-length olive shorts; white ankle socks and heavy white sneakers added jock appeal. His tanned legs, covered with a perfect layer of sheer blond fuzz, were spread wide while the palms of his large hands rested on his knees.

The lecture came to a halt at noon for a half hour break, and the entire class made a quick run for a pair of glass doors at the back of the lab leading to a small concrete courtyard that connected to the student union building. Noah, unaware of his surroundings, followed four hapless students who had been sitting at his lab table to a round wooden picnic bench as though he'd known them all his life.

"I need a cigarette," said one woman in white cotton Capri pants and pale blue vinyl mules. She looked older, maybe in her late thirties; the type that goes back to school when the kids are old enough to take care of themselves.

"Me too," said the guy with the great legs. And then he turned, with a cigarette dangling from his thin lips, and offered one to Noah. He wasn't too tall; maybe five ten at the most. He stood with his legs spread wide, as though bouncing on the balls of his feet.

"Thanks, dude," Noah said, taking the cigarette. He didn't smoke, but somehow couldn't refuse the offer either.

The small group sat down and began to converse, people who normally wouldn't have bothered to know each other outside of a summer biology course. And while Noah pretended to puff away he learned that the guy's name was Larry, Larry Cochran, and he only lived about a mile from where Noah lived.

"Cool, man, I live on Dupont Lane," Noah said, "My family has a summer place there, on the lake, and they won't be up at all this summer." Lake Mount Saint Arlington was an expansive lake, with many coves, in the far northwest section of New Jersey. Noah had spent every summer of his life there, but this was the first time in his life he'd ever been alone.

"I'm down lake a bit," Larry said, "But we're year-round. I envy you being alone all summer. I have four sisters who drive me crazy, man."

Noah smiled. "We could commute. I mean why not share the forty-five minute ride and save on gas. We could just alternate from week to week." Where he'd found the voice to suggest such a thing he didn't know, but there, he'd said it. Larry looked like the captain of the football team and the guy all the cheerleaders wanted to date in high school. You could almost imagine him standing on a street corner smoking with his buddies while he spit into the gutter every so often. Why would he want to ride with Noah?

But Larry said, "Cool, man," taking a long drag from a Parliament that was pressed hard between his index finger and thumb, "I'll drive the rest of this week. What's your address?" He wasn't enthusiastic; didn't even smile; just shrugged his shoulders and blew a thick cloud of smoke into the warm summer breeze.

"132 Dupont Lane," Noah said, "white clapboard toward the end of the lane, with a sign that says 'Irene's Cabin.' My grandmother's name, she bought the place originally back in the 1940's and it's been in the family ever since."

The next morning Larry parked in front of Noah's house at nine o'clock sharp, gently tapping the horn of a black, older model corvette, and Noah jogged down the brick sidewalk to meet him. He had thought about wearing shorts to school that day, but just didn't feel comfortable with his legs exposed. So he wore his usual white polo shirt and faded jeans; no socks, and worn docksides. Larry leaned over and popped open the passenger side door from the inside, "It sticks sometimes," he warned. And when Noah pulled it shut he gave it a small push, just to make sure it wouldn't pop open while they were on the road.

Larry drove too fast and chain-smoked, while hard rock music blasted from the CD player...a later addition to a car that had originally been produced with only a cassette deck. He didn't talk much either. When Noah asked, "Are you a full time student here?" Larry only grunted, never taking his blue eyes off the road, and said, "Nope, I'm a full time business management major at University of Maryland; just here for the summer cause it's close to home." To which Noah replied, without being asked, that he was a full time student at Brown and that he was an English major, while Larry continued to grunt and nod his head. Noah gripped the seat until his knuckles turned white, but he was exhilarated, too, speeding down the highway with Larry at the wheel. The rugged odor of the worn black leather seats mixed with Larry's spicy morning aftershave...the way his strong hands gripped the steering wheel at the very top; his large athletic feet tapping the pedals; how he spread his hairy legs so wide and masculine. His right knee actually rested against the handbrake in the center console and Noah had to hold back from reaching out and placing his palm on it.

That day Larry and Noah became lab partners, and though Noah was far from proficient in biology, he pretended to be extra stupid so Larry would look like the brightest guy in the room. When it came time to read the first experiment Larry said, "I'm going to let you be in charge...you seem so much better at this." And when Larry made a mistake while lighting the Bunsen burner, but then corrected it quickly, Noah couldn't help mentioning, "You're so smart, dude; I'd never have been able to figure this out without you, man." The more helpless Noah pretended to be the more Larry couldn't resist offering assistance. On the drive home Larry actually said to Noah, "Tomorrow we have to do that blood test lab experiment on ourselves, where we have to draw a drop of blood with a razor blade. You'd better let me take charge; you might hurt yourself with the razor." Noah agreed wholeheartedly, and then folded his hands on his lap and smiled.

By Friday Larry and Noah began to speak openly about their lives on the ride to school. Larry worked part time at a boat marina on the lake, every weekend, from eight in the morning until nine at night, so he didn't have much time for a social life that summer. And Noah had a part time job working for a web site, getting paid to interview and review bloggers and web masters for a web site directory. So when Larry dropped Noah off at the house that Friday night Noah didn't hesitate to remind him, "Don't forget, I'm driving next week."

On Sunday morning Noah put on a tight pair of white shorts

and a skimpy black tank top for a full day of sun on the old family boat, a 1960 twenty-four foot Chris Craft sportsman, one of those old wooden classics with a slow inboard motor that gurgled and rumbled like the smooth even beat of a soft drum. You could barely break a wave with the old beauty, but when Noah sat on the dark red leather seat behind the great white steering wheel and started the engine he always felt as though he were about to embark on an adventure. And that morning the adventure was to stop at the marina where Larry worked to fill up the gas tank. He could have gone to any one of four marinas (he did have a favorite; not Larry's), but it was the perfect excuse to stop by and say hello to his new lab partner while wearing a pair of tight shorts.

Noah slowly pulled the old boat toward the marina's dock, maneuvering with care so he'd look as though he knew what he was doing...Noah, in fact, despised driving the boat; he never could master it and would have lived his whole life without ever going near water. Larry was at the other end of the dock holding the gas hose, finishing up with another customer so he didn't notice Noah right away. But as Larry stuffed some cash into the back pockets of his navy shorts, while the idiot customer pulled away abruptly, there was a sudden surge of large waves that hit the dock and ruined Noah's smooth entry. By the time Larry saw Noah trying to tie the boat to the dock, fighting to hold his balance while the waves splashed and tossed him from one side of the boat to the other, a smile formed on Larry's serious face; he ran to help calm the rocking boat and to keep Noah from falling overboard.

"I guess it's now official," Noah said, while Larry grabbed the boat's windshield and stopped it from rocking, "I'm just as inept with a boat as I am in biology class. You must think I'm a moron."

Larry laughed. "No, man. That guy was an asshole; he shouldn't have pulled out of here so fast. He needs a kick in the ass."

"Well, thanks for helping out," Noah said, moving toward the back of the boat. His sheer white shorts were soaked by then; Larry stared at the outline of Noah's white briefs as he innocently bent over to open the gas cap. It occurred to Larry that Noah was a bit needy and helpless. But more than that, Larry had never seen such a great ass on a guy; and the way Noah's back arched made Larry bite his bottom lip.

"You want her filled?" Larry asked, lowering his head and turning much too quickly so that Noah wouldn't suspect he'd been staring as his backside.

"Please."

While Noah filled the tank they talked about the weather, school and how crowded the lake seemed that day with so many weekenders; just small talk, but Noah sensed Larry was glad he'd stopped by for gas, and to say hello. Larry's rugged smile, the relaxed way he mentioned how much he liked the Chris Craft, and the fact that he only charged Noah half the amount for the gas impressed Noah. "Just ten bucks, man," Larry said, "I get a discount for family and friends and I never ever use it."

"Thanks," Noah said, starting the engine.

"I'll untie you and give a push so there aren't any accidents," Larry joked.

Noah creased his brow. "Thank you."

"See you at nine sharp, tomorrow morning," Noah shouted. He couldn't see the expression on Larry's face as he slowly drifted away; but he would have enjoyed it. Larry was standing with his hands on his hips, shaking his head slowly with his lips pursed as though he were about to whistle. The way any horny young guy stares when he sees something he wants.

On Monday Noah showed up fifteen minutes late. He told Larry he'd overslept, but the truth was he wanted to wear a new pair of low-rise jeans but didn't remember until the last minute that he'd left them in the trunk of his Honda. Noah apologized and Larry said, "No problem, dude, but you'd better let me drive; I don't want to be late. I have this quirk about always being right on time."

Noah hesitated and raised his eyebrows; his grandfather had always said, "Never let anyone else drive your car." But, then again, his grandfather had never had a hot guy like Larry Cochran ready to take the wheel. So Noah got out, walked to the passenger side, and Larry lifted his left leg and climbed into the driver's seat. By that time, though Larry was a very fast driver, Noah trusted him. Larry handled a car in such a way you never felt a bump or pothole, and Noah loved the way he spread his legs while he drove, as though pressing them together might be too painful to endure.

For the next three weeks, whether it was Larry's Corvette or Noah's Honda, Larry did *all* the driving.

By the end of the fourth week of summer classes, after taking a mid-term that lasted the entire Friday, Noah's brain almost hurt from memorizing all the scientific terms and phrases he knew he'd only forget once the course was over. With three other classmates, Noah and Larry had been studying all week in the school library, and it was time for a break. But it wasn't planned when Noah asked Larry, "Would you like to come over to my place tonight to watch that new horror film on DVD (Noah could never remember the names of films)? I put it on reserve at the video store last night." The question simply flew out of his mouth in italics.

Larry hesitated, but then answered, "Cool, dude, what time?"

"Come over around seven; I'll order a pizza, too."

"I'll bring some beer."

"Cool," said Noah. Though he wasn't much of a drinker, and the taste of beer made him sick to his stomach. But his breathing grew heavy at the thought of hanging out with Larry and drinking beer.

Larry knocked on his front door at seven sharp, with a six-pack under his right arm and one dangling from his left hand. His jaw was clenched, and when he put the beer down on the kitchen counter he didn't know what to do with his hands so he put them in his pockets. Though this was supposed to be a casual night of movie watching, Noah noticed Larry's hair was still damp from the shower, and his face so smooth, smelling of Balenciaga aftershave; new white sneakers on his feet without so much as a grass stain. Noah was freshly showered, too, wearing a clean white T-shirt that hugged his torso and torn, faded jeans with a large chunk of his tanned thigh showing; a hole wide enough so anyone could slide the palm of their hand up inside and feel his bare behind if they wanted to. His body was smooth; like any part time weight lifter who shaved every single hair except for one small black patch above his groin shaped like an arrow.

Noah ordered a large pizza with pepperoni and Larry insisted on paying for it, which in a way turned out to be fair because Noah only ate one slice while Larry finished off the rest in one sitting.

"Where do you put it all?" Noah asked, "And you never gain a pound. If I ate like that I'd be fat as a pig."

"I'm a growing boy," Larry said, gulping his third beer and patting his flat stomach.

"Are you still hungry?" Noah asked, "I picked up a cheesecake for later, but if you want some now I'll get it."

"Cool," said Larry, "I love cheesecake, but not until later, dude. Let's go watch the movie." The beer had clearly relaxed him; his face wasn't pinched anymore; jaw loose and calm…his movements weren't planned in advance.

It was a luxurious, but casual, summer/weekend house; a large kitchen dining area open to the family room where an outsized brown leather sofa faced a flat screen TV that had been built into the wall above the walk-in fieldstone fireplace. Noah's mother, a professional interior decorator, liked to practice on the house with all the latest trends in design. Noah inserted the DVD and Larry sat on one end of the sofa. There were other chairs in the room, but the best view of the TV was from the sofa, so Noah sat on the other end and put his feet up on the matching leather ottoman. It was large and square, with a solid tray in the center to balance drinks and food, and Noah told Larry it was meant to be used and that he should feel free to put his feet up and get comfortable. By then the sun had set and the room had ballooned into a collection of shadows.

"I'll put on a light if you want," Noah said, "but I like watching in the dark."

"Me too," said Larry. He kicked off his sneakers and propped his hairy legs on the ottoman. Now on his fifth can of beer while Larry was still sipping his first.

The beginning of the movie dragged, which created an awkward silence. Once they stopped talking and joking around and started watching the movie it became difficult to speak. From the corner of his eye Noah saw that Larry had unbuttoned his pants; too much pizza (or too much beer?), but he was terrified to look in Larry's direction. He tried to concentrate on the film, but couldn't stop thinking about Larry's unbuttoned pants. And then, about twenty minutes into the horror film, there was one scene that caused Noah to literally jump in his seat and shout. Larry had just finished taking a sip of beer and when Noah screamed the beer went up his nose and he began to roll around on the sofa laughing.

"Fuck, dude," He shouted, holding his stomach.

"Hey, it's not funny," Noah whined, "This shit is getting creepy and I've got to stay all alone in this house tonight.

Larry smiled, crawled over to where Noah was sitting, and put his arm around him, "Don't worry, baby, I'll protect you from the monsters and vampires lurking around Irene's Cabin."

No sooner did Larry finish the sentence than there was another scene, gruesome and bloody, with dead bodies, and Noah screamed again. But that time he didn't jump, he sank down into the sofa and rested his head on Larry's chest while Larry screamed with laughter and pulled him closer.

"Dude," Larry joked in a quasi Transylvanian accent, "I am a vampire and I'm going to suck your blood." He was speaking to the top of Noah's head and Noah could smell his beer breath.

Noah rested his palm on Larry's strong thigh; the line had been crossed and there was no turning back. So Larry slowly lifted Noah's head and whispered, "Dude, you are so hot, I've wanted to hold you like this since the first day I saw you." Then he sank his mouth into Noah's neck and began to suck; just playful biting...rolling his tongue around. In no time both young men were kissing and sweating...jeans and T-shirts and sweat socks flew into the air until both guys were completely naked; ending with Noah stretched flat on his stomach, pinned to the sofa by Larry's strong hairy body. But Larry was gentle and precise and it only hurt for a split second when the big thing entered. Noah spread his legs, closed his eyes, and gasped; he wanted to like this. Larry said, "Just relax, baby, I'll make this good for you," and he didn't start to rock and pound with full force until he knew Noah wanted more of him.

The next morning they were in Noah's bed. When Noah opened his eyes and realized Larry's hand was resting on his buttocks. He reached down between Larry's legs, took a handful into the palm of his hand and began to gently squeeze. For the first time in his life he actually felt attractive.

Larry moaned. "That's feels great, baby boy."

Noah felt him swelling; three times the night before and ready to go again first thing in the morning.

"Are you okay?" Larry asked, "Hope I didn't get too rough with you last night."

"I don't know if I'll be able to walk today, but other than that I've never been better," Noah joked.

"Are you okay with this…with what happened last night?" Larry asked.

Noah shrugged. "Yeah, I'm glad it finally happened."

Larry sighed; he was fully erect again; all Noah had to do was touch him with one finger. "Dude, I don't know where this will go, but if you're okay with it then so am I."

Noah turned, went under the covers, and put his head between Larry's legs.

"I have to get to work," Larry moaned. "You're gonna make me late."

"You'll get there on time," Noah said from beneath the covers, "And with a smile on your face."

They had their first fight toward the middle of August. Noah pulled up to the marina for gas one Sunday afternoon wearing a skimpy black bikini he thought Larry would like, but instead Larry went crazy when he saw how another guy at the marina was staring at Noah's ass. He banged the side of the boat and said things that hurt: "What the fuck is this? Looks like you're showing your ass off for other guys. I don't walk around like that; it's fucking trashy. You're not supposed to be showing that ass off to anyone but me." Though Noah was mad because that hadn't been the intention, his eyes filled and he had to control his body from breaking into tears with all his strength. Without even trying to defend his position he started the boat, forgot about getting gas and pulled away while Larry clenched his fists and continued to rant.

Noah didn't hear from Larry for the rest of the day, but that night there was a knock on the door and Larry was there with Noah's favorite wine and a box of expensive chocolates.

"Are you here to scream at me, to call me a slut?" Noah asked. He'd gotten over being hurt and now he was mad as hell.

"No, baby," Larry said, his blue eyes staring at the black door-mat, "I'm here to apologize. I shouldn't have said those things. Can I come in?"

Noah hesitated. "Of course you can come in…idiot."

Larry opened the door and placed the wine and candy on a small table and as Noah turned to walk down the hallway toward the kitchen Larry grabbed him by the waist and pulled him to his chest. "I'm so sorry," Larry said, kissing Noah's mouth and shoving his tongue all the way in, "I was a jerk…I'm an idiot…but I fucking love you. I don't know what else to say. I just can't stand the thought of other guys looking at you like that, baby. You make me crazy."

Noah, though he wanted to, could not remain mad at Larry for long. The way Larry's eyes begged, like a puppy dog that wanted to play, made his heart melt.

"Are we okay?" he asked Noah, sliding his palm down Noah's pants and squeezing hard as though he were reclaiming lost property.

"Yes, we're okay," Noah said. "And I won't go around half naked in public anymore either. I just thought you'd like how it looked. I only did it for you."

"I did like it, man, but so did all the other guys on the dock," Larry said. "That's the problem. I think even some of the straight guys wanted to get into your pants today."

"Get out of here," Noah said, "I think that's just your imagination. My ass isn't that great."

"Oh yes it is," Larry whispered, grabbing Noah by the waist and placing his hand on the small of Noah's back, "But the rest of you is pretty damn hot, too."

"Did you mean what you just said?" Noah asked, "About being in love?"

"Every word," Larry said, "I really do love you…you make me crazy."

Noah rested his head on Larry's chest. "I love you, too."

FRATELLI

LEWIS DESIMONE

HIS HAND, OF COURSE—the one that held the stone—was huge, veins bursting through the skin like the roots of ancient trees pushing up through pavement. I walked slowly around the pedestal, past the big toe jutting out invitingly, and continued to the back, where bulging leg muscles climbed up toward firm buttocks the size of cantaloupes. The sun hit his face directly and he seemed to be squinting as he gazed across the piazza, on the lookout for giants.

"There he is!" cried a middle-aged woman just entering the square. She sped past me, her overweight husband wobbling behind her as though drawn by magnetic force. His camera, suspended from a strap around his neck, bounced against his plaid shirt, just above the rounded shelf of his belly. The woman held a guidebook open in her hand, but her eyes were locked on the statue. Oblivious even to the people bustling around her, she staked out a position directly in front of the pedestal, where the surprisingly small penis seemed to retract in fear.

"I can't believe we found him so easily," she said in a thick Brooklyn accent. She turned back to her husband, who was still ten feet away. "You said he was on the other side of town."

Her husband caught up to her, breathing heavily. "That's not him," he said.

"Whaddya mean it's not him? Look at him—just like in the pictures." The woman scrunched her nose and inspected the toes just above her head.

"It's not him," the man repeated. "It's a copy."

"A copy? You're crazy. It looks like the real thing to me."

David's head was turned to the left, emphasizing his marble indifference to the squabble beneath him. It was still my first day in

Florence. I had scheduled my visit to the Accademia for the last day, to make David the climax of my trip. I hadn't known about the copy—like Mrs. Brooklyn, I had merely stumbled upon it. It was smaller than the original was supposed to be, the stone worn by weather and bird shit.

I followed David's gaze out of the piazza. In the shadow of the Uffizi, I was suddenly confronted by a folded newspaper, just inches from my face. Behind it, I could see the head of a child—dark skin, greasy hair, wide expressionless eyes. Beside him stood another child, younger but with the same vacant look. Yet another was making her way behind me. It took me a moment to realize what they were after. Quickly, I reached down for my wallet. It was still there.

"*Vada via!*" cried a deep voice behind them. "*Chiamero la polizia!*"

Suddenly, the urchins scattered, running toward the bundled gypsy women who stood quietly on the corner with silent babies in their arms. In their stead I saw a man's face, crowned by a wild sweep of curly blond hair. He moved slowly toward me.

"You must watch out for the gypsies," he said, an almost maternal tone in his voice. "Offer them half a euro and they will grab your whole purse."

I smiled, glad for the concern of a stranger in a strange land. "So I've been told," I said. "Thank you."

"Someone must to watch out for the innocent," he said, smiling enigmatically. There was only a trace of an accent in his voice, his Italian origins betrayed primarily through his syntax. He was in his twenties, around my age, and about my height and weight, though a bit thinner at the waist, a bit broader in the shoulders.

"You are from America?" he asked, pale blue eyes just a few inches from my own.

"Yes," I replied, "Boston."

"Boston." He seemed to be trying out the word. His *O*'s were round and long, lending an exotic sound to the syllables.

"It's near New York," I offered.

"Ah, New York." His eyes brightened—the way an American's would at the sound of *Firenze*.

Like the gypsy children, he had closed me in against the wall of the museum. I had to keep reminding myself that this was not Boston: people were friendly in Italy.

"And where do you go now?" he asked.

"I'm not sure," I said—too quickly to realize it was precisely the wrong thing to say. "It's only my first full day here. I was just walking around to get my bearings."

"Your bears?"

I laughed. His innocence came through in the puzzled look on his face. This man would not hurt me. "My bearings," I repeated. "A sense of where things are."

"Ah!" His grin widened. "I show you everything," he said, flicking his head to the side to point the way. "Come."

"I—I wouldn't want to take you away from anything. You must have things to do. You were probably on your way to work. ..."

Now it was his turn to laugh. "Work? No. Life is my work."

How perfectly Italian, I thought.

We walked slowly through the narrow, winding streets of Florence. "I am so rude," he said suddenly. "I have not asked your name."

"Jonathan."

He smiled. "Jonathan. Giovanni. That is my name, too. I am Giovanni." He laughed. "We could be *fratelli*, no?"

Yes, I thought, in a very strange family. I smiled halfheartedly, incredulous. It was a common enough name in any language, I supposed, but surely the chances were slim that this "Giovanni" was telling the truth.

We seemed to traverse the entire city in an hour—past museums, public squares, and churches upon churches. The famous spots came upon us so quickly, I couldn't help thinking I was still looking at pictures in a guidebook, that somehow I wasn't really here. At times Florence felt like a movie set; at others, I half-expected Michelangelo himself to appear in a church doorway, chisel or paint brush in hand.

The Ponte Vecchio was thick with tourists in search of gold, streaming in and out of the jewelry shops overlooking the sluggish Arno. I stopped at the middle of the bridge and snapped a few photos.

"You like I take your picture?" Giovanni asked.

The sun was in my eyes. I held a hand as a visor on my brow and watched the crowd flow behind him.

"I take your picture, here." He moved closer, his hand outstretched for my camera.

"No, thank you," I said, clutching the camera protectively. "I've taken enough."

"But none with you in them. How your friends will know you are really here?" He smiled again; he clearly knew the irresistibility of his smile. "Please," he said. "I like to do it."

He took two pictures—one overlooking the river, the other with the city in the background. "There," he said, passing the camera back to me, "now you have proof."

"Thank you." As I accepted the camera back my fingers grazed his soft skin, and his eyes stared a second or so too long into mine.

"Let's see," I said nervously, both hands on the camera. I checked out his photos on the display screen, startled by how relaxed I looked.

"Good, no? You are an excellent subject. Very photo—" He searched for the word.

"Photogenic," I said. "And usually I'm not."

"*Impossibile*," he said. The sudden reversion to Italian struck me. That one extra syllable turned a mere word into music.

"You like gelato?" he asked.

"Yes, of course."

I followed him to a tiny place on the other side of the Arno, in the shadow of the Pitti Palace. He motioned to a table in front and sat down.

"*Due tartuffi*," he said to the waiter, who quickly disappeared into the restaurant. "How do you like Italy so far?" he asked.

"It's magnificent," I admitted. "I feel like I'm in a fairy tale."

"You are," he said. "Especially in Firenze. Firenze is magical."

The waiter returned with two sinful-looking desserts. I broke the hard ice cream with my spoon and took a tiny bite. The cold sent shivers through my teeth, but it was a welcome relief from the summer heat.

"You like?" Giovanni asked, smiling inquisitively at me.

"Yes," I mumbled, a piece of the cookie coating still lodged in the corner of my mouth.

"Tell me about America," he said softly.

I wasn't sure what to tell him, so I just described Boston, the well-worn streets of my childhood. He listened attentively, as if the red brick sidewalks in my story were the yellow brick road in Oz. It amused me that America was exotic to him, that he could be surrounded by this classic beauty and yet crave sterile modernity.

We lingered at the café long after the ice cream was finished. Giovanni ordered wine and we continued to talk. "What will you do tomorrow?" he asked, refilling my glass.

I sat back, savoring the wine, the calm inside and out. "Perhaps I'll visit the Uffizi. I'm dying to see the Botticellis."

"Ah!" Giovanni said loudly, his palm gesturing sharply beside his head. "I know what we must do. When I first saw you, you were in the piazza—admiring the copy of David, no?"

He had been watching me. "Yes," I said, as though in a trance.

"You know it is just a copy?"

"Yes," I told him. "I was planning on visiting the real one in a couple of days."

"No," he said. "I take you tomorrow. David cannot wait. David *is* Firenze."

I was in no position to argue. I no longer cared to.

Twilight began to fall over the square. The natives, on their way home from work, came to join the tourists at the café. The air was suddenly full of the boisterous, lilting melody of Italian words, voices spilling over one another as if language were meant to be spoken but not heard, as if the sense of the words were less important than the sheer sound. Somehow, the meaning still came through: it was in the infamous gestures, the tone of voice, the expression of the eyes.

"It is getting late," Giovanni said, taking a final sip of wine. The bottle sat empty on the table between us. He called out to the waiter, who was passing by the first row of tables. "*Il conto, per favore.*"

The waiter bowed and disappeared again into the restaurant. I pulled out my wallet to pay the check, but Giovanni insisted, laying a firm hand over mine. "*Prego,*" he said, "allow me."

His hand lingered warmly upon mine for a moment. At first I couldn't be sure whether he was flirting with me or just displaying a peculiarly Italian physicality—until he whispered, leaning in closer, "You have very beautiful eyes." I looked up, showing him my eyes, searching for his in the dying light.

A sudden breeze rippled my shirt, and I shivered with the abrupt change in temperature. Only my hand, lying beneath Giovanni's, seemed to escape the approaching cold.

✦

WHEN I ARRIVED in the piazza the next day, Giovanni was already waiting beside the fountain. A corona of light burst through the cascading water behind his head. "*Buon giorno, caro mio,*" he said, taking my hand and pulling me toward him. His lips grazed one cheek, then the other, then pressed firmly against the first once more.

This was Italy, I reminded myself. Men kiss in public.

The Galleria dell'Accademia was several blocks away. We found David at the end of a long hallway, beneath a vaulted ceiling and bathed in natural light. Fourteen feet tall, he dwarfed the copy in the piazza. From the end of the hall, when he first came into view, I was struck by the peacefulness of the image. This was a man who was about to kill a giant and become a king, and yet, in the moment, he looked so gentle, at ease in his nakedness.

I kept my eyes on him as we approached: the musculature of the legs that planted him firmly, effortlessly, atop the pedestal; the waves of abdominals; the gentle curve of his chest. Finally, up close, the marble took on the look of skin—a white layer of protection for the veins and muscles that seemed to pulse within it. Only the eyes—sharp slits carved into the stone to define the pupils—revealed any emotion. Unlike the body, so calmly poised, the eyes signaled the full weight of the moment, an anxious watchfulness.

"He is magnificent, no?" Giovanni whispered in my ear.

I couldn't speak.

"That is the beauty of man," he said, his breath warm against my neck. He took my hand then, clasping it as tightly as David did the rock. "Come," he said, "there is something else you must see."

I reluctantly turned my eyes from David and followed Giovanni back into the hallway. "They are called 'the prisoners,'" he said, gesturing to a group of unfinished figures against each wall.

We stood before one of the statues, life-size and situated upon a small pedestal. I might have been eye to eye, if the figure had had eyes. Instead, one arm was draped over his face, as though he were hiding in shame or blocking the sun. His head, in fact, was unfinished, stopping at the hairline. Similarly, his bent leg emerged from the stone at the calf, his invisible foot still trapped inside.

"Michelangelo believed that he did not *create* his figures from the stone, but *released* them," Giovanni told me, standing close. "They were already inside. All he had to do was chip away the— *come si dice*—extra."

"Excess," I said, turning my head to look more closely. The figure seemed to be straining against the stone, forever half in and half out. There was something tragic about it. I wondered if he would prefer to be still completely inside, untempted by the world that passed before him, the world he couldn't reach.

Giovanni's hand still clenched mine as I turned to look into his eyes. His blond curls crowned his head like David's, but his eyes were less strained. His eyes were calm, soothing.

He led me silently outside. Within a couple of blocks, he took a sharp turn and the stream of tourists began to thin out.

His apartment was not far away, on a narrow street with burnt sienna buildings and green wooden shutters covering the windows. Inside, as Giovanni lifted his shirt over his head, his arms fully extended to reveal small tufts of hair, I studied the lines of his naked form. He was not as chiseled as the sculptures in the Accademia— no rippling muscles over his abdomen, no rounded pectorals or thickened thighs—but his body still reminded me of those struggling souls in the hall, his clothes the confining marble. As the top came free, revealing once again the face, the unkempt mop of blond hair, he seemed Michelangelo's dream incarnate, a new David—no, an Adam, ready to discover the world.

Naked at last, he stood still for a moment, his eyes staring intently into mine. There was a strange purity about his body—an uncorrupted smoothness of line, an imperfect perfection. Unlike most Italian men I had seen parading shirtless on the summer streets, Giovanni had only a few strands of blondish hair dividing his chest. Only several inches lower, below the navel, did the hair grow thicker and a shade darker, coursing down to form the triangle above his cock.

There was a full-length mirror behind him, half lit by the sun-

light peeking through the slats in the closed shutter. On one side
of it, shaded, I could see Giovanni's broad back, tapering down to
the thin waist and then flowering out into the valentine shape of
his buttocks. And beside that vision, there appeared a frontal view
as complement—the skin a bit lighter; the hair a bit darker, more
abundant on the chest; the legs beginning an inch or two lower. I
studied my own reflection with as much curiosity as I had granted
Giovanni's. It was as if this discovery were just as new, just as surprising.

Slowly, the vision was displaced, the back overtaking the front.
And then there was no reflection at all—only Giovanni in the flesh,
standing before me, moving closer, one hand reaching out.

✦

"YOU MUST LEARN TO RELAX," he whispered, still caressing my chest. "You are most tense when you should be most at
ease."

I stared up at the ceiling. The paint was peeling in various
places, hanging like the sword of Damocles. I reached for Giovanni, but immediately he grasped my wrists and forced them
above my head. My body tensed against the mattress; I wasn't sure
whether to struggle. "Relax," he repeated, more vehemently now.
"Trust me. You must learn to trust me—trust your body."

He released my wrists and turned again to my chest. His tongue
darted quickly along my sternum and then slowly across to my
right nipple. Gently, his mouth closed over it and I could feel it
harden with the soft flutter of his tongue. The pleasure was almost
unbearable. I squirmed on the bed, fighting the urge to pull his
head away. I closed my eyes and steadied my breathing, keeping my
fists clenched beside my head.

He moved slowly downward. At first touch, each part of my body
recoiled instinctively, as if it were all nerve, no skin to absorb the
sensation. I kept my head flat on the pillow, afraid to look down,
not really needing to after a while. As he lingered—on my chest,
my belly, my thigh—the sensitivity abated, giving way to pleasure,
and finally to an irrepressible, agonizing desire.

It seemed to go on for hours; I no longer had any sense of time.

When he lifted his head at last, I felt a cool draught assault my legs in the place he had abandoned. I opened my eyes to see him hovering over me, his face inches away from my own. I drew my hands up at last to caress his hair, and pulled him down to kiss me.

"Tell me about your lover in America," Giovanni whispered in the darkness later, as we lay still.

"My lover? What makes you think I have a lover?"

"I see it in your eyes," he said. "He is with you, even here."

"No," I replied, matching his dry tone, "no, he's not. We broke up a month ago."

"Why?"

I laughed. The question seemed so naive. "We had different priorities," I said at last.

"I don't understand," Giovanni said.

"Neither did I."

After a while, I stopped feeling the need to answer questions and Giovanni stopped asking them. We simply held each other, language—whether Italian or English—finally exhausted. At some point—I have no idea when—I fell asleep with the warmth of his chest against my cheek and the gentle clasp of his fingers on my side.

✦

I SAW THE REST OF FLORENCE through Giovanni's eyes. Together, we strolled through the bright courtyard garden of San Lorenzo, and stepped into the dim light of Santa Croce to pay our respects at the tomb of Michelangelo. We climbed Giotto's tower for a spectacular view of the entire city and the rolling hills beyond. With Giovanni at my side, I felt less like a tourist, my American constraint somewhat diminished. I practiced my lumbering Italian with him, further enclosing us, setting us apart from the crowds that jostled for a peek at the sights of the city, a taste of the living Renaissance.

When pressed, Giovanni finally explained his mysterious freedom. He had no job. He had left school a year or so ago with an impractical degree in literature and moved to Florence to think about what to do with his life. There was no rush; his family's money could keep him comfortable indefinitely.

"What would you like to do?" I asked over espresso around the corner from the Duomo. In America, that was the first question you would ask at a cocktail party. In America, what you do is who you are.

"I'm doing it," he said, smiling, gesturing at the cup, the café, the bustle around us.

"Surely you'd get bored sitting in cafés all day," I said.

He laughed. "I haven't so far."

I postponed the next leg of my vacation—losing a day or so in Rome seemed a small price to pay. For the rest of the week, I shared in Giovanni's adventure. In the mornings, we rushed through the tourist attractions, but the rest of the day was just for us. He showed me the real Florence—the side streets where the tourist babble gave way to the music of the people.

We walked arm in arm through the city, the electricity of his touch masked under the Italian ordinariness of the gesture. To me it was a kind of intimacy out in the open, a declaration that no one heard. I floated through the city as if the streets were gentle currents, Giovanni's arm a lifejacket supporting me, holding me aloft.

✦

THIS IS NOT A LOVE STORY. Even in *my* pathologically romantic imagination, five days is not long enough to fall in love. Back home, it would have been ample time to develop an obsession, time enough to entertain fantasies of forever. But here, in Florence—which was, itself, a kind of romance—I had no illusions. Here, I learned to simply enjoy what was happening—*as* it was happening.

In a love story there would have been a crisis: an argument, a disappointment, an epiphany of disillusioning. Giovanni and I didn't have time for any of that. In the moment, we could pretend that our time together was its own kind of forever. We could pretend that forever was measurable: forever, in Florence, lasted five days, six hours, and thirty-nine minutes.

✦

THE VIEW FROM the Boboli Gardens was the most spectacular of all—no wonder Giovanni had saved it for my last day. Framed by the cypress trees that lined the garden, the city glowed silently in the late morning sun, the only signs of life an occasional curl of smoke wafting from a chimney. It might as well have been the Florence of 500 years ago, frozen in time.

"You will love Roma," he said.

I sat on a bench beside him, gazing at the Duomo, whose wide curve seemed to cushion the sky. Rome was something I was trying not to think about. I kept my eyes on the horizon, the ancient tile roofs of the city, the earth tones that threw the heavens into greater contrast. Behind the city, the hills were alive with light, colors as vibrant as those on a Renaissance painter's palate—brighter and sharper than real life was supposed to be.

"I can't imagine anything more beautiful than this."

"Oh, Roma is not *more* beautiful," he said. "It is beautiful in a different way."

I finally turned to face him. The wind was playing havoc with his hair, tossing the blond curls over his forehead, one completely unfurled and bouncing before his eyes. His skin was smooth, as if untouched, and I had to remind myself that I had indeed touched it—all of it. I conjured the images back into my brain—the curve of his hip, the sensitive spot just beneath his navel that made him gasp when my finger brushed against it. I took his hand—warm, veiny flesh—and squeezed it hard, interlocking my fingers with his, sealing the memory in stone.

INVOKING THE PAST

S.J. FROST

DERRICK STARED DOWN at the small boulder adorned with a white rope that had a wooden plaque inscribed with kanji. According to his tour guide book and the sign nearby written in English, this was one of the 'love stones' of Jishu Shrine, a Shinto shrine located on the complex of Kiyomizu Temple. The stones were believed to be able to bring good luck in love to anyone who could walk the distance from one stone to the other with their eyes closed.

Derrick glanced to both sides, behind him, in front of him, at all the people milling about the packed grounds of the shrine. Normally, he would feel like a total idiot for doing something like this with other people around, but he guessed that was the beauty of being in a country half the world away from his home in Michigan, he'd never see any of these people again. Besides, he needed all the help in love he could get.

He adjusted his backpack on his shoulders and took his place in front of the love stone. He scanned the distance to the other straight ahead. It didn't look that far. Probably only eighteen meters give or take, so he should be able to make it. And what was the worst that could happen if he didn't? If he failed in securing good luck in love from the stones, that wasn't anything he wasn't used to already. He inhaled a deep breath, closed his eyes, and took the first step.

✦

DAISUKE STEPPED OUT from the shrine, freezing in place at the sight before him. A blond haired guy was making the walk between the love stones. He couldn't see the guy's face, but if he looked as good from the front as he did from behind, then there was a lot of promise there.

Daisuke glanced back into the shrine. He had come to Jishu-*jinja* to offer his prayers to *Okuninushi no Makoto*, god of love and matchmaking, to help him find a good partner. But the problem wasn't that he couldn't find anyone to have sex with. That was easy. He could get laid ten times a day by ten different people if he wanted, but lately, his casual encounters had been growing in emptiness to where even his physical satisfaction had diminished, leaving him wanting more than any of his partners had been able to give.

He looked back to the guy still making his journey to the other stone, each step so slow and cautious. Daisuke walked forward, making his footfalls come light and silent, reading the guy's back-pack as he approached, University of Michigan. He must be a uni-versity student, which meant he'd probably be close to his own twenty years of age. He saw a tag on the backpack with his name, Derrick Cassidy, and American address.

He noticed pins on Derrick's backpack of various male idols, ac-tors, and musicians. The sexy actor and singer, Kato Kazuki, whose idol DVD, *55mm*, had been a guilty pleasure purchase of his, but had certainly been worth the money to watch Kato-*san* roll around on a beach. Another pin featured the adorable actor, Fujiwara Tat-suya. A couple others were of the super cute guys in the pop group KAT-TUN. And the one who Derrick had the most pins of, the beautiful and musically gifted rock star, Gackt, who was also his fa-vorite performer. Besides the fact that it was a little overly fanboy for Derrick to be brandishing the pins, at least it cleared one thing up for him: most guys that preferred women wouldn't display a col-lection of so many lovely men.

Daisuke moved beside him. Derrick wavered in his stride, seem-ing hesitant to take the next step. Daisuke walked forward, looking over his shoulder to see Derrick's face. He smiled and turned around, sending a silent thank you to *Okuninushi no Makoto*.

He headed over to the torii gate to watch Derrick from a dis-tance. He had seen people make the walk before, but never had he seen anyone with the concentration on their face that Derrick had, as if he were truly putting all his hope on the ritual being successful. It was really quite heart wrenching, and he wondered what would make someone so attractive so desperate for love. But then, his situation was no different. Since it seemed the ancient god was at work, he hoped Derrick would complete his journey successfully. He only had three more steps to go.

Derrick took another step. He figured he had to be getting close now. It felt like he had been walking forever. He took a second step. He couldn't lose focus. He needed to concentrate on what he wanted. A boyfriend who wouldn't cheat on him, lie to him, or use him. Someone that when he woke up beside them in the morning, he'd smile at seeing their face, and would want to wake him so they could begin their day together, not feel trepidation at what deception would come from the other's mouth as soon as he woke up. He had been putting so much focus on those thoughts, he could have swore just a moment before that he had smelled the most delicious cologne, and wondered if it was a sign that the ritual was working.

Derrick brought his foot forward for another step and bumped it into the second stone. He snapped his eyes open, ready to punch the air in triumph and stopped, his gaze locked on the gorgeous Japanese guy standing near the torii gate. The guy smiled, applauding softly for him, then turned and descended the stairs.

Derrick stood motionless. The heat of the day was nothing compared to the embarrassed flush rising in his cheeks. He had just seen the hottest guy in his life, and he was walking away probably thinking that he was the most pathetic thing in the world to be asking some old rocks to help him find a man. He lowered his eyes to the love stone. Then again…

Daisuke meandered down a path heading in the general direction of the garden in the southeast corner of Kiyomizu-*dera*. He knew he had given Derrick enough of a welcoming smile that if he was interested he would follow. He paused, pretending to admire the architecture of another small shrine and peeked out the corner of his eye. He grinned and began walking again.

Derrick lingered back trying to be as inconspicuous as possible. He had managed to catch up to him, but now what? He had never been good at making the first move since his shyness kept him back, but this was a whole other dilemma. To say his Japanese was shoddy would be complimenting it, and it'd be his perfect luck that the guy couldn't speak a word of English. He was pretty sure he could use the universal hand and mouth sign for blow job, but that would either get his point across in a good way, or earn him a fist in the teeth.

One thing he had noticed while tailing him was the way the guy walked. At first, he had been too preoccupied with staring at the perfect curve of his ass to notice, but then he saw the confidence with which he moved, as if the whole of Kiyomizu Temple belonged to him. He couldn't help but wonder if the guy would bring that same confidence into the bedroom, then decided without a doubt he would. A man who moved like that had complete self-assurance no matter what his situation, and would take claim to any area he set foot in, which was just one more reason he'd been holding back. The only place he had confidence like that was on the tennis court. He didn't even know how to begin talking to someone like that.

He remembered his language books in his backpack and shook one strap off his shoulder. He rummaged around inside and retrieved a book with a hot pink cover titled *Making Out in Japanese*. Despite the book being filled with colorful phrases for getting it on, it also had more polite conversational lines. Maybe he could find a good opener that he might actually be able to pronounce without slaughtering the language.

He walked with his eyes flashing over words that brought his mind to a screeching halt in complete confusion, making him wonder why he had turned his friends down when they invited him to go with them to Mexico. Oh, that's right. He decided it'd be more fun to zip across the world in a tin can sitting in economy for thirteen and a half hours to a country where he couldn't even ask where the restroom was, let alone hit on a guy.

Derrick glanced up from the book. There was the guy, on a bridge arching over a small pond. He leaned forward with his elbow propped on the railing, his chin cupped in his hand, his dark eyes as serene as the water he gazed at. He wore a short-sleeved black shirt with the top few buttons undone to reveal his smooth chest. His black hair was long to the middle of his neck in back and styled with the sides brushed forward to frame the elegant features of his face. With his hair parted so the majority of his bangs laid to the left, they would occasionally fall over his left eye, and he would push them back, sometimes flipping the top layers giving it a cute tousled look.

Derrick stared at him; glad he had decided to not go to Mexico.

Daisuke looked at Derrick from under his eyelashes, taking a long moment to drink him in. Derrick wore his light blond hair brushed back and the golden strands of his bangs fell to the sides of his forehead near his hazel eyes. He drifted his gaze down Derrick's lithe body to his defined quad muscles peeking out from under the khaki shorts, and the toned musculature of his calves.

He rolled his eyes when he noticed the white T-shirt Derrick was wearing had *baka gaijin* written in kanji. Derrick probably thought it was funny to wear a shirt calling himself a "stupid foreigner", and maybe he did get a couple chuckles from school kids, but it was really bad taste. Still, he shouldn't hold his poor choice in clothing against him. If anything, he could use this since Derrick had decided to remain stubbornly shy.

Daisuke cleared his throat and called out in English, "Hey! You don't look like a stupid foreigner to me. Am I wrong, or is your shirt right?"

Derrick clenched the book and looked down at his shirt, shocked not only that the gorgeous guy had called out to him, but had done so in excellent English edged with the sexiest accent. "Um, I guess it's a matter of opinion."

Daisuke leaned his hip against the railing and folded his arms across his chest, giving him a scrutinizing look. "Then I'll have to talk to you more to form an opinion." He waved for Derrick to come closer.

Derrick quickly shoved the book into his backpack. He climbed onto the bridge, and as he approached, he caught the scent of sandalwood and spice cologne, the same he had smelled when he walked between the love stones. He breathed it in and bowed deep to him. "*Watashi wa* Cassidy Derrick *desu.*"

Daisuke choked down a laugh. Derrick's pronunciation was really bad. Though, it was adorable that he had tried. He even introduced himself putting his last name first instead of keeping with his Western tradition of the given name before surname.

Daisuke inclined a slight bow, then held out his hand, deciding that he'd try to keep the conversation in English. "It's a pleasure, Cassidy-*kun*. I'm Nakamura Daisuke."

Derrick smiled and took hold of Daisuke's hand. "It's nice to meet you, Nakamura-*san*."

Daisuke kept Derrick's hand in his. "Please, feel free to call me Daisuke, or Dai for short. We can let propriety slide, and you're American, who are known more for being casual, am I right? That was my impression when I visited there last year. But my English was even worse then than it is now."

"Your English is perfect. You speak it better than me," Derrick chuckled, watching Daisuke glow from the compliment. He wondered if Daisuke was going to let go of his hand and hoped he wouldn't. "Did you like the States?"

Daisuke shrugged. "Some of it was nice, but quite a bit wasn't what my friends and I thought it would be. And we got arrested, and that didn't make us very happy since it wasn't our fault." He released Derrick's hand only to grab his other and gave it a tug. "Walk with me."

Derrick stumbled to walk at his side, startled by Daisuke's boldness. He glanced from all the people strolling around them, down to their hands joined together. He looked at Daisuke walking as if nothing was capable of fazing him, least of all holding hands. He had always been too self-conscious to hold hands with any of his past boyfriends in public, but there was something about Daisuke's confidence that made him feel so comfortable.

Derrick tipped his head back, gazing up at the three-storey pagoda towering above with its gracefully sweeping tiers. "You said got arrested. For what? Where were you?"

Daisuke walked slow, leading Derrick back toward the main hall of Kiyomizu-*dera*. "We were in Los Angeles, me and two friends. We had spent the evening going to clubs, and were walking back to our hotel when this car with four guys in it sped up beside us. They started throwing rocks and eggs at us, but what pissed me and my friends off most, besides how cowardly they were, was when they drove off, they called us "Chinese faggots." Can you believe that? I'm Japanese damn it! If you're going to insult me, get it right. I was so pissed, I threw one of the rocks at their car, and it broke their back window.

"They turned around and jumped out. I guess they thought they were going to beat us up, and were yelling at us to show them some of our kung fu. But since we don't know kung fu, we improvised by educating them in jujutsu. Unfortunately, someone must have seen the fight and called the police. When they arrived, the fight was over, but since the four guys were lying on the ground crying, we were the ones who got arrested, and we hadn't even really hurt them. We just defended ourselves and tossed them around a little. But we got out of it okay in the end. At the police station, we just pretended like we didn't understand English. They couldn't find an interpreter at that hour and got so frustrated that they let us go."

"That's awesome!" Derrick burst out, then quieted his voice. "I mean, it's not awesome that those guys were hating on you like that, but it's awesome that you kicked their asses."

"I suppose, but I don't think it taught them anything. People like that have a vision of the world as one would have looking through a straw with one eye closed. They see nothing outside of what they want, and have no desire to expand their world. But I've tried to not let that experience taint my view of the States. In fact, I'd like to study there for a while if I could decide on a school. I saw on your backpack underneath all your buttons of beautiful men that it says University of Michigan. Is that a good university?"

Derrick winced inside at the twinge of embarrassment for blatantly displaying a few of the men he'd love to get on their backs, their knees, their stomachs, pretty much any position so long as they were naked. "Yeah, that's where I go to school. It's got a very good reputation."

"Do you know if they teach biochemistry? That's what I'm studying now at Kyoto University."

"I'm sure they do. My major is computer engineering. I'm hoping to get a job as a software programmer for video games someday."

Daisuke looked at him with a bright smile. "I love video games. I'll kick your ass in tennis on my Nintendo Wii anytime."

Derrick laughed. "I doubt that. I'm vice-captain of the varsity tennis team."

Daisuke moved his gaze down Derrick's body as they climbed a set of stairs leading to main hall. "That's why you look so beautifully fit." He leaned closer, putting his lips to Derrick's ear and softening his voice. "But I think I can keep up with you if you come over to my apartment to play. I was captain of my tennis team when I was in high school, and I've worked very hard to not lose any of my stamina."

Just as his heartbeat had begun to calm down as he got comfortable talking to Daisuke, it shot back up, and seemed intent on sending the majority of his blood between his legs. Derrick took a deep breath and wet his lips. "You don't waste much time, do you?"

Daisuke climbed the last step and stopped inside the entranceway to face Derrick. "I just assumed I don't have much time. You're only visiting, right? When do you leave?"

"In seven days. I'll be in Kyoto a couple more days, then I was going to head up to Tokyo for the rest of my trip."

"Then I only have two days to convince you that I'm more interesting than anything in Tokyo."

Keeping Derrick's hand in his, Daisuke reached out with his other, caught the top of Derrick's shorts and gave him a sharp pull forward. Derrick staggered the single step between them, bumping into Daisuke. Before he could recover, he felt Daisuke's warm hand on his cheek, his thumb under his jaw tipping his head back. In less than half of one of his rapid heartbeats, Daisuke's lips were pressed against his.

Derrick tensed, the voices of tourists and visitors making their way into the hall seeming impossibly loud, reminding him how many people were around them. As he thought to pull away, Daisuke's tongue traced over his lips, and the voices of the people began to sound quieter. He parted his lips to Daisuke, and at the feel of Daisuke's tongue gliding into his mouth, the only sound he heard was the soft groan that passed from Daisuke's mouth to his.

Daisuke eased back from the kiss, smiling. "Don't you think that was far more interesting than anything you'd see in Shinjuku or Shibuya?"

Derrick nodded slowly.

Daisuke tugged on his hand. "Come on. I'll show you how beautiful Kyoto is."

Derrick walked beside him, his head still spinning from the kiss. Daisuke guided him to the massive veranda of the main hall that jutted out over the hillside. Kyoto spread out far below, nestled among the deep summer green forested hills and mountains.

Derrick stood at the thick wooden railing, his eyes moving slowly across the view as his mind worked to store each wild cherry tree and maple, the shape of the city and its buildings, the lay of the hills and rivers. "It's beautiful," he whispered in awe.

Daisuke placed a gentle kiss on his cheek. "It's better than Tokyo."

Derrick glanced at him, then, turned his gaze back to Kyoto.

Daisuke sensed the withdrawal in Derrick's mood. "Or maybe it's not."

Derrick shook his head. "No, it's not that."

Daisuke's slender brows furrowed closer in confusion. "Derrick-*kun*, why were you doing the love stone ritual? A guy that looks like you and seems to have such a kind heart shouldn't have any trouble finding a lover."

"Yeah, well, my so called kind heart is the problem. You see, I have this little issue of never wanting people to be mad at me, which means that I'll do pretty much anything anyone asks of me to keep them happy, which in turn means I get walked all over, and it's taken every guy I've ever tried to have a relationship with about a nanosecond to figure out that I'm an easy target.

"Not that I can put the blame fully on them. I'm the one who hands over my car keys if they need to go somewhere. I'm the one who shoves my credit card in their face if they're short on cash. I'm the one who opens his door if they can't pay their rent, only to have them screw somebody else in my bed while I'm in class. I'm the one who believes all the lies like "It'll never happen again" and "You're the only one"."

Derrick faced him, locking his eyes into Daisuke's. "And if things between us keep going in the direction that they seem to be heading, there's no way I'd go to Tokyo. I know how I am. I'd stay with you for my whole trip, and then when it'd be time for me to go back home, I'd end up staying a few more days until I absolutely had to leave. You should know now, I'm about as clingy as they get. I'm twenty years old, and I already have major dependency issues." He took a deep breath, exhaling fast as he ended his rant.

Daisuke stood silent for a moment, blinking at him. "What kind of car do you drive?"

"I just bought a Pontiac Solstice a couple months ago. Why?"

"I just want to know what I'd get to drive if I come to the States." Derrick's mouth dropped open.

Daisuke laughed and gave him a playful shove on the shoulder. "I'm teasing you! If you're trying to scare me away, you'll have to do better than that." He took Derrick's other hand so he held them both. "I think you view yourself too poorly. You shouldn't let men of such low character determine your self-worth. I understand your concerns about having to leave, but that's something to worry about when the time grows closer. It could be that at the end of seven days, you may be running for the plane to take you back to the States to get away from me."

Derrick smiled. "Somehow, I doubt that."

He closed the distance between them, bringing their chests and hips together, and covered Daisuke's mouth in a deep kiss, no longer caring what people who saw them thought. He pulled his hands from Daisuke's and wrapped his arms around him, feeling Daisuke's arms go around him at the same moment.

Daisuke slipped one hand up the back of Derrick's shirt and caressed his lower back. With their hips pressed tightly together, he shifted so his erection rubbed Derrick's through their clothes.

Derrick drew back from the kiss, briefly sucking Daisuke's bottom lip. "Does the invitation still stand for going to your place to play?"

Daisuke nodded. "But I'll warn you that my apartment is very small, so we won't have any choice but to be on top of each other, and my air conditioner doesn't work good, so we'll get very hot and sweaty if we play with lots of energy."

"That sounds like the perfect way to spend the rest of my summer vacation." Derrick brushed his lips over Daisuke's. "I guess invoking the past really does work."

"Ancient gods and love stones can only do so much. You had the courage to walk in the steps of the past for the hope of creating a beautiful future. Keep that as a memory that you are a strong person."

Derrick looked into his eyes and met Daisuke's lips again, knowing that half the world was not a great enough distance to keep him away from the sincerity he had seen in Daisuke's gaze.

SECOND CHANCES

WILLIAM HOLDEN

I SAT AT what had become my spot, a small wooden bench on Kite Hill overlooking the city. In the distance I watched with sadness as the pride flag twisted and turned in the bay breeze, standing tall and proud at the corner of Market and Castro. The cooling temperatures meant only one thing to the residents here, the end of summer and for me the end of my stay, and the end of what had become one of the happiest times of my life.

I never meant for any of it to happen. After all, I had someone waiting for me back home. But something happened to me the day I stepped off the plane three months ago. I don't know if it was the warm ocean air, the electrifying energy of the city, or my own loneliness for never having made the life for myself I had always hoped for. Whatever it was, it let me forget my life back home and live for the moment; a moment that has lasted the entire summer, and now sitting here by myself with the soft warmth of his lips still lingering on mine, I'm not sure if I can board that plane and go home. We've already said our good-byes and had one last cry in each other's arms. But as the taxi drove away, I knew there was one last good-bye I had to make—Kite Hill. So here I sit on the bench, as I have done almost every day since arriving here, staring off at the city below me one last time. My eyes wander out across the city, as I imagine him alone out there in the streets missing me like I was missing him.

❖

IT WAS MY FIRST NIGHT of what was to be a three-month research trip. I had quickly settled into the guesthouse I had rented and was already enjoying the sights and sounds of the Castro in the late afternoon. The sun was shining brightly, yet over the hill I could see the edge of the summer fog beginning to roll in for its evening visit, blanketing the city with its cooling touch. I was sitting in the upper loft of Twin Peaks sipping my rum and coke and looking out of the small window as people came out of the Castro Street Muni Station. It was then that I noticed him for the first time, just below my little window.

He was sitting on the sidewalk with his back against the glass of the bus stop. I couldn't take my eyes off of him from the minute I saw him. I'm not sure what came over me, all I know is in that moment, my heart went out to him—I could tell he was homeless. His face was ashen and dull. His hands were rough and covered in the grime of the city, his clothes ragged. He wore a grey baggy sweatshirt. His jeans, covered in the same dirt as the rest of him, were torn, exposing parts of his legs and red-flannel boxers. I continued to watch him, my eyes exploring the condition of his exposed body. His legs, which appeared bruised and scarred, were covered in dark hair. He smiled at everyone that passed him, asking them for loose change or a cigarette—they ignored him. His smile made him look youthful behind the filth; an expression of lost innocence and hope was hidden in there as well. I'm not sure how long I sat there watching him; it was as if time had completely stopped for me, yet everyone else continued to move through his or her own world. His movements and facial expressions told stories that no words could have. A warm sensation started in the pit of my stomach. It floated upwards filling me with feelings and emotions I had thought I had lost somewhere in the past. The warmth touched my heart, surrounded it, and then gripped it like nothing ever had. I knew at that moment my life would never be the same.

I finished my drink, left the bar, and walked over to him. He looked confused as I knelt down next to him, pulled out my pack of cigarettes, and lit one. I handed him one and held out my lighter for him. He puffed a few times till the embers began to glow, then pulled his face away. When I didn't leave, he spoke.

"What do you want?"

"Nothing, I just wanted to say hi." I replied, not sure exactly what to say. "What's your name?"

"Why do you want to know?" His eyes glanced over my body trying to figure out my purpose. "Look man, I appreciate the smoke, but I don't want any trouble."

"I don't plan on giving you any trouble." I paused. "Look, let me start over. I'm Matt. I was watching you from the window." I pointed up to where I was sitting, "I just wanted to say hi and talk for a bit. I hated watching everyone walk by you like you weren't even there."

"You shouldn't worry about it. Besides, I'm used to it. I don't exist to people. They only see what they want, and I'm not something they want to see. T.J."

"Excuse me?"

"You asked what my name was, it's T.J." He looked up at me and smiled. Our eyes locked. Neither of us made any excuses to move or to say something. The moment was all we needed.

I'm not sure what it was that actually happened between us at that moment, all I know is that it had never happened to me before and I doubt it would ever happen again. We never spoke of that moment during our time together, we didn't need to; the moment itself was all that mattered.

The ringing of my cell phone brought us back from where we were. I reached into my pocket and pulled it out. At first I didn't recognize my own home phone number, then reality came rushing back—my boyfriend was calling from home. I looked up at T.J. then back to the phone. I turned the ringer off and slipped it back into my pants. Guilt began to creep into my mind as I thought of Michael sitting at home alone, thinking about me; and here I was on the other side of the country getting ready to do the unthinkable—break my commitment of fifteen years. It wasn't that I didn't love him, I did—more than I thought possible but it was a love that should never have been. We both had been on different paths when we met and somehow we ended up taking the same detour, a detour that kept us both from living the lives we had wanted. I became numb during those years, locking away my sadness, emotions, wants and desires; to keep what we had for no other reason than to have someone in my life. Now, without expectation, without notice it came back to me a dull faded memory—the path I'd once been on and the hope I had felt for my own future.

I watched as the ember of T.J.'s cigarette flare as he inhaled. His exhale brought smoke swirling around us. I lit one for myself and took a deep inhale trying to relax my body as I asked the question, I shouldn't have been asking.

"Would you have dinner with me tonight?" I could tell by the look on his face that he was as surprised by my question, as I was fearful of his answer. Would I be able to stop what I put in motion—but more importantly, would I want it to stop?

"Look man, that would be great, and I would like to say yes, but unless you want to eat out here on the street with me, I think I'm going to have to pass on the invite."

"Why?"

"Do you have to ask?" He looked down at himself. "Look at me. I'm dirty, my clothes are old and torn, and I smell." He looked up at me and smiled again, perhaps to hide his own distaste of the situation he found himself in. "No one is going to welcome me into their restaurant like this, and I don't blame them." He paused as if wanting to say more but instead he crushed his cigarette out on the pavement and sat there silently.

"So you'll have dinner with me, as long as it doesn't require us to go anyplace?" I reached out, and picked up his hand in mine and squeezed it. It was the first physical contact we had made. He seemed a bit uneasy with it at first, but yet he didn't pull away. He just sat there motionless, looking at his hand in mine. "Stay here and I'll be back in a few minutes, okay?"

"Why are you doing this?"

"Because I want to," I paused, "isn't that enough. Now promise me you'll be here when I get back." He looked up at me and nodded his response. A smile appeared on my face. "I won't be long." I stood up and headed across the street to get dinner on order while I finished the rest of my unexpected errands. Thirty minutes later I walked up to where T.J. was waiting with my arms full. He looked up at me in disbelief as the extent of what I had done washed over him.

I slowly knelt down and placed our supplies on the sidewalk, then went to work quickly to get our makeshift table together before the crowds picked up. I shook out a blue-checkered tablecloth then laid out the plastic cups and plates. A candle was next out of the bag. The cool breeze rushing up the Castro made it difficult to light, but finally the wick caught, casting dancing shadows across our faces. I looked over at T.J. who just sat silently as dinner was laid out before him. With the pizza between us there was one last thing to do. I pulled a bottle of wine out of the bag, popped the cork, and poured us each a glass. As I settled down, I took my glass of wine and raised it up to give a toast. I looked over at T.J., a tear was running down his cheek making a clean path of skin from the layers of dirt that covered his face.

"You okay?"

"Yeah, I'm fine." My voice seemed to have brought him out of his thoughts. He quickly wiped the tear away. "It's just ... no one has ever done anything like this for me."

"Well maybe its time someone has."

"But why? Why me and why now?"

"Does it really matter why?" I paused and touched my plastic cup to his. We watched each other take a sip of the wine. "I don't know why. Can't we just enjoy it and not question it."

"I'm sorry. I don't mean to sound unappreciative; it's just that over the years I've learned to questions people's motives. I guess it's just something I've picked up during my time on the streets." He took another drink of the wine then picked up a slice of pepperoni pizza and took a big bit out of it.

"So what happened?" I took a bite of my own slice. "I mean that forced you to live on the streets."

"That was over ten years ago and believe it or not you're the first person who has ever thought to ask me that." He looked up at me. "My parents."

"Your parents did this to you?"

"I was sixteen years old when it happened. I had known for some time that I was gay and like most people probably struggled with it before telling anyone else." He finished off the wine that was in his glass. I refilled it for him as he continued. "After I turned sixteen, I decided that I needed to tell my parents. I hated having to hide who I was and I really thought if anyone would understand it would be my folks. So one night at dinner I told them and in that split second, my whole world changed." His hands began to tremble from the memories.

"I'm sorry. I didn't mean to ..."

"No, its okay. It feels good to finally tell someone." He took an-other sip of wine then continued. "My father's first reaction was to hit me and accuse me of lying to them just to hurt them. He picked me up and shook me, screaming at me to tell them I was lying. I had never been so scared in my entire life and these were my par-ents I was scared of, the ones who were supposed to love and pro-tect me. In an instant that fear turned to hate and I shouted back that I was gay and that I was proud of it. My father threw me against the wall and told me that I had one hour to pack my things and leave. I've been on the streets ever since."

◆

THE WINDS ON KITE HILL chilled the tears that began to form in my eyes as I replayed our first evening together. I remem-ber the emotions and feel of every moment of that dinner on the street as if it had just happened. Yet that dinner was only the begin-ning. Neither of us knew it at that moment, but the night was far from over. In fact that first night, the first stare, the first kiss lasted for the next three months. My heart began to ache at the thought of leaving T.J. I could almost feel him in the air of the city as the wind whipped and caressed my body.

◆

WE SAT ON THE SIDEWALK and talked for hours, eating the pizza that continually got colder and drinking the wine that got warmer, as if nothing else existed. The growing number of people wandering around the Castro was nothing more than a backdrop to what was going on between us.

"That was so good. I can't remember the last time I ate a com-plete meal." T.J. spoke as he looked around at the empty bottle and pizza box.

"You sound as if the evening is over. I thought you might come back to my place after this. You could shower and get cleaned up, then who knows." The glimmer I had seen in his eyes just moments before vanished, leaving emptiness in its place. The tone in his voice became tense yet somehow shallow.

"So that's it, isn't it?"

"That's what?"

"All of this, the wine, the dinner; bringing it all to me on the street. You just wanted to get me into bed." He stood up and grabbed his duffle bag. "You're no different than the others." He began to walk away.

"Wait!" I shouted as I stood up and grabbed his arm. "Please, wait. What just happened?" He turned around and looked at me, but didn't say a word. "Look, I know you're not used to trusting people, but I didn't do all this just to get you into bed. I did this because I wanted to. If sex was all that I wanted I could have gotten that from just about anyone out here, but that's not what this is about. I thought you knew that?"

"I don't know what to believe." He paused and brought his hands up to his face and groaned frustration into them. "Okay, look. If sex is all you want, please, just say so. I'll understand and we can just end this now, before I let myself get carried away again thinking that somehow there is more here than there really is."

"T.J. Please, come back to my place with me. You can take a shower and get cleaned up. If at that point you just want to leave and not take a chance on whatever this is, then I'll let you go. No strings, no catches." I could tell he wanted desperately to reach out to me, to have someone feel something for him, but still he hesitated. "I think I may be falling for you." The words spilled out of my mouth, before I could stop them. It was one thing to think those words about someone who wasn't your boyfriend, but to say them out loud, shocked even me.

"But…"

"Please, let me finish." I gave him a soft smile trying to reassure him before continuing. "T.J. since the moment I saw you this afternoon, I've not been able to think of anything else but you. I see a part of myself in you. A part of myself that I gave up many years ago." Tears began to well up in his eyes as he listened to me. "Don't you get it? It's not about the sex. I was watching you earlier today as you sat here alone being ignored by everyone around you and yet I could see something in you, a distant glimmer of hope that you held on to. It was in that hope of yours that I found mine again."

"What's the point, Matt? Why should we let whatever this is happen? You're here for what, three months and then you'll get back on a plane back to your boyfriend and I'll go back to living on the streets. Why go through all of that?"

"I don't know what will happen, but even if it works out the way you just described, I'm willing to take that risk to have three months of happiness with you." I grabbed his hands in mine. "Please just come back with me. No promises, no false hopes or dreams. Just tonight and nothing else."

I let go of his hands and began to pick up our sidewalk dinner table. As I tossed the remaining garbage into the trashcan, he came up to me with his duffle bag over his shoulder.

"No promises." He said.

"No promises." We walked among the crowds on Castro as we headed towards 18th Street. As the crowds began to thin I felt his fingers intertwine with mine. We walked back to my place in the mission, holding hands in silence.

✦

I LOOKED DOWN AT MY HAND as if expecting to see it held tightly in his. I rubbed my fingers and thumb together to force myself to realize that I was alone up here on Kite Hill with only my thoughts of him to help with the loneliness. I looked back at the cab still patiently waiting for me to finish my business here, but I couldn't turn my back on the city and on T.J. somewhere down there walking the streets. I wondered if he was back sitting where I first saw him, under the window of Twin Peaks. I had offered to keep the payments up on the rental so he would have a place to stay, but he refused, saying that he'd rather go back to the streets then to stay in the apartment without me. I understood his reasoning but it didn't make thinking about him back on the street any easier.

Tears fell down my face as I thought of our first night together and the moment I saw him come out of the bathroom freshly showered with only a towel wrapped around his waist. He was as beautiful on the outside under all that dirt as he was on the inside.

His blond, uncut hair hung loosely over his face. It was damp and stuck to his skin in seductive curls. His torso was hairless and pale from lack of care and sun. A small trail of dark hair curled around his belly button and fell below the white terry cloth towel. I walked over to him. The scent of his clean body overpowered me. I became lost within him. He looked at me. His blue-grey eyes pierced my soul and touched a part of me that hadn't been touched in a long time. What was left of the brick wall I had surrounded my heart with for all those years finally began to crumble under his gaze. Emotions held captive all those years flooded out of that sealed room. I couldn't control myself and brought my lips to his. We kissed for what seemed like hours, but in reality were no more than a few minutes. I brought him over to the bed and laid him down next to me, holding him in my arms. There were no words between us that night. No hesitations, no fears, or hidden agendas. We came together naturally and perfectly in every way. I let him enter me, something I would never have let anyone else do. We gave ourselves to the other without question, without guilt.

◆

I BECAME SO LOST in my own thoughts of that night, that I thought I could hear his voice being carried by the wind all the way up here on the hill. I looked around and saw T.J. standing there with the darkening sky behind him. In disbelief, I shook my head to clear the vision away, but the vision of him remained. I walked towards him, expecting with each step that he would disappear and I would once again be standing here alone. We walked slowly towards each other as we spoke.

"I had to come up here to say good-bye."

"I thought you might." We were only a few feet away now and I could see the tears in his eyes, his chest moving in and out quickly from the rush of the moment. "I had to try to find you."

"I can't go through another good-bye T.J." I took another step closer. He did the same.

"I'm not asking you to." He took another step, I followed his lead. "I can't loose you. This summer started something that I'm not ready to let go of." We now faced each other. I could feel his sweet breath against my face. I took a deep breath and brought his scent into me, calming my nerves. "Remember our first night you told me that you saw a glimmer of hope in me, even though I was homeless and people ignored me, you could see it."

I began to cry. "Yes, I remember."

"You also told me that there was something between us, something that brought you back to a time when you had that same hope. Well I'm here to tell you not to turn your back on that hope a second time. Don't make the same mistake you made fifteen years ago by settling with something you know isn't what you want. Allow yourself to hope. Give yourself that second chance you know you want. Do it for the both of us and come back with me. Don't get on that plane."

He reached his arms out towards me. My mind flipped to my boyfriend anxiously awaiting my return, then I felt T.J.'s arms around me and I knew where I wanted to be. Michael would be okay without me, as I would be without him. We stood there in silence with the city's lights sparkling beneath us and the cool autumn winds blowing our fears and doubts out into the bay.

THE RIGHT THING

CURTIS C. COMER

THE DAY WAS ONE OF THOSE miserably hot days that only seems like a good thing later as a memory, one of those days that is so hot everything seems to stick to your skin and nothing is moving. Jon and I had braved the heat only long enough to escape to our usual spot by the river, atop a large flat stone that had been rubbed smooth by the current of the river, a spot hidden from view of the nearby road by a large outcrop of land that supported a large oak. This spot by the river was favored by the local Baptist church for its baptisms due to the relative shallowness of the water, deep enough to immerse the converts, yet shallow enough that nobody could be swept away while finding Jesus. I glanced over at Jon, who had his eyes pulled tightly closed against the mid-day sun, and wished that this wasn't his last day in town. Jon's dad was a preacher from another town and, as with the past two summers, Jon was in town visiting his grandma for two months.

The scent of sycamore trees and river mud filled the air like heavy incense, and cicadas droned overhead from their hiding place in the canopy of the twisted oak. Jon twitched his foot as a dragonfly, the first movement I'd seen in an hour, landed on his big toe. He was finally able to coax the dragonfly to move, and it hovered above us for a moment, almost as if trying to figure out who was stupid enough to be out in the stifling heat. Its body was the same brilliant blue as Jon's eyes, and I told him so.

"Yeah?" was his only response, flashing his eyes at me before clamping them shut again, almost as if letting me make sure I wasn't mistaken.

We had met two summers earlier at a summer camp out in western Kansas, and neither his parents nor mine knew what we had done in the shower that first summer, or why he suddenly had an interest in staying with his grandma for weeks on end each summer thereafter. It was the same each summer; we would continue our clandestine affair at summer camp as if months hadn't passed in between, and then Jon would come to my town and stay with his grandma for another couple of months before heading back home. I lived for this time of year; where most of my classmates couldn't wait for the summer because of anticipated vacations and swimming pools, mine was an urgency born of a growing sexual awareness.

This year, both of us eighteen and out of high school and too old to attend the summer camp where we had first met, were making do with these two weeks. Jon had convinced his parents, despite their demands that he get a summer job, that his grandma would miss him if he didn't visit, a claim, luckily, she didn't deny. While I was thrilled that he had been able to accomplish this, my elation at seeing him was met with his usual coolness, replying that he had only come to see me before I left for college and he was shipped off for basic training in the army. To Jon, our "thing," as he called it, was something that happened in the summer, a mere diversion. I never pressed him about whom he saw or who his friends were back home, though his rare letters in the fall and winter sometimes hinted at girls he was seeing. I didn't care; if summer was all we had, then I was fine. At least in summer he was all mine. Though he wouldn't actually come out and say it, I know that Jon had actually decided to join the army as an act of revolt against his strict father, who really wanted him to follow in his footsteps and become an ordained minister. I tried, unsuccessfully, to convince Jon to apply to the state college I had been accepted to, but this apparently wasn't far enough away from his father to suit him.

"I'm roasting," I finally said, admiring the white circles left on my chest by the pressure of my fingertips.

"Get in the water," Jon suggested, not budging from his spot.

"I'm not getting in that water," I replied. "I think I saw a water moccasin."

"You probably just saw a stick floating by," laughed Jon, surveying the surface of the water through slits, his own cheeks red from the sun.

Neither of us moved, remaining immobile on our flat rock, like two snakes sunning themselves, wearing only cut off jean shorts, our T-shirts and shoes cast aside.

Tired of supporting my torso with my elbows, which were digging into the stone, I laid back, staring into the cloudless sky, which was nearly white from the sun.

"You'll still write, won't you?" I asked, my question more a plea than a query.

"Sure," he replied without looking at me.

I turned my head toward him, wondering what he would look like in the army with all of his shaggy hair cut off. He, too, had fully reclined onto the stone and had cupped his hands behind his head. I watched beads of sweat glistening in the wiry hairs of his armpit and wanted to reach over and touch him, but I knew that, after our earlier romp in the bushes, he was probably done for awhile, weighed down by his guilt and the persistent voice of his father that never seemed to give him peace.

"I'm going to miss you," was all that I was able to manage.

"It's going to be like it always was," replied Jon, exhaustion in his voice.

He had sat up, his legs drawn up to his chest, and was tossing pebbles into the water.

"I'll try to make it back here next summer," he said, skipping a rock across the surface of the slowly moving water.

The impatience in his voice embarrassed me and, fearing I had gone too far—especially on his last day here—I playfully kicked him.

"Maybe I won't be here next summer," I replied, forcing a smile.

Jon glanced at me over his shoulder, his expression stony, then resumed tossing pebbles into the river.

"I hope not," he said, his voice low.

I nervously cleared my throat, knowing fully well what he meant; all either of us wanted was to escape our small towns, to find a place where we felt that we belonged.

"Trust me," said Jon, his voice tender, "we're doing the right thing."

I looked up at him and had to shade my eyes from the sun, which was obscured by his head, creating the illusion that he was wearing a brilliant halo. Wanting to do nothing more than to change the subject, I asked Jon what he wanted to do on his last night in town.

"You're coming over to grandma's house for dinner," he replied, matter-of-factly.

"Okay," I replied, trying to match his indifferent tone. "But I've got to ask my parents first."

Jon smiled at me as if I was crazy, knowing full well that my parents didn't give a damn what I did, a newfound luxury since turning eighteen.

"Whatever," he said, rolling his eyes.

He stood up abruptly and began gathering his things.

"I'm done getting sun," he said, pulling his white tee over his burnt torso.

"Me, too," I agreed, putting on my flip-flops, but opting not to wear my T-shirt over my burn.

We walked up the embankment to my car, a 1965 Mustang convertible, and climbed in. We had left the windows rolled down to keep the car cool because the top was a real bitch to get up and down, but the car was still ghastly hot. I turned the ignition and winced as I touched the steering wheel, which was almost soft to the touch from the heat, while Jon turned on the AC, which only blew warm air in our faces.

"Let it cool down first," I said as I steered the car onto the gravel road and headed toward town.

I let Jon out in front of his grandma's house, a quaint white-washed two story, with a large wrap-around porch, which sported pots of red geraniums hanging from its woodwork. Jon's grandma was in her eighties and, like most people in our town, wore a crucifix around her neck, sporting it as if it were a weapon, a warning to outsiders. Fortunately, though, she liked me, not only because I attended the same church as she did, but also because I mowed her lawn for her. I didn't mind hanging out at her house because she was nearly deaf; anything whispered near her was most likely going to go unheard.

When I got home Mom was sitting in the living room working a crossword puzzle from a paperback she had bought at the grocery store, a hobby of hers. She looked up as I entered the room.

"I'm going over to Jon's grandma's house for dinner," I announced.

"That's nice," she replied, smiling. "What, with this being his last night in town, and all."

I nodded, doing my best not to let myself betray any sign of emotion and walked from the room, climbing the stairs and stripping off my clothes once in my room. I climbed into the shower and turned on the water, which felt good on my burnt skin. I rubbed on copious amounts of lotion to keep from peeling, though the humidity made it nearly impossible to dry of. The lotion became an odd consistency as I rubbed it over the sweat covering my body. I walked down the hall, a towel wrapped around my waist and, once in my room, removed it, relishing the feeling of nakedness. I lay down on my bed, knowing that, in the humidity, the sheets would only remain cool to the touch for a short while. A few feet away on my dresser sat a framed snap-shot of Jon and me from last summer, and the sight of his face stirred me. I closed my eyes, imagining us somewhere else, somewhere the sun was always shining, happy, and free to be together always. Jon's earlier words about how we were doing the right thing kept playing over and over in my head; how, I wondered, could our not being together be the right thing?

I got up from my bed, sweat already beginning to collect on my face and chest, and began dressing, opting for a pair of khakis and a white button down. After kissing Mom goodbye I paused at her flowerbed beside my car and snatched a handful of daisies before heading to Jon's grandma's house. He met me at the screen door, and actually blushed when I presented the daisies.

"You're a freak," he said, but smelling them anyway before passing them off to his grandma, who went in search of a vase.

"I just love daisies," she said, retreating to the kitchen. "Such a simple, yet underappreciated flower."

The aroma of fried chicken and corn on the cob filled the house, and I collapsed onto the sofa and Jon re-took his seat, an overstuffed armchair facing the television, which was loudly blaring *Jeopardy!*

"Dinner smells good," I offered.

"Why the hell are you so dressed up?" asked Jon, a smirk on his face.

"Shut up," I replied, the only reply I knew was necessary.

Jon's grandma said grace before we ate, asking for God's blessings on me and Jon as we "set off into the world," and asked that, though we will be going to different places, He keep our friendship strong. I nudged Jon's foot under the table and, through half-closed eyes, saw him smile. After dinner, Jon and I cleaned off the table and did the dishes while his grandma sat in front of the television in the living room watching the news.

"Looks like a storm may be heading this way," she announced as we walked into the room.

I looked at the screen, which displayed a mass of clouds, dotted with red and orange, moving in our direction.

"Maybe you should just spend the night here," suggested Jon, and his grandma agreed.

I nodded my consent and called my parents to tell them I wouldn't be home. Jon's grandma announced that she was going to bed and asked that, should the weather get bad, we wake her up before we went to the storm cellar. We assured her that we would and bade her goodnight, before heading out to the front porch with ice teas in hand, and settled onto the hanging porch swing. Lightning illuminated the sky to the southwest, and a slight breeze, the first in days, rustled the leaves on the trees. We had turned off the porch light to avoid attracting mosquitoes, but crickets sang from a thicket alongside the dirt road and lightning bugs hovered above the landscape of the yard, their tiny bodies twinkling like miniature constellations.

"I really wish you'd reconsider going to my school," I said, softly, not looking at Jon.

He didn't reply immediately and, for a moment, the only sounds were of the crickets singing their discordant melody and the porch swing creaking beneath our weight.

"It's too late," he said, finally.

"But you don't officially sign up until tomorrow," I replied, excitedly.

I had worked it all out in my head; he just wouldn't show up, could easily get financial aid to attend my school and we could spend the next four years together.

"It's not going to work," he said, his voice calm.

"Why not?" I asked, my voice catching on the words.

Jon suddenly stood up and strode from the porch into the yard. I put down my iced tea and followed, cautiously.

Lightning flashed across the sky and was followed by the low rumble of thunder. A sudden drop in the temperature chilled me as I stood there waiting for Jon to say something. He suddenly turned to face me, his eyes hollow.

"We're doing the right thing!" he shouted, over the increasing wind. "We can't change the way things are, no matter how much we want to."

I don't know what happened but, suddenly, I lunged at him, taking him by surprise and knocking him to the ground and punching him hard. He easily rolled me over and returned my punch, hitting me hard in the mouth. I could taste blood as torrents of rain were suddenly released from the clouds, the storm finally upon us. With a Herculean surge of energy, I flung Jon off of me and pinned him beneath my weight, holding his arms down.

"I love you!" I shouted over the storm. "Don't you understand that?"

Jon heaved me off of him and we both sat, exhausted and wet, in the grass, breathing heavily.

"I love you, too," he said, his voice barely audible over the gale.

Blood trickled from his lip and his messy hair hung wet in his face, but I was so stunned by his words that the details were hardly noticeable. It took me a moment to realize that he had stood up and was offering me his hand, which I accepted, and we made our way to the front porch where we stripped off our wet clothes before entering the house. Despite the fact that she was nearly deaf, we crept carefully up the stairs for fear of waking Jon's grandma and made our way to the spare room where Jon was staying. We stripped off our wet underwear and stood, staring at one another, as lightning flashed outside the window. Jon reached over, and with a trembling hand, stroked my chest. Though my cracked lip ached, I kissed Jon hard on the mouth. He pushed me onto the wrought iron bed and pushed his cock into me with such force that I momentarily forgot about my sore lip. Each thrust was hard and fast, as if he was taking out all of his frustrations, all of his hurt and sorrow on me, a sensation not totally unwelcome.

"I do love you," he whispered, his breath hot on my skin.

"This...this is the right thing," I said, my body wrapped around his. "Let's just get out of here."

We lay on the bed talking until we fell asleep, the sound of the storm growing fainter outside. Soon only the sound of rain on the window was to be heard, along with the sound of Jon's snores, and I fell into a deep, deep sleep.

Jon awoke early the next morning, emerging from between the sheets and pulling on a pair of gym shorts, whispering that I'd better get up before his grandma barged in. I pulled on a pair of Jon's shorts and a T-shirt, and we began throwing everything he owned into a large duffle bag. After a breakfast of scrambled eggs and bacon, Jon hugged his grandma goodbye and promised to write, and we jumped into my Mustang and headed to my parents' house. They were still sleeping when we arrived and Jon waited in the car while I went inside, retrieving the money I'd saved from my part-time job and throwing a few things into my own bag. I quickly wrote my parents a note, telling them that I would call as soon as I could and not to worry, and left it on the kitchen table where I knew they would find it.

The sun was rapidly rising by the time I emerged from the house, so I lowered the top on the Mustang, not caring how long it would take to put back up; the day was going to be a hot one and we were going to be on the road for awhile. As I pulled out onto the interstate, headed west, it occurred to me that we had no idea where we were headed, but it didn't matter. Jon turned up the radio, a smile on his face and, for the first time ever, I knew that I was doing the right thing.

AIN'T GOING NOWHERE

STEPHEN OSBORNE

"YOU'RE GOING, BRAD," Denny said as he folded his arms across his chest with finality. "You need to get out and have some fun."

"It's true," Bob chimed in. Unable to talk without moving his hands, Bob nearly spilled some of his iced tea all over his overly tacky Hawaiian shirt. He cocked his head at me in much the same way my mother used to when I was twelve. "Honey, it's been three years since John died. He wouldn't have wanted you to join a nunnery. It's time to meet people and get some sun. You're so white you look like the belly of a frog."

I knew there was some truth to what my friends were saying, but I wasn't sure that Gay Day at Huntington Beach was the answer to all my prayers. I figured I could put them off the idea with some sound, non-John related arguments. "I can't spend a day at the beach," I protested. I pulled up my T-shirt. "Look at this stomach. My abs are buried under mounds of fat. I'd scare the fish, let alone any guys that might be around. I ain't going nowhere."

Denny shook his head. "You're not fat. You just don't have a six-pack. It's not that big a deal."

"You're skinny," Bob insisted. "And don't let a slight belly keep you from a day of surf and sand. God knows the only six-pack I've ever had bore the Bud Light label. Christ, you're thirty-seven, Brad. You're allowed to look human. And with your looks, no one's going to care."

"I can't swim," I said.

Bob frowned. "Who the fuck goes into the water? Certainly not me. There are things swimming around out there! We'll just go out and lie on our towels, and soak up the sun, and watch the cuties walk by."

I had other reasons to stay at home but they were all quickly shot down. Before I knew it the cooler was packed with sandwiches and drinks and we got into Denny's beat up VW. The sun was already blazing overhead, and the interior of the car was like an oven. Denny's air conditioning had long since given up the ghost so we drove with all the windows down. Bob, in the passenger seat, stuck his head out of the window and sort of resembled a curly-haired spaniel. I almost expected his tongue to hang out of his mouth as he enjoyed the rush of air blowing into his face.

I sat in the back and sullenly watched the palm trees as they flew past. I knew I shouldn't have come. I would be grouchy and just a whole lot of no fun. I'd bring down any chance of Bob and Denny having a good time. Hell, the seagulls would keep away from me knowing that close proximity would result in my sour mood rubbing off on them. I could be blamed for whole legions of seagulls committing suicide.

When we arrived at the beach Bob and Denny bounded out of the car, all smiles and enthusiasm. I slowly climbed out of the back and fanned the back of my shirt where the sweat had plastered it against my skin. As Denny pulled the cooler out of the trunk I watched some guys leaving their own car and making their way down to the beach. One of them reminded me of John. At least, he looked a little like John before the cancer had taken its toll on him. The guy was tall and muscular and had short blond hair that was nearly obscured by a red baseball cap. One of his friends said something and the guy laughed. His laugh was even similar to John's. My heart sank. I'd never fool anyone like that into falling in love with me again. Accidents like that happen only once in a life-time.

Bob's flip-flops managed to make noise even on the packed dirt of the parking area. I marveled at how he always seemed to be making a sound of some kind. If he wasn't talking, some noise had to come from somewhere, it seemed. He hummed as we trudged down to the beach.

It was crowded as hell. Everywhere you looked, gay boys were either sunning themselves, swimming, playing volleyball, or making out. My eyes immediately looked the other way whenever they saw two guys kissing. It's not that it embarrassed me. It just made me a .

little jealous, knowing that such an activity was lost to me now forever.

Denny miraculously found an unoccupied area big enough for
us to put our towels down. He and Bob settled next to each other
and began to smear each other with sunscreen. They worked the
thick oil into their bodies with the unashamed ease that comes
with being lovers for many years. Wordlessly, Denny indicated a
spot at the back of his neck that Bob had missed. Bob put a little
glob of oil onto his fingers and rectified the situation.

I sighed heavily and put on my sunglasses. Maybe I could just
sleep through the whole ordeal. Before I relaxed, though, I knew
I'd have to smear myself with the SPF 30 I'd brought. Bob was
right. I was fish-belly white, and if I didn't coat myself I'd be lobster
red in no time.

I was just about to squirt some of the junk onto my hand when I
heard a voice say, "I can do that for you, if you like."

I looked to my side and my first reaction was that the speaker
was a long-haired teenager. He was thin, with no chest hair and
very little on his arms and legs. As if to make up for this, he'd
grown his hair out down to the middle of his back. There was so
much dark brown hair that it seemed if the guy shook his head the
weight of it would snap his skinny little neck. He also had a pro-
nounced overbite. I smiled politely and shook my head.

"I can handle it, thanks."

He grinned back at me. "I don't doubt that, but it's more fun if
someone else does it for you."

I lowered my voice. I didn't want to embarrass the kid. "I appreciate the offer, but I'd feel awkward having someone half my age
rub lotion on me. Thanks just the same."

A momentary flash of anger showed in his eyes. "I'm twenty-
seven," he said defensively. "I can't help it if I look like a kid."

I looked at him briefly over the tops of my sunglasses. There
were some tell-tale lines around his eyes, so I figured he was telling
the truth about his age. I swallowed the impulse to tell him he'd
look more his age if he cut his fucking hair. Instead I told him, "I
can manage it, thanks."

He shrugged and settled back onto his towel, opening a John
Grisham paperback.

Next to me, Denny must have caught part of our conversation. He leaned in to me and whispered, "Why didn't you let him oil you up?"

I made a dismissive noise. "He's ten years younger than me, and besides that he's not my type. I don't go for twinks."

"Oh, that's right," Denny replied sarcastically. "You only go for the big, beefy types. If they don't remind you of John, you're not interested."

"That's not true," I said defensively. I started rubbing the sunscreen onto my arms.

"You're right. You don't go for anybody, period." Denny didn't wait for my reply. He and Bob shuffled around, finally ending up on their stomachs to allow their backs to tan first.

Done with oiling up, I fished my own book out of my beach bag. It was a Michael Crichton thriller. I noticed the long-haired guy stealing a glance at the cover. He smiled briefly before returning to his own book.

When I flipped a page over, I stole a sideways glance over to the guy. He was engrossed in his own book. I shrugged inwardly. After I'd finished a chapter, I found myself looking again. Unfortunately he chose that moment to look over at me. Luckily my eyes were obscured by my sunglasses. I returned my gaze to the book. I felt like I'd been caught doing something naughty.

Something gnawed at the back of my brain. Why did I keep looking over at the twink? I shook my head and began to envision John as the hero of the Crichton book. That seemed to work. I forgot about the long-haired wonder as I immersed myself in the thriller.

✦

"YOU KNOW I CAN'T PLAY VOLLEYBALL," I protested.

"You don't have to be good," Denny said. He had his hand firmly on my elbow and was leading me over to the game getting ready to start. "The idea is to have fun and meet new people."

"If the idea is to embarrass myself in front of strangers who'll laugh at how bad I am, then I'm your man. Otherwise..."

"I'm going to play," Bob said breezily, "and I suck at it."

I gave him a deadpan look. "You surprise me."

Denny looked at the group that had formed around the net. They seemed to be choosing sides. "Got room for three more?" he asked.

Suddenly I spied the long-haired guy on one side of the net. He pointed at me. "Sure thing. He can be on our side." He gave me a sly smile.

Bob and Denny ended up on the other team. I found myself positioned next to the skinny guy right up at the net. My heart was racing in anticipation of the disaster that was to come. Nervously I said, "I can't play volleyball."

"No one cares," the long haired guy said. "I'm Jeff, by the way."

"Brad."

"Well, Brad," he said with a grin, "if you don't think you can hit the ball back, just shout out 'yours' and I'll hit it over for you."

I was about to reply when the game started. The ball began to fly back and forth over the net, and I began to pray that it wouldn't come anywhere near me. Suddenly, there it was: Sailing over the net right at me. I tried to knock it back over, but it refused to go forward. It went to the left, right to Jeff. He leaped up, his hair flying everywhere, and blasted the damn thing over the net. The other side failed to return it, so I guess we scored.

"Nice pass," Jeff told me, slapping my back.

"Um...yeah." I wasn't about to tell him it hadn't been intentional.

Jeff was a really good player; although how he managed to see anything I have no idea. Every time he jumped up to hit the ball, his hair billowed out like a dark brown cloud. I found myself watching his chest as he smacked the ball. For a skinny little bastard, he didn't have a bad chest.

While I was daydreaming, the ball smacked me right in the forehead. Everyone laughed. I must have turned twenty shades of red. Jeff touched my elbow. "That was my fault," he said. "I should have got that one."

He was lying, of course. It had been totally my ball, but I appreciated him trying to take responsibility.

Finally we came to the moment I was dreading. It became time for me to serve the fucking ball. I recalled all the failures of gym class as I got into position. Then I thought of John. He could play any sport. He didn't worry about things, he just did them. I pictured John in my mind and gave the ball a hit. It flew off to the right, not even coming close to the net.

I watched it roll across the sand. "Fuck," I muttered.

Jeff, in his baggy red swimming trunks, retrieved the ball. He brought it to me and was suddenly standing right behind me. Close behind me, in fact. Very close behind me. "Let me show you how to serve," he said.

Someone on the other side of the net shouted out a protest.

"Hey, fuck off!" Jeff yelled back. To me he said, "Ignore everyone else. Just hold the ball like this, and your other hand should come up like this." He directed my hands. I hit the ball and it went right over the net. "See?" he said, grinning.

✦

HIS SKIN WAS TOUCHING MY SKIN. His cheek brushed my shoulder. I glanced at his face and he looked like an angel. I couldn't recall the last time I'd seen anyone so beautiful. Even his overbite was gorgeous.

He hugged me suddenly. I don't know what happened, but all I know was suddenly I was sporting the biggest erection I'd had in years. Blushing, I broke away from him. I wasn't ready for this. Tears filled my eyes as I ran as fast as I could away from the game. I vaguely heard Bob shouting after me, but I didn't stop. I couldn't stop. I just ran.

✦

THE SUN WAS GOING DOWN, and the horizon was fiery mix of reds, oranges, pinks, and blues. It was beautiful. I'd found myself miles down from where Bob and Denny and I had entered the beach. Frankly, I wasn't sure just where I was. Somewhere in my wanderings I'd discovered an unmanned cooler containing half a bottle of Jack Daniels and knowing the beach had a no-alcohol policy I confiscated it. Knowing the mood I was in, I drank it.

I stood clutching the empty bottle, staring off into the sea, feeling like I'd let John down somehow.

A mist seemed to be forming before me. I don't know if it was an actual mist or if my drunken eyes were clouding over. The mist almost had a human shape to it. It reminded me of John. John, who'd always been my rock.

I sniffed and said to the mist, "It's nice seeing you again."

The mist refused to answer.

"I guess it's no secret that you're a tough act to follow," I went on to say. "I've never really gotten over you leaving me like that. You were the strong one. You should have survived."

There was a sound behind me, but I was too intoxicated for it to really register in my mind. I went on.

"I was wondering...if you'd mind if I was interested in someone new. I need to know if that would bother you."

If anything, the mist seemed to get somewhat thicker.

"He's nothing like you," I said. "He's skinny. He's a twink, I guess you'd say. And he's got too much fucking hair. But there's something about him. I'd like to find out what that is, if it's okay with you."

I swear to God the mist nodded. Tears began to stream down my cheeks. I felt someone hug me from behind, and there was Jeff. That explained the sound I'd heard. I wondered how long he'd been standing there. Then I realized I didn't care. He rested his head on my shoulder.

"You're drunk," he said. There was no accusation in his tone.

"Yes," I admitted. "Yes, I am."

He looked out to sea. The mist was gone. "You must have loved him very much," he said softly.

Unable to stop crying, I nodded. "I did." I'd have said more, but it was hard enough to get out just the two small words.

We stood, his arms around me, for what seemed like an eternity. Finally Jeff said, "I hope I'm the skinny twink you were talking about."

I turned and ran my hands through that mass of hair. "You are," I said. I kissed him softly on the lips. I wanted to kiss him again, but something made my legs wobble and I nearly stumbled. I've never passed out from drinking before, but I knew I was close this time.

Jeff held me up. "You need someone to take care of you," he said, laughing lightly. "You're a mess."

I knew he was referring to my drunkenness, but I spoke of my life. "It's a huge mess. Not something to be undertaken lightly."

Jeff smiled. "I ain't going nowhere," he said.

We walked back down the beach with him helping me walk. The sun was quickly dying and it was growing darker and darker. I didn't take much notice. I only knew this skinny guy had his arms around me and that was okay by me.

SUMMER KISSES AND ICE CREAM DREAMS

J. M. SNYDER

I'M ON BREAK, leaning against the counter behind the soda machine and stirring a drink more ice than soda, when the bell above the door chimes. "Back to work, Sean," my boss Chad tells me.

Ignoring him, I glance at the customers. Three friends—a Romano from the pizzeria down the boards, and with him, a couple. The girl is pretty in her bikini top and shorts but the guy, with his arm draped around her shoulders, is only *the* sexiest boy I've ever seen. I told myself I wasn't going to do it again, fall for someone in the summertime, but before his ice blue eyes even glance my way, I'm gone.

"Welcome to the Good Shoppe Lollipop," Chad announces. I groan into my drink; I hate the name of this place. "What'll it be tonight, guys?"

I watch the stranger with his arm around the girl as he looks over the menu. His neck curves gracefully, his Adam's apple a fleshy knob I want to suckle. I can imagine what it'd feel like to trail my fingers down that smooth throat, to brush that short blond hair up from his nape and kiss behind his ears. I'm going to have wet dreams about him tonight, I just know it.

"We're thinking," the Romano kid says, leaning over the ice cream case. Tony, I think it is. Big and burly, head full of dark curls. Nothing like the lithe blond and his girl. When he sees me staring, Tony asks his friend, "Hey Andrew, what was that thing you wanted to try?"

His name is Andrew. He looks at me dead on, then clears his throat and shrugs. "Something warm and sweet," he says, his gaze burning into me. "With lots of cream." He turns to Chad. "You have anything like that?"

God.

Chad frowns at the menu. "Well …" If he tells them about the hot fudge sundaes, I'll just die. *Warm and sweet, lots of cream.* And he's already *got* a girl? Damn. "How about a hot fudge sundae? Perfect way to end a perfect day, don't you think?"

I roll my eyes. Of *course* I have to work for Mr. Comedian. Andrew stands there smiling because he knows he wasn't talking about the sundaes, and he knows *I* know he wasn't talking about ice cream … hell, from the smirk on her face even his *girl* knows what he's talking about, and if I wasn't already hiding in the corner behind the soda fountain, I'd sink into the floor and just disappear. My knees are weak from that pale gaze, that deep voice, and any moment now I could melt away like chocolate. I imagine myself as chocolate beneath his hands, melting into his touch, moaning his name, his lips like cherries on my skin, his tongue a swirl of sensation across my body. Tony's as oblivious as Chad. "Fudge sounds good."

Andrew shrugs as I shake ice from my drink into my mouth. "Maybe I'll go for something hard," he says. The ice cracks loudly between my teeth when I bite down on it.

Tony frowns. "You want something warm and hard?"

Damn it the hell I'm blushing, I know it, flushed and red—I'm *not* prepared for this. Any other night I'd flirt back; it's summer and there are a million guys on the boardwalk, but this one makes me ache as if I'm waking from a good dream, one I don't want to lose in the daylight. If he didn't have a girl with him, if the Romano kid wasn't here, if *Chad* wasn't here, maybe I'd flirt back. If I could even look at him and remember how to speak. Tony squints at the menu and has the audacity to ask, "You want a Popsicle or something?" Looking around Andrew, he asks the girl, "You want to split a sundae with me, Lori?"

"Sure." She ducks out from under Andrew's arm and, with a twitch of her hip, bumps him over as she squeezes in between her friends, edging him closer to my end of the counter. "Move over." Andrew complies, sliding down a little, down towards me. To Chad she says, "We'll get a sundae then, and give this boy something hard to suck on."

Just let them leave already. Get me through the rest of this night and get me home before I come just thinking about this guy, and Jesus please don't let Chad say— "Are you done your break yet, Sean? 'Cause I need a sundae."

"With nuts," Lori says, winking at me, and Andrew laughs. "And lots of cream."

Fuck.

I busy myself making the sundae, trying to ignore them as I work, but I feel hot stares on my ass when I bend over for another can of whipped cream and his girl laughs again, just a little breathless giggle. When I set the sundae down on the counter, I don't look up. My cheeks are red and I'm not going to look at him, I can't, I *won't* …

He touches my hand as he takes the sundae and I wait for him to say something but he's silent. Finally I look up at him, and he smiles slightly. "Thanks, Sean."

His friends are seated at a table on the other side of the room, Chad scoops out a cone for a little girl, and we're alone at the counter right now. *You're welcome,* I want to say, but I'm lost in his eyes and when I open my mouth to speak, nothing comes out. Then his smile widens … how stupid do I look? Standing here staring at him, his hand warm over mine, the ice cream cold through the metal bowl beneath my fingers. "Anytime," I whisper. It's all I can muster.

"I'll keep that in mind." As he joins his friends, his girl waves my way, just a little wiggle of her fingers that makes me hate her, because tonight she'll be in his arms and I'll just have my empty bed and my hand, and the memory of the short time he was here.

✦

HE HAUNTS MY DREAMS, like I knew he would, and I wake up angry because I'll never see him again. It's only June but my whole summer is shot to hell—I'll ache for him every night, and anyone I meet won't live up to what he could have been to me. Yeah, I've had boyfriends before, guys I met on the beach or on the piers when the rides were in full swing and the summer night stretched away like taffy, that sweet and sticky. But there was never anyone who made me hurt just looking at him the way Andrew does. I never imagined I wanted another summer fling or sweet God, something *more*, not until he came into the Shoppe and tore my world out from beneath me before disappearing into the ebb and flow of the crowd.

As I walk to work the next day, I look in every face I pass for his, hoping to see those light blue eyes, so much like clear sea-glass winking in the sun. Even though I tell myself it's stupid, he's gone, give it up already Sean, forget about him. My heart quickens whenever I see short blond hair or hear the deep bass tones of rich laughter. By the time I get to the Shoppe I'm pissed because I didn't see him and it's my own fault for even looking. Who am I to him? The boy who made his girl's sundae. At work Chad glares at me when I come around the counter. "You're late."

"Five minutes," I tell him. Before he can say anything else I push through the double doors to the back room and sit down on the closest milk crate. I need to forget Andrew. He said what, three words to me? Maybe five? And I've had a hard-on ever since. I can't move without my pants chafing my crotch and my mind is filled with thoughts of him naked and glistening above me, his hands like a promise on my skin, his teeth biting my nipples. I can imagine him entering me, I *feel* it, a rush of desire that curls through me until I want to cry because how can I live knowing he's somewhere in this world and not with me?

Chad kicks open the door. "Customers, Sean."

I push myself up wearily. "I'm coming."

Tying on my apron, I'm about to shove through the door to get to work when I hear a familiar giggle. A bright, girlish voice says, "Hi there! Remember me?" My heart catches in my throat and I step up to the doors, pressing my nose against the dingy glass ...

It's her.

Andrew's girl. Lori. Leaning over the counter, smiling up at Chad, who has a clear view down her tank top and doesn't try to hide the fact that he's looking. "How could I forget a face like yours?" he asks, turning on the charm. Who's he kidding? It's not her face he remembers.

But she laughs again and gives him a coy look. "That boy you had working here last night." She means me. When Chad nods, she asks, "Sean? Is he here?"

To my surprise Chad shakes his head. "He's not in yet."

Liar. I'm tempted to push through the doors and prove him wrong, but what's she want me for, anyway?

Maybe she's asking for Andrew.

Because that thought twists my stomach into knots and flutters my breath, I don't let it go any further. The idea that Andrew sent her in here looking for me is too much. It's too wild ... I shift to the window in the other door and try to see if she came in alone. I tell myself I'm not disappointed when I don't see anyone else but her and Chad and ...

And Andrew outside, leaning against the window, watching her closely.

Shit. I duck down and try to think, but my mind's not cooperating. *He's outside. He's outside waiting for her and he sent her in here to ask about me and —*

No.

Thank God there's a reasonable voice somewhere inside me, even if it's just a tiny little squeak. *No, he's with her, I don't know what they're doing back today but it's got nothing to do with you.*

Then why did she ask for me?

I have no answer to that.

Why *did* she ask for me? I hear her tell Chad to give me this number only she doesn't say it's *her* number, she doesn't say to call *her.* I'm reading too much into this, into everything. Why would he be interested in me?

For the same reason you're into him. He saw you and fell just as hard only you don't know it, you won't know it until you go out there and Chad gives you the number and you call it to see who answers. And I bet it's not her.

I wait until I hear the bell ring and Chad kicks at the door again, telling me to get to work. When I push through the doors there's no one in the Shoppe, but I can see Andrew and Lori through the window as they walk away down the boardwalk. Even though I know the answer I have to ask, "Who was that?"

"Some girl." Chad tosses me a napkin with a tight feminine

script on it. '*Not who you think,*' it reads, written in red ink, with a local number and an '*A*' like a scarlet letter written on it. *Andrew*. So it *is* from him. He really *did* send her in here looking for me.

I fold the napkin into my back pocket, and when Chad asks if I'm going to call, I shrug like I don't know, but who am I kidding?

✦

WHEN NIGHT FALLS, the boardwalk comes alive outside our windows. The rides light up the darkness and vendors call out to the tourists, win one for the little lady, step right up, give it your best shot. As Chad props open the door, I pick up the phone and dial the number I've already memorized. The phone rings in my ear and I watch Chad struggle with the placard that proclaims we have the best sundaes on the boards. I count four rings, five, I'm just about to hang up when someone answers. "Romano's," a man says, the Brooklyn thick in his voice … she gave me the number to the pizzeria?

"Um," I don't know what to say. "Is Andrew there?"

"Just a minute." The phone knocks against the counter as he sets it down. "Andrew?" I hear him yell. "Tony, tell Andrew he has a call."

My heart pounds in my ears, the rush of blood loud as the surf, drowning out the rest of the world, and then *he* picks up the phone, his voice as deep as I remember it, a little breathless because he hurried to answer. "Hello?"

What am I supposed to say now?

"Hello?" he asks again.

I hang up. I can't even say hi, I'm a wuss, he gave me his number and I called it and chickened out. *Fuck*. Chad comes in and frowns at me. "You can at least look busy."

"There's no one here," I mutter. I can't believe I hung up on Andrew. "How about we close up and go home?"

Chad laughs. "How about you watch the place while I run out for dinner?" When it's just the two of us working, Chad makes a run down the boardwalk for something to eat—we both get sick of ice cream after a while and we're only a few blocks from the midway, with its numerous fast food joints and hoagie shops and …

Romano's Pizzeria.

Once Chad leaves maybe I can get up the courage to call Andrew again. Maybe this time I can think of something to say.

But I'm scared he knows it was me who called. He'll wonder why I hung up, and I can't bring myself to try again. So I lean over the counter and doodle on one of the napkins, writing his name over and over like some lovesick schoolboy. He gave me his number and that means he likes me, right? I draw a heart around his name and color in the edges with my red pen, wishing I could call him again and not feel like a fool.

"Hey there."

I look up to find him standing in front of the counter. I ball up the napkin before he can see his name scribbled across it but from the smirk on his face, I think he already saw. "Hey."

Why didn't I hear him come in? *The door's open.* So he knew it was me, he had to or he would've never walked down here to see me. Trying to remember my manners, I ask, "What can I do you for?"

His smile widens—that didn't come out the way I wanted. My cheeks heat up and I roll my eyes, he probably thinks I'm an *idiot.* "I mean …"

He leans across the counter and pins me down with that crystalline gaze of his, trapping me. I can't move, can't think, can't breathe, and his voice is low and husky when he asks, "What do you have in mind?"

Right now a lot of things swirl through my mind but they all involve the two of us naked and sweaty and locked in a passionate embrace, writhing in throes of lust and desire and the way he's grinning makes me think his mind is full of the same sordid things. Playing it safe, I ask, "Did you want some ice cream?"

He shrugs, a little roll of his shoulders that makes me want to reach out and touch him, just to see if he's real, but I don't dare. "I guess."

I get the impression that's not what he wanted me to say. *But you have a girl.* And where exactly does she figure into this? What girlfriend goes out of her way to hook her boy up with another?

I don't ask. Instead I suggest, "Try the Mocha Almond Fudge." He stares at me and I can't look away, I know I'm blushing but I have to add, "It has nuts in it. Do you like nuts?"

That deep laugh again, and the twinkle in his eye tells me we're thinking the same thing. "Are they hard?"

God. "Yeah, but the chocolate melts in your mouth, it's so good."

He raises one eyebrow. "How good is it, Sean?"

"Wouldn't you like to find out?" I tease.

"How about a sample then?"

Are we still talking about ice cream? Because I'm not. Not by a long shot.

I feel him watching me as I open the freezer and scoop ice cream into one of the tiny sample cups. I hope he sees my taut muscles and wonders how it would feel to be held in my arms, because they ache for him right this second.

It's more than the usual sample but then again, he isn't the usual customer, is he? I smash the ice cream into the little cup, getting it all over my hand in the process. It's cold and creamy and I'm going to lick it away the minute he takes the cup from me. But when I hold it out he leans forward, lips closing over my fingers with a warmth and softness that feels heavenly. He stares at me, daring me to say something, and I can't because his tongue is licking between my fingers and doing horrible things to my stomach, making my groin throb, making me *hurt* from wanting him. He takes the cup from my nerveless fingers while his lips stay latched to my hand, his tongue tasting my skin. Then he slips my fingertips into his mouth and oh my God I *can't* pull away, not now, not ever.

Finally he lets go and smiles at me. "I like the way it tastes." Is he talking about the ice cream or me? "Very sweet."

"Do you want more?" I ask, my voice thick.

He smiles. "When do you get off tonight?"

Almost got off just now, I think, but he doesn't need to know that. "Ten."

"Can I come by then?" he asks. "Walk you home?"

"Please?"

✦

WHEN MY SHIFT ENDS I'm out the door, looking through the crowds for Andrew but he's nowhere around. Crossing the boardwalk to lean against the railing, I stare past the lights and noise from the piers into the darkness beyond, where the sea mutters to itself. There's a strong breeze coming off the shore that makes me wish I brought a jacket. Maybe Andrew will put his arm around me and pull me close. Maybe he'll come in—my apartment's a mess but I don't think the lights will be on for long. I can't believe he wants to walk me home. *Me.* I wonder if he thought about me last night, if he woke up with my name on his lips, my eyes behind his. I wonder —

"Hey," Andrew says, right behind me, his lips brushing against my ear as one arm snakes around my waist. I turn to find myself caught up in his arms. His eyes reflect the neon lights of the boards and his hand is so warm on my back that I can't keep from grinning. "Sorry to keep you waiting."

"No problem." The night around us has disappeared, the crowds, the rides, everything is gone but him and me and the railing I'm leaning against, his arm behind me. He's wearing a shirt that says *Romano's* on it, and I tap against the word with one finger. "You work there?" I feel his nipple harden beneath the fabric as I trail my finger down his chest.

His smile widens. "I've known Tony forever." Leaning closer, he whispers, "You smell sweet, Sean. Like dessert." His breath tickles my neck, and his hand clenches at my back, balling my shirt into his fist. "A perfect way to end a perfect day."

I laugh, embarrassed. "God, you and Chad." When Andrew snickers against my neck, I place my hands flat on his chest as if to hold him back. "Can I ask you a question?"

His hand tightens against my back. "She's just a friend."

Am I that easy to read? "How'd you know that's what I was going to ask?" But my heart races—she's just a friend, he's practically holding me in his arms, he's going to walk me home and she's just a friend, that's it.

"You're cute," he says, leading me away from the railing. "Tell me you don't have someone waiting up for you."

"I don't." His arm drops from my waist as we walk through the crowds, but my back tingles where he touched me. I can imagine what it would be like to make love to him, to have those hands touch every inch of my body, igniting my flesh and setting my heart aflame. We walk through streets still busy this late because it's summertime and morning may never come. It's just the two of us together, him close beside me, his elbow brushing my arm.

Once we're away from the boardwalk, he takes my hand without a word, lacing his fingers through mine. Just when I think there's nothing to say between us, Andrew laughs. "I never thought I'd do this."

"What do you mean? Do what?"

He glances at me, that smile on his face hard to see in the darkness. "I saw you last night and haven't stopped thinking about you since. You're like the sea, Sean. You've gotten inside me and I don't want to get you out." His hand squeezes mine in a reassuring gesture. "I just met you, I know. You think I'm a freak."

"I think you're beautiful," I say before I can stop myself, but it's the truth. I want to lose myself in him—if anyone's the sea it's him, I want to drown in him and never resurface. With a tug on my hand, he reels me in, his arm settling across my shoulders as if there's no place else it belongs.

When we finally reach my apartment, I don't want to let him go so soon. "Want to come in?"

"I'd love to," he says. "But we've got the whole summer ahead. I don't want to wake up tomorrow and hate myself because we rushed through this."

"What's this?"

"Us."

He leans forward, eyes shut, until his lips close over mine in a kiss that will keep me warm all night. "Can I come by tomorrow?" His breath feathers across my cheek and I nod because I don't trust myself to speak.

He smells like musky cologne and pepperoni, and his hands are strong on my waist, his lips soft on my own. With his mouth over mine, I admit, "I'm going to dream of you tonight."

"Sweet dreams then, Sean," he says, kissing me again. As he pulls away I steal another kiss, and another. I can't stop myself—he's addicting like candy, sugary and more sweet than any flavor in the ice cream case back at the Shoppe. "I'll see you tomorrow."

He kisses me once more before turning away. I can't wait for tomorrow to come.

KC AT BAT

TOM MENDICINO

I SPENT THE SUMMER before last answering to the name Buddy. My social security card, my driver's license, my passport, all the official documentation of my existence, still confirmed my identity as Charles Beresford. But no one on the crew wasted any time or effort trying to remember if I went by Charlie or Chuck or Chad. Or Bill or Mike or Dave for that matter. I was beneath contempt, the lowest of the low, the worst possible brand of sausage, their name for the college kids who swelled their ranks from May through August, the peak months for America on the move. Meat, that's all we were. Dead meat if we slowed down the job or otherwise screwed up.

My uncle, an officer at the savings and loan, had persuaded Oliver Ryan, his golf partner and the local franchisee of the nation's largest long-distance moving company, to put me to work until I departed for Hanover, New Hampshire. "What the fuck am I supposed to do with you?" Mr. Ryan sputtered, obviously expecting someone who weighed more than a hundred forty pounds. Below-prime interest rates and generous loan repayment terms being powerful incentives, he suppressed his natural instinct to spin me on my heel and send me home before I had an opportunity to make a claim on his worker's comp insurance. The dispatcher, however, didn't appreciate being told to featherbed his crews with a pale scarecrow constructed of toothpicks and rubber bands. The drivers threatened an uprising, objecting to being forced to pick up the slack and carry any deadweight assigned to their trucks, but Mr. Ryan laid down the law, crushing the revolt by 6:45 AM .

"The kid will put on some muscle by July and, until then, have him do most of the packing and make him clean the shit out of the basements and attics. Think you can handle that buddy?" he asked, grinding a Marlboro Red between his teeth.

Maybe Dartmouth was a cruel tease, a macabre joke. I was certain I'd never live to pass through its ivy-covered gates. Even on light duty, I ached in places I'd never known existed. My crime was needing tuition money and the sentence was long days loading the contents of the split levels and ranches of Schenectady and Albany for a one-way trip to the Sunbelt, rarely finishing before dinner time, sometimes not until after dark. I crawled home to a tube of Ben-Gay and was sound asleep by ten, still exhausted when my mother pulled me out of bed before sun-up and pushed me out the door, thermos in hand. It was a miracle I'd survived through Thursday. The first four days had left me a broken man. There was no question the next three months would kill me. I decided to resign at the end of the week. Sweating over deep fryers at McDonald's seemed like paradise compared to this living hell.

Friday morning I was assigned to a load-and-deliver cross-town move. My last hurrah was going to be a twelve-hour day with the driver cracking the whip because it wasn't a job transfer and the client was paying out of his own pocket. The hell with it I thought. Why suffer any further when I was quitting today anyway? I summoned my courage and tried to overcome the onset of dry mouth. I was minutes away from announcing my intentions when a hand clasped my shoulder and a sympathetic voice promised solidarity in misery.

"Looks like we pulled the shit end of the stick. Guess it's you and me today buddy."

My knees went wobbly, my voice tight. The name on his birth certificate was Kevin Conroy, but he'd been called KC since his first Little League season. His ability behind the plate and his prowess in the outfield were almost mythical; his batting average and number of errorless innings were legendary, The Mohawk Valley High School yearbook had entire pages dedicated to the Mighty KC, the winner of every prize awarded by his graduating class. Best Athlete. Best Looking. Most Likely to Succeed. I was as awestruck as I had been a few years earlier, when I was a sophomore, my puny existence unworthy of acknowledgement, and he was a junior, emerging from the steamy mist of the locker room, his thick black chest hair slick from the shower, his big brown eel slapping against his thigh, snapping a towel at a dude he affectionately called his shit-bag.

"You want one of these?" he mumbled through a mouth full of Boston Creme, offering me the doughnut box.

It was going to be a long day and the crew was small, just KC and me. Squeezed into the cab, I kept nudging closer to Bruno, the driver whose easy-going nature had been rewarded by being saddled with me three days running. I was intent on avoiding even the slightest physical contact with KC who was too engrossed in manicuring his nails to notice me squirming.

"You ain't getting that shit all over my truck are you, Superstar?" Bruno grunted.

"Relax, bro. It's cool," KC said, tossing the clippings out the window.

Cool was his birthright. Not cool as in 'hip' like the assholes who told you they were into the band you'd just discovered before it became so passé that only the worst geeks were downloading their music. KC was the real thing, cool as in Bond, James Bond, cool. Capable, confident, slightly distracted as if he occupied an entirely different space than ordinary mortals and the rest of the world was only occasionally worthy of his attention.

The load-and-deliver was easier than expected, no Victorian armoires to maneuver, no king-size mattresses to grapple. I did my fair share of humping, the professional terminology for hauling shit in and out of the van on your back. I hustled all day, carrying weights I couldn't have lifted a week ago, driven by the fear of being thought inadequate by KC. Not that he would have cared. KC knew only one work speed. Slow. Bruno could only mutter snide remarks under his breath because KC, like me but for different reasons, was off-limits. Driving back to the depot in the hazy summer dusk, Bruno made a pointed comment, the highest praise for sure, sincere but also meant to embarrass the member of his crew for whom such compliments would not be forthcoming.

"You know buddy, keep working like that and you'll be a hell of a humper soon."

KC acted as if he hadn't heard but I saw him rolling his eyes as

Bruno dropped us at the warehouse. Not knowing how to talk to a legend, I kept my mouth shut while we waited for Bruno to park the truck and unlock the front door so we could punch the time clock. KC helped himself to a pinch of chew and offered me the bag. I waved it away, clueless about what to do with it.

"Smart guy," he said. "I'm trying to quit."

The brown juice would have turned my stomach if it had been dripping off anyone else's chin.

"Where'd you go to school?" he asked.

"Mohawk Valley."

"Me too," he said, as if I wouldn't know.

A chorus of Jiminy Crickets serenaded the full moon as it emerged in the darkening sky. I heard KC's casual question as Bruno strolled toward us, keys in hand, but was too stunned to kick start my tongue and answer.

"So, you wanna hang out tonight?"

Me? Hanging with KC? Impossible. I'd be exposed in an hour. I couldn't play pool. The only card game I knew was hearts. I'd never done tequila shots and hadn't drunk enough beers in my sorry eighteen years to make a six-pack. I'd pass out on the spot if some girl pulled up her blouse and offered me a feel. I'd embarrass him in front of his posse. He'd be forced to humiliate me to save face. Shitbag would be the kindest thing he'd call me.

"Sure," I said, stuttering, as if I had a choice.

So I was relieved, and more than a little disappointed, when KC's idea of a big Friday night was chugging liter bottles of warm Pepsi and watching *Field of Dreams*. His parents had a cabin on the Finger Lakes where they spent every summer weekend so we had the house to ourselves. He had an American Legion game Saturday at noon, then a night game in Newburgh at seven. He needed eight hours of shuteye to be at the top of his form. There was still time for a couple hands of blackjack or a game of Nintendo after the credits rolled. I pulled Stratego from a stack of board games and challenged him to a match.

"No way buddy. I always lose that fucking game. You have to think too much."

So we settled on video games and, of course, his quick reflexes and hand-eye coordination made short work of my offensive moves. It didn't help that I was distracted by his hairy legs and barely concealed crotch.

"You gonna spend the night?" he asked as nonchalantly as if the invitation had already been accepted.

My dad, whose mission in life was to protect me from temptations like water bongs and keg parties, was convinced that bad influences lurked in the shadows. But when I called to say I wanted to stay at Kevin Conroy's, "yes, THE KC," he told to have the car back by noon and to ask if KC was interested in playing in his softball league.

"Cool," KC said when I told him I'd gotten the green light. "Man, it's time for sleep." He tossed me a pillow and blanket to make up a bed on the couch. I slept like a baby, dead to the world. Hours later, in the middle of the pitch black night, I woke up, sure I was still dreaming, not believing until he was almost finished that the Mighty KC in the flesh and blood was lying on top of me, grinding and rubbing, skin on skin, panting in my ear.

"Shit buddy, it feels so fucking good."

◆

"EIGHT MORE HOURS buddy and you'll be looking at Ryan Moving and Storage in your rear view mirror," the dispatcher said after giving me my last assignment. By six o'clock, KC and I would be doing seventy-five on the Thruway, headed for Jersey.

Old Man Ryan had been right. The work had gotten easier after the first brutal weeks. If I hadn't quite turned into Charles Atlas, at least I had the suggestion of pectorals and biceps. My acne had disappeared except for a spray of pimples across my shoulders. I was absolutely certain my voice had dropped an octave or two even though there was no scientific evidence that chewing, as opposed to smoking, tobacco thickened the vocal cords. Ten weeks of humping had made a man of me and by humping I didn't mean hauling refrigerators and chests-of-drawers.

Every Friday afternoon, KC asked the unnecessary question: "So, you wanna hang out tonight?" The only variation in the routine was ordering pizza or Chinese takeout. KC slouched in his father's recliner, dangling his bare legs and slugging Pepsi, absorbed in *Bull Durham* or *Bang the Drum Slowly* or *Major League*. The night

would end with an encore of *Field of Dreams* or an hour of Game
Boy or Texas Hold-em while Ricky Nelson chirped be-bop-baby on
the sound system. KC had a decent music collection, a lot of Pearl
Jam and Soundgarden, but mostly he listened to records that had
belonged to his dad—Gene Pitney, Dion, and especially Ricky Nelson. I knew all the lyrics of Ricky's *Sixteen Greatest Hits* by the Fourth
of July. After KC called lights out, we'd wrestle on the sofa until our
briefs were around our ankles and he'd pinned me to the cushions. I let him put his dick in my mouth and his finger up my butt
after he promised I could do the same to him. He'd head up to his
bedroom when we finished and I would toss and turn, unable to
sleep. I'd known from the first night KC and I were different. We
wanted the same thing but we wanted it in different ways. I wanted
KC and he wanted someone to rub up against, someone peripheral
to the things that meant most to him, someone too timid and
grateful to expose him. We talked about it only once, the Saturday
KC reluctantly agreed to let me drive him to his game after his car's
accelerator fluttered and died.

"You're not going to embarrass me, are you?" he asked, not entirely persuaded I wasn't going to pull out the pom-poms and start
cheering his name on the third base line. But KC was as supersti-
tious as every other ballplayer and insisted I come to every game after he had two home runs and six RBIs that afternoon. And if there
had been any doubt that I was a better good luck charm than a rab-
bit's foot, he hit for the cycle the next week, impressing the Mets
scout looking at prospects. He played the game like an artist, gracefully and effortlessly, capable of feats no one else on the field
would even attempt. His teammates idolized him; he was gracious
and humble and if he seemed unapproachable and a bit distant
they assumed it was because of the wide gap between their abilities.
KC didn't snap towels at his buddies anymore and kept to himself
off the field. He never called his teammates to check out *wassup*
and he always had an excuse if they invited him to hang and party.

Which is why I never expected to find Jay Delduco, the catcher
on his Legion team, in the back seat of KC's car as we headed for
the Meadowlands.

"Because Delduco's the one who scored the Pearl Jam tickets after the show sold out," KC explained.

"What's that shit you're playing?" Delduco complained two songs into the *Sixteen Greatest Hits*. "Who's that fag singing?"

"Ricky Nelson, a-hole, and he got more in pussy in a week than you'll see in a lifetime," KC said, trying not to sound irritated as he tossed the CD case over his shoulder.

"I don't know man. This dude looks pretty gay to me," Delduco concluded after a quick study of the cover photo.

KC hit the eject button and loaded a bootleg Pearl Jam. Delduco was too busy trying to match Eddie Vedder note for note to notice that KC's knuckles were white from gripping the steering wheel and that he was grinding a plug of chew between his molars. KC didn't relax until we were sitting in traffic on the Garden State Parkway, Delduco snoring and farting in his sleep, and I slipped Ricky back into the player.

"Sorry about the asshole, buddy," he apologized. Subject acknowledged and just as quickly closed, he turned up the volume and hit the repeat button, playing "Lonesome Town" again.

We found a Travel Lodge in the industrial wasteland outside Elizabeth, New Jersey that only charged sixty bucks a night, a cool twenty dollars each. Delduco took one look at the pair of double beds and announced he didn't care where we slept as long as it wasn't in his bed since he wasn't going queer tonight. I said I'd take the floor. The rough carpet and the rumbling traffic speeding down the highway kept me awake. I spent most of the night pounding my thin pillow and rolling from side to side.

"Hey buddy, you okay down there?" KC whispered.

"Yeah."

"You wanna change places?"

"I'm okay," I said, suddenly content when I realized KC couldn't sleep either.

Saturday afternoon, Delduco insisted we meet up with his cousins before leaving for the stadium. They were sisters and the older one, Elise, looked like the chick on the television show that married Van Halen. She latched onto KC, asking him stupid, flirty questions, teasing him and giggling when he caught her sneaking one of his fries. Delduco and his cousins passed a joint and, once the band started ripping through its set, Elise grabbed KC by the arm, jumping up and down with the music and pushing her tits in his face. He didn't seem to mind, but he didn't look enthusiastic when, during "Alive," she tried to force her tongue past his clenched teeth. There was a party in Teaneck after the concert; she promised KC a wild time and, yeah, I could come too. Delduco thought KC had lost his mind when he begged off, saying he wanted to go back to the motel. Suit yourself, he said before driving off with his cousins, just make sure you don't leave before I get back in the morning.

"That girl wanted to fuck you," I said, as surprised as Delduco that he'd passed on the invitation.

"You know what? Let's find some beer," he said as we walked to the car.

I couldn't have gotten served by a blind bartender in the darkest, crummiest dive in New Jersey and KC was carded the first place he tried. But the kid at the liquor outlet store didn't hesitate to take a twenty for two sixes of cheap beer.

"Buddy, we're gonna get drunk tonight," KC promised as he pulled up to the Travel Lodge.

Sixty bucks a night only gets you basic cable, so after the recap on *Baseball Tonight* the only thing on television was a rerun of *Porky's* with no tits and asses, the dirty words bleeped and a ten-minute commercial break every six minutes. The high school sluts in the movie reminded me of Delduco's cousin. Half-loaded for the first time in my life and liberated from my inhibitions, I turned to KC and, emboldened, asked him a question.

"Have you ever fucked a girl?"

I wasn't the only one in that motel room feeling the effects of alcohol. KC fell back on the bed and sighed at the ceiling.

"If you tell anyone I'll have to kill you," he said.

"I won't."

He propped himself on his elbow and, staring me in the eye, solicited a solemn promise.

"You swear?"

"I swear."

He flopped back on the mattress and looked away.

"I tried it a few times. It didn't work. I guess I wasn't very interested."

I had nothing to say. I'd never even tried it, never had the opportunity.

"Tell me the truth," he said. "Do you only like Ricky Nelson because I do?"

"No man. I really like him,"

"Good," he said, smiling. "I get real sad when I think of him going down in that airplane. I hope he didn't feel anything. Hey, did I ever show you something?"

He pulled a frayed baseball card from his wallet. It was older than we were, Topps 1961 issue, Mickey Mantle, No. 475, personally autographed to Paul Conroy, *Best Wishes, the Mick.*

"My dad gave it to me when I hit my first Little League home run. He'd been saving it for me since before I was born."

He finished his six-pack and started working on mine. I was dizzy and the only way to stop my head spinning was to close my eyes.

"Hey buddy, you're not crashing on me?" he asked as he lifted the sheet and crawled into bed beside me, naked with his equipment fully working. But instead of grinding against me, he pulled me close, sliding his hand between my legs and slipping his tongue in my mouth. He must have been as drunk as I was to admit what he told me next.

"I'm really gonna miss you when you leave, Charlie."

✦

THE FIRST THING I DID after registering for classes was sign up to volunteer at the college radio station. By Thanksgiving I was one of those assholes who was into the band before they became so passé that only the worst geeks were downloading their music. I called KC's house when I was back in Albany for Christmas break but he was still in Arizona where he'd been invited to play in the fall league. On a freezing wet night in February, the phone rang and KC was on the line. He was back in Albany and maybe he could drive over to Hanover Saturday. My roommate was spending the weekend in Killington and I had the room to myself.

"Hey buddy," he greeted me when I met him outside the dorm.

He was unprepared for the New Hampshire winter, shivering in his nylon official Tempe Thrashers windbreaker.

"So this is where you live?" he asked, waiting for an invitation to come in out of the cold.

He tried to sound excited when I told him I had tickets to see a new band from Montreal playing on campus. KC didn't say a lot at the concert, being quiet by nature, and more so whenever he felt self-conscious. His team jacket glowed like bright red neon among the thrift shift overcoats favored by the Dartmouth underground.

"You wanna check our coats?" I asked, hopefully.

"Naw, I'm okay, buddy."

I didn't introduce him to my friends because none of them asked his name. When he went to the bathroom, a girl from the station told me he was cute, but she couldn't get past the haircut. The program director asked where I found the bobblehead doll. The consensus was KC was Classic Rock and could never appreciate the band's virtuosity with feedback.

"Do you still listen to Ricky?" he shouted over the noise.

I kept nodding my head to the music, pretending I hadn't heard.

Later, back in my room, he crawled under my roommate's blankets and turned his face to the wall. I laid on my back, working up the courage to ask if he wanted to sleep in my bed. "Hell, yes," he said, rolling over and tossing off his covers. For the next few hours it was still last summer and nothing had changed. We spent the night on that tiny mattress, KC sleeping in my arms. But in the morning, he said he had to leave early, before breakfast, that he remembered he had something he had to do.

"See you on the vans this summer?" he asked as he stood by his car.

"Sure," I said, knowing I'd already made plans to intern at a radio station in Boston.

I called his house when I was in Albany the week before the fall semester. His mother said he was in Kingsport, Tennessee, finishing the season in the Instructional League.

"We're real excited," she said. "The Mets drafted KC in the seventeenth round. He's doing real well in the rookie league. He might even get invited to spring training next year if he keeps it up in winter ball. He'll be back after Labor Day. I know he'd love to hear from you."

I left my number, but I never called back and neither did he. I think about him if I'm sad and lonely and when I feel like the pathetic loser I was before Dartmouth. When I do, I log onto the *Baseball America* web page, following his progress through the minor leagues. Someday soon, I'll turn on the television and see him in a Mets uniform, poised, waiting for the fastball down the middle, the perfect swing, a walk-off home run, the Mighty KC at bat.

A RAVENSWOOD SUMMER

J. SARKIS

"AN ANTIQUE." That's what everyone called my computer. Well, everyone except me. It was ten years old, but I knew how to use it, and it had never broken down before. I was a writer with a deadline looming, so I had to act fast. I grabbed the slim yellow pages for Ravenswood, North Carolina and began my search. I had been living in Ravenswood for six months, transplanted from Manhattan, a city that seemed claustrophobically small after my ex dumped me for a neighbor. So I decided to make a major life change, and headed south. I had visited Ravenswood years before, to experience the stunning vistas of the Blue Ridge Mountains, and found I genuinely liked the town. It was a dichotomy of progressive and conservative influences, home to a mix of retired northerners, gays and lesbians, artists, neo-flower children, holly rollers and mountain folk. I was dumbstruck when I found a copy of Jean Genet's *Thief's Journal*, in the original French no less, at the local independent bookstore. That this quaint town could sustain a book store that carried literature this far out of the mainstream made a lasting impression on me.

◆

I PULLED INTO THE PARKING LOT at Point & Click, a computer store I had picked at random from the phone book. It was in one of the many strip malls that proliferated on the outskirts of town. They were eyesores, but were framed by breathtaking views of the mountains. I stared at a majestic range as I carried my computer across the parking lot. Then my attention was diverted by something more interesting, a slim guy, early 20's, entering the building. Too young for me, which I used as justification to engage in some innocent ogling. He wore baggy jeans, hanging low on his hips, showing a hint of a white waistband. His light brown hair was cut long on the top with a slight curl at the end, and sheared close to the scalp below, exposing his slender nape. My mind drifted to thoughts of that nape stretched out below my mouth. I imagined his bare back and the delicacy of his angel bones, which I could almost make out under his thin T-shirt.

I followed his path into the building, carrying my computer, but when I got inside, he had disappeared. Perhaps it was just as well I never saw his face. There weren't a lot of beauties in this neck of the woods. Better to be left with my fantasies than disappointed by reality. I approached the guy at the desk and placed my computer on the counter. He hooked it up to one of their monitors, and began punching keys. Different things flashed on the screen, and he shook his head repeatedly. Then he got on the phone, said something in computer-speak, and told me to wait. There was nothing to read but computer magazines, which I flipped through out of boredom. I couldn't even understand the advertisements. Finally, out comes their troubleshooter, and who is it but the kid I had followed into the building. Without even glancing my way, he put a disk into the computer and punched more keys. I took a look at him. He was cute, in that skinny-assed sort of way. His eyes were dark and slightly almond shaped, his face thin and pale, his lips full and sensuous. One ear was pierced with a small silver hoop. Another hoop, slightly larger, hung on a black cord, snug around his neck. I imagined leaning across the counter and taking that hoop in my teeth. "So what's wrong with it?"

He continued to hit various keys. "This thing is so ancient, it's hard to say. You'll have to leave it overnight."

I took his continued refusal to look at me as a challenge. I had to say something to get his attention. "Aren't you a little young to be working?" A lousy line, but it was the best I could muster.

He lifted his head to look at me, scowling slightly. At first I thought he was annoyed, then I realized he was giving me the once over. He slipped a finger under his leather choker and tugged on it with what seemed like studied insouciance. "I'm twenty-two, legal for work and anything else." I was shocked at his boldness, even though no one was close enough to hear. "So how old are you?" he inquired, so seductively I felt a small tremor pass through my body.

"Thirty-one."

I didn't know how he'd react to this, but he merely asked, with a teasing drawl, "Does Mr. thirty-one have a name?"

"Guy."

"Guy," he snorted. "Is that like 'Bubba'?"

"What?"

"Bubba. You know, what kids call their big brothers." I gave him a blank look. "You're not from around here, are you?" There was a mocking lilt to his voice.

Embarrassed and feeling suddenly very much out of place, I backed away from the counter. "You'll call me when it's ready, right?"

"Yup. Soon as you give me your phone number." I couldn't tell if he was flirting, or being a smartass. I handed him a card from my wallet. He caught it between two fingers. "OK, Guy. See you in a couple of days."

He didn't call me when it was ready, someone else did. When I came in, the woman at the counter said there was no charge because Eric, that was his name, fixed it on his own time, being that we were cousins.

"Hi, cuz," I said when Eric emerged from the back. He was wearing a faded white T-shirt that said "zoom, zoom, zoom," and painter's pants so large they seemed to float around him. I had a terrible urge to strip him naked.

"Thanks for fixing the old clunker. You didn't have to do it for free." He shrugged. "Can I repay you with dinner?" I was surprised at my assertiveness. This was the South and I wasn't even sure he was gay.

"Boy's gotta eat," he responded coyly, his eyes lingering on mine. There was no mistake, this was a date.

That evening, after work, he came by in his truck. I'd never seen anything quite like it. It was as much of a relic as my computer. It had cost him $500 plus a new engine, which he proudly told me he put in himself. I'll have to admit, I found that kind of sexy. I thought about saying so, but had a feeling he wouldn't understand.

We drove to the small downtown area in my "vehicle" as they call it here, emphasis on the middle syllable. It was the first car I owned. Never needed one in New York.

We dined at a cozy tapas bar that rivaled, if not bested, any in New York. In a land of chain restaurants, it was a true find. While waiting at the bar we popped through a bowl of mixed olives, fragrant with oil and spices, which we washed down with glasses of ice cold Chilean wine. The bartender carded Eric, which didn't bother him, but caused me some discomfort. What the hell was I doing? Eric was way too young for me. But then, I told myself, it was summer, time to relax and enjoy whatever comes.

I watched Eric's cheeks pucker as he rolled an olive around in his mouth, and wondered if he had just come along for the meal. Then I remembered he had fixed my computer for free. Why would he do that unless he was interested? I always had a hard time believing that someone I was attracted to would reciprocate the feeling. Perhaps it was because the men I found good-looking were so different from me. Take Eric for instance. Tall, leggy, and boyish, he was undoubtedly smooth all over. I, on the other hand, was average height, muscular and moderately hairy. Once I had shaved my chest in an attempt to look more like the kind of man I found attractive. My ex had a conniption, saying I had shaved off my best feature. I suppose there's truth to the saying that opposites attract. I hoped it would hold true with Eric.

As we waited for our table, Eric asked me about my life in New York. He seemed curious, although not envious, as I had expected. In turn, I asked what it was like to grow up gay here. "Could have been better," he responded unemotionally, "could have been worse."

"Were you out in high school?"

He looked at me suspiciously. "You mean, did I go around telling people I was gay? I didn't have a death wish."

"Does your family know?"

He took a gulp of wine. "Unfortunately, yes. A couple of years ago my dad found a copy of *The Front Runner* in my room. Not porn, just a regular book. But it was gay, so he went ballistic."

I stiffened in my bar stool, feeling suddenly protective, imagining a middle-aged redneck screaming as he waves around a tattered paperback. "Did he hurt you?"

"No, but he busted up the room bad, punched out a wall. It was pretty scary. I left for a day, but had no place to go, so I came back. Now we just pretend nothing ever happened. Most of the time it's OK, but I have to keep my private life under wraps. I want to get out of there, but I'm working my way through school, and can't afford rent and tuition."

"Aren't there other college kids you can share an apartment with?"

"Like what, with a bunch of frat boys? I'd have less freedom than I do now."

"There are other gay college students. There are even gay frats."

He looked at me like I was from another planet. "Not in this town."

We were escorted to a small table decorated with a votive candle that flickered against the rough terra cotta wall. It was romantic, yet not ostentatiously so. Our waiter was about Eric's age, with a similar build and angelic blond curls. While he took our order he looked at Eric the way a kid looks at a Popsicle on a hot day. When he left, I commented jovially, "I bet he wouldn't mind sharing an apartment with you, a bed either."

Eric chuckled. "Maybe, but way too pretty for me. I go for the more rugged type." He looked at me flirtatiously.

He thinks I'm rugged?! My confidence instantly skyrocketed.

The rest of the meal passed enjoyably. Later we strolled in the mild evening air—it never got really hot here in the mountains—and peaked in at the art galleries that stayed open late during tourist season. Then I drove him back to my house.

As I pulled up I asked, "Would you like to come in for coffee or something?"

"I'm not ready for 'something' yet."

"That's fine. But you can still come in."

"Maybe another time."

He was difficult to read. Perhaps he hadn't had much sexual experience. I was ready to conclude the venture a waste of time, but there was nothing else happening in this town, and I kind of liked him. "Can I at least kiss you goodnight?"

He nodded, but as I leaned in, he put a hand on my chest, stopping me. "Make it a first date kind of kiss, OK?"

I was tempted to tell him that by this time on the first date I'm usually in bed with the guy. "Why don't you kiss me instead, so I'll know what you want."

"No." Out came that fetching smile. "I want *you* to kiss *me*."

Normally I hated this kind of game playing, but in this instance it was getting me really hot. I grabbed his head with one hand, pulled him towards me, and kissed him long and hard. It took him a moment, but he warmed into it. Then I broke away, exited the car, and walked into the house. If he wanted to play games, I could play them too. A few minutes later I heard him get out of my car and into his, then pull away.

My gut told me I'd hear from him again, and I was right. A few days later he called and we chitchatted while I waited for him to suggest we get together. Then I remembered he liked to be the one pursued. So I asked him to a movie. Although I suggested one showing at the local art theater, he wanted to see something silly and forgettable at the multiplex, which we did. Afterwards we went to the town's one gay club. We started in the pool room, shooting a few rounds with a couple of boisterous lesbians. Later we moved to the dance floor, where we kissed. I wanted to continue in a more secluded spot, and when we found one I got pretty aggressive, pulling him against me and letting my hands have the run of his body. I felt him come alive under my touch, but it wasn't long until I felt resistance too. "Guy, I like you," he said between hard breaths, "but I need to go at my own pace."

Clearly that pace was very slow, but this time it didn't bother me. We danced some more, smooched some more, then returned to our respective homes.

The next time I called him I was surprised but pleased at his suggestion that we spend the evening watching videos at my home. After we settled in, and I set up the movie, I knocked the pillows off the couch and stretched out horizontally. It was large, and there was plenty of room for the two of us. Eric lay down with his back towards me, and I threw an arm over him as we watched another mindless piece of Hollywood junk. After a few minutes he snuggled against me, scooting his behind against my crotch. "If I were you, I wouldn't do that," I warned.

"Why not?"

"Keep doing it and you'll feel why not."

"I already feel it." He snuggled closer. "It feels good."

This was a change. "If you're teasing me, it's not very nice."

He flipped onto his back and looked up at me. "I'm not teasing you." He seemed almost hurt that I would suggest it. I leaned over and kissed him. His mouth tasted sweet and salty from the honey-roasted peanuts he had been nibbling. A moment later I was on top of him, and we were making out in a way I hadn't done since college. He tugged at my T-shirt. I pulled it off and tossed it aside. He touched me tentatively, running his fingers through my chest hair and pressing the muscles underneath. "Wow," he exclaimed softly, the word emerging in a small puff of air. I had been with guys who made an ostentatious display of fawning over my muscles. I won't say it didn't please me, but it often seemed more show than substance. But that little "wow" was so genuine and spontaneous that it overshadowed every other compliment I'd ever been given. I started to lift his shirt. He pulled away.

"What, is there something pierced you don't want me to see?" I asked playfully.

"No. It's just—I have an ugly, skinny chest. You won't like it."

I smiled. "I'm sure it's not ugly. Let me see."

"Can we shut the lights?"

I reached past him to turn off the lamp, and the TV, then removed his shirt. Yeah, his chest was skinny, but I liked that. His skin was flawless, his nipples tender. I tweaked them gently as we kissed. Soon I could feel his erection pressing against mine. "Can we go to your bed?" he asked earnestly, as if there was a chance I would say no.

Once we got there, his hands went immediately for my belt. He opened my fly and reached in to stroke me. There was nothing tentative about his touch now. We finished undressing each other in the small space between my bed and the wall. His pants were so loose that they easily fell to the floor before I got the zipper halfway down. Underneath were old-fashioned boxers, adorable on him. I teased him a bit through the thin cotton, then pulled them down and away with the rest of his clothing. I made an appreciative murmur as I dropped my mouth onto his cock. After a few minutes I pulled away, and turned him around to face the wall.

The room was dark, but a shaft of light came in from the hall, illuminating the golden down on his back. I had been dying to get a look at his ass since I first saw him in the Point & Click parking lot. It was even better than I had imagined, round and smooth, perfectly perched on top of long, graceful legs. I could have fucked him right then, but there were other things I wanted to do first. I was sitting on the bed, my mouth level with the middle of his back. I started there with my tongue, moving slowly down his spine. When I reached his ass, I pulled his hips towards me and pushed my tongue inside. He made a small sound, then leaned forward so I could go deeper. I took my time, feeling him with my tongue. Eventually I reached around to stroke him. He moaned, a sexy, guttural sound, but after a few moments he took my hand away. "You gotta stop," he choked out, "or I'm going to come."

"What's wrong with that?"

"I want to come while you're fucking me."

If it was possible for me to become any more aroused than I was, that did it. He turned around, pushed me back on the bed and gave my chest little licks, like a randy puppy. He worked his way down to my cock, but stayed away from the head, I assumed for safety reasons. It didn't matter, what he was doing felt great. Before this evening, I had been wondering if Eric was a virgin, but now it was clear he was not. He was surprisingly self-assured and genuinely affectionate, a quality lacking in most of my recent sexual encounters.

He asked for a condom, which I happily supplied. After he wrapped and lubed me, he stretched out on his stomach, turning his head to the side. A pinpoint of light reflected in one pupil. "No rough stuff, OK?" It was more a question than a demand.

I wondered if he had had a bad experience in the past. "Don't worry. Not my style." Although I entered him gently, he still tensed up. I waited for him to relax, then eased the rest of the way in. He was wonderfully tight and sleek. I took it real slow at first. After a while he shifted his body so he was on his hands and knees, bringing me up with him. His head hung down between his shoulders, heavy as a piece of overripe fruit. I could see the knot of leather at the back of his neck and the flash of silver in front. I loved this position. Not having to support my body weight, it was pure pleasure with minimum exertion. There was also something incredibly arousing about having a man assume such an undignified position for me. It seemed a reflection of both trust and raw sexual need.

He started moving with me, thrusting back against my hips. I took this as a signal to pick up the pace. I did, driving faster and deeper inside him, but kept the rhythm smooth and even. His sexy groans coupled with his continuing backward thrusts threatened to push me over the edge. I held myself back as I reached around for his cock. When he came, warm and sticky in my hand, I let myself go, falling into the abyss.

I pulled out carefully, discarded the condom, and grabbed us each a towel. He relaxed on his back, lazily patting the towel over his flat stomach. Meeting his eyes, I was overcome with tenderness. As we kissed, he leaned into me, and I felt a kind of aftershock as our bodies met, delightful and unexpected. I held him until I started to drift off to sleep. Then I felt a stir.

"What's the matter?" I murmured.

"Sorry, but I need to go."

I was awake, suddenly and unpleasantly. "But it's late. Can't you stay?" Now it was my turn to show naked need.

"I want to stay, but, you know, I live with my parents . . ." He trailed off without finishing.

I tried to reign in my emotions. "Come on, Eric, you're over twenty-one. If you don't want to stay, just say so. Don't make up excuses."

"It's not an excuse." He seemed to struggle for a few moments. Then, still conflicted, he cuddled back against me, mumbling into my shoulder, "I'll deal with them tomorrow."

We had a lovely morning together, and he left in a good mood, but when he called that evening he was clearly upset. "I can't take this anymore. My parents totally flipped because I didn't come home last night." I had no patience for this, and was about to tell him that when I heard how pained his voice had become. "I don't know what to do. They're going to throw me out if I don't follow their rules, but then how will I see you?" His voice fell to a soft whisper. "I've been going crazy all day thinking about you, the stuff we did last night, and this morning." I flashed back to the morning, the elegance of his Adam's apple bobbing above that leather choker as he straddled me, the sunlight illuminating magnificent expressions of pleasure on his face.

"I want to see you too," I echoed, but had no solution to offer. Then he had an idea. A few days a week his shift didn't start until noon. He could see me those mornings, at a time of day that was above suspicion. I agreed, but felt ridiculous. I hadn't taken part in this type of closeted sneaking around since I was in high school, and I was not interested in revisiting it.

We carried on this way for about a month. As much as I enjoyed the morning sex, I hated how limited our time was together, and how restricted our activities. And I seethed at the idea that a couple of homophobes were dictating how I conducted my love life.

The summer came to a close and Eric prepared to return to college. He told me that between his classes, his job and his home situation, we'd only be able to see each other once a week. That was not acceptable to me. The "situation" had to be corrected, and that meant doing one of two things. I could help him out financially, which I feared would create a very bad dynamic between us. The alternative was to ask him to live with me, which was so premature it would likely doom our burgeoning relationship. Perhaps, however, there was a middle ground.

A week later I invited him over and led him into the basement of my house, where a previously empty studio apartment was now modestly furnished. Eric looked around the bright, above-ground space with astonishment, seemingly unsure of what was being offered. "You're welcome to stay here until you can afford your own place," I explained, "but getting your own place does have to be a priority. Everyone needs to learn to live on their own." He nodded thoughtfully. "The apartment has a separate entrance. You can come and go as you please, have over anyone you want, including other guys, although I can't promise I won't be jealous."

He wrapped his arms around me tightly. "You're the only 'guy' I want."

Despite what I had told him, this pleased me. "Eric, I'm really starting to care about you. Should I put the brakes on, or is that something we could explore?"

He held my eye. "I'm all for exploring." Then he pulled me down to inaugurate his bed and his new found freedom.

SUMMER STOCK

SIMON SHEPPARD

"SO YOU'VE HEARD of Sam Sullivan, then?" Winslow and Matti were strolling down beside the oh-so-scenic canal in New Hope, Pennsylvania.

"Yeah, sure," Matti said. "Kind of." She wrinkled her nose, looking cute, just in case anyone approximately as cute was approaching the opposite direction. For girls like Matti, Winslow mused, looking cute came easily. He, on the other hand, had to work on it.

"But you did see *Paths of Pain*, right?"

"Um, maybe on TV. A long time back. Hang on, I want to go in there."

"I'll wait out here."

"Just for a second." Matti ducked inside the impossibly pricey boutique. Winslow was left out in the stifling July afternoon, wondering—not for the first time—how someone with Matti's microscopic knowledge of, and interest in, the finer points of theater had ended up apprenticing for the summer at the Bucks County Playhouse. True, not everyone possessed his encyclopedic familiarity with the minutiae of Sondheim's career. But if Matti's ambitions in the theater arts went no further than longing to play Christine in a major revival of *Phantom*—and, face it, he himself had grown up prancing around in front of the rec room mirror while lip-synching Bobby's songs from *Company*—well, Matti was proving to be a hard worker and a pretty good friend.

He looked at his reflection in the shop window. OK, maybe he could be thought of as pretty cute himself, at least from certain angles. And by guys who preferred their sex objects on the chunky side. At twenty-two, he also sometimes caught the lustful stares of the older men who drove down from New York or up from Philly, though he suspected that it was usually his mere youth that was carrying the day. But Matti...Matti was undeniably a dish, so much so that he sometimes, walking alongside her, felt like Sebastian Venable in *Suddenly, Last Summer*, dangling estrogen-soaked bait in front of the sometimes-hunky tourists who would have to serve as the Mexican urchins in this particular, shaky simile...

"Gosh, I just saw the most darling shoes in there. Come see."

His reverie broken, Winslow sighed. Being a fag hag's fag could sometimes be hard work: He was a *lot* more interested in Bob Fosse than Manolo Blahnik.

"Do I have to? It's so fucking hot today. I just want to go home and lie down."

Matti wrinkled her nose at the obscenity; it was hard for Winslow to believe that she'd been raised as a fundamentalist Christian. But she had, and to atone for his dirty word, he accompanied her into the blessedly air-conditioned store.

The shoes were strappy little things that must have cost a hundred dollars an ounce.

"Kinda overpriced, huh?" he said. The salesgirl looked like she wanted to kill him.

"Not to worry. My dad will buy them for me. I'll just have to whine a bit."

And there it was.

✦

THERE IT WAS: the Bucks County Playhouse, its barn-like hulk hovering in the sticky heat of mid-afternoon. The sign on the side read "COMING ATTRACTION: ANNE BARKSDALE & SAM SULIVAN IN WHO'S AFRAID OF VIRGINIA WOOLF?"

"Dammit, Levine, they left an 'L' out of my fucking name."

"So we'll fix it."

"The decline and fall."

"We'll fix it," Levine said, gripping the steering wheel.

It was depressing, really, when Sullivan thought of what he once had been. Not the young, handsome part of it. He knew well enough that he'd been lucky to be born with his face, and that time works its unseemly magic on us all, even those who've had quite a bit of work done. No, it was the knowledge that he'd once been thought a shoo-in for an Oscar for *Paths of Pain*, and now he was playing summer stock.

"*Tatelah*, it's not so bad," Levine said, as though he were a mind reader. "It's the Bucks County Playhouse, for heaven's sake. Prestige. It's not like you're playing cruise ships."

"Almost." The Playhouse had once been known as a place where Broadway stars could pick up a little spare change during the slow season. Julie Harris had played there, Walter Matthau, the legendarily loony Frances Farmer. Colleen Dewhurst had starred there in *Virginia Woolf*, but that had been way back when Samuel Sullivan had yet to reach puberty. In recent decades, the Playhouse had been stuffing their seasons with cash-cow musicals cast with unknown, and therefore inexpensive, actors. Who needed a big name when you had *Joseph and the Amazing Technicolor Dreamcoat*...year after year after year? At least the Playhouse management had agreed to let Sullivan act in a real play, not one of those Andrew Lloyd Webber monstrosities. Falling chandelier, indeed.

"Yeah, Levine. Could be worse." Damn scandal. The kid had sworn he was eighteen. Sullivan had managed to dodge jail, but his career was never the same after that. Not nearly.

◆

"MR. SULLIVAN, it's an honor to meet you."

It was, too. Winslow knew all about the actor's past, of course—who wouldn't? But Sam Sullivan was the biggest star he'd ever met, excepting when he was standing outside a stage door, *Playbill* clutched in one hand, ballpoint in the other.

Sullivan shook his hand, seeming genuinely pleased, but also a little...what would the word be? *Tentative?*

"So how old are you?"

"Twenty-two, sir."

Or maybe "horny."

◆

"AND THE BOY? I saw you giving him the eye, Sammy."

"Worry not. I can take care of myself."

Levine raised one bushy eyebrow. As Sullivan's one-time lover and current manager, his impulses were a tug-of-war between protectiveness and cynicism. "So it's nice to be out of New York, *nu?* I bet the blacktop has melted on the Great White Way."

Sullivan kept shifting clothes from his suitcase into the suitably colonial dresser of the room in the self-consciously quaint bed-and-breakfast that the theater had booked for him. So Levine tried again. "It's a nice place, New Hope, huh? Even the name is nice."

"Levine, I'm OK, all right? Yes, you're right. Better here doing Albee than slumming in that damn soap opera." Sullivan's character on *Many Loves*, Dr. Leo Crane, had recently been killed in a plane crash in the Andes, where he'd gone on a noble mission to cure some fictional South American disease. The producers had assured him, though, that if his attempt to recover artistic cred tanked, he'd be welcome back as Dr. Crane's evil twin. Was that a good thing or bad?

"Sammy, I'm *shvitzing* here. Can we please close the window and turn on the AC?"

Sullivan gave him one of his *Do you always have to act the Jewish stereotype?* looks. "Sorry," he said, "but I'm enjoying the sweltering heat."

"You're thinking about that boy, aren't you? I've been with you long enough to know that he's your type."

Sullivan pulled off his shirt and, his still-toned body naked from the waist up, walked into the bathroom and switched on his electric razor.

"Exactly your type," Levine called over the shaver's buzz, "Precisely exactly."

◆

"OK, SULLIVAN SEEMS NICE ENOUGH, I guess," Matti said. "Only when he's around you, he seems kind of like a...letch." Another sunny day having given way to a balmy, tourist-filled evening, she and Winslow were strolling down Mechanic Street before heading off to work. "I'd watch myself if I were you."

"You jealous, Matti?"

"I don't *think* so." Only she was, kind of. After all, *she* was the one who was supposed to be attracting the attentions of the rich and famous. OK, Winslow was, she had to admit, kind of cute in a geeky way, but he hadn't even lost his baby fat yet. And he could be really snotty about things like show tunes.

"Anyway, Sam Sullivan is an attractive man and an accomplished actor. That's all. It's not like he's ever going to pay much attention to me." He slapped at his thigh. Mosquito.

"Honey, I know about men. He already is paying attention to you." No, she wasn't jealous, only protective. Except...it wasn't fair.

◆

WINSLOW WAS BUSY doing tech work, while the first read-through was taking place onstage. To his ears, it sounded pretty good. But then, Sam Sullivan was a good actor, and Winslow had heard enough rumors about Anne Barksdale to know that she was a natural choice for the part of a drunken harpy. The actors who played Nick and Honey were locals who were also in the current production, *Pippin*. They were OK, though they certainly weren't up to Sullivan's level.

At last, Martha confessed to George that she was indeed afraid of Virginia Woolf. The director, a way cute, ostensibly straight guy from Philly, said, "OK, gang, that was great. See you tomorrow." But Winslow still had tech work to do. He was absorbed in switching out the gels in the follow spots when he heard footsteps behind him.

"Hard at work?" Sam Sullivan said. "Or hardly working?"

It was an old joke, but Winslow chuckled nonetheless. "Somewhere between the two, Mr. Sullivan," he said, looking over his shoulder.

"Sam. Call me Sam."

"OK, Sam."

"I hope I'm not being presumptuous, Winston, but..."

"Winslow."

"Sorry...Winslow..."

"No problem, happens all the time," Winslow said, even though it didn't.

"Winslow, would you care to have dinner with me tonight?"

"I'm sorry, Sam. I'm working tonight. Concessions." Damn *Pippin*. Damn juice boxes. "An apprentice's day is never done."

"Impressive. But regrettable." Sullivan was beginning to sound like he'd learned his dialogue from some 1940s movie, one with George Sanders, maybe.

"I won't be doing anything afterwards, though."

"Ah."

"So if you…"

"How about I pick you up when the show is over?"

"A little later, actually. I have to help clean up. 10:45?"

"Excellent. At the stage door? That is, unless you would rather not be seen…"

"No, I'd love to be seen with you. Stage door it is."

And that was that.

✦

"soooo…"

Matti set her bagel down on the kitchen table.

"So?" Winslow was playing dumb, apparently.

"What time did you get in last night?" She'd seen him leave the Playhouse with Sullivan, a man old enough to be Winslow's father. At least.

"We went back to his room, if that's what you're asking. And talked."

"Just talked."

"Yeah, that was all. He's a nice man. Interesting."

But when it came to repressing a blush, Winslow was no good at all.

He would have liked to think the boy was a "revelation," or some such pretentious nonsense. He wasn't, of course. He was just a cute, somewhat *zaftig* kid, sweet enough, with a hankering for show biz, and therefore—Sam Sullivan hoped—for him.

The evening had gone well enough. He'd established early on that Winslow was self-defined as gay, and that he wasn't a virgin—both good things in terms of avoiding trouble. And if he hadn't ended giving the kid either his autograph or his dick, well, that was probably a good thing, too, seeing as how they'd be working in close proximity for the next month or so.

He looked at himself in the mirror, the towel from his shower still around his waist. Nope, not bad, considering. And if he was into somewhat younger men—OK, let's face it, *much* younger men— well, that wasn't a crime, was it? As long as the boys were legal.

And Winslow was.

✦

WINSLOW HAD ALWAYS BEEN attracted to older men. Not just because of their experience, or their maturity, or, as in Sulli- van's case, their fame or fortune or whatever. Oh sure, it would be nice to be taken out to dinner at a nice restaurant—Winslow was nowhere as well off as, say, Matti. But he wasn't a gold digger. Not of 1935, he thought puckishly, not of any year. He simply found older men, sometimes much older men, attractive. And if it wasn't *really* simple, well, when it came to desire, what was?

Sullivan had been very sweet that first night, almost as if he were afraid of Winslow or something. Truth to tell, Winslow would have liked it to go further than just some talk and a semi-chaste good- night kiss. But Sullivan hadn't pressed matters, and Winslow was re- luctant to, not wanting to be seen as a slut. They did, though, agree to get together again in the next few days.

And sure enough, the following Monday, when the theater was dark and the apprentices had a well-deserved day off, Sullivan took him to Chez Marie. Let the other diners think what they wanted to—that he was Sam's son, or Sam's kept boy, or whatever— Winslow felt proud and pleased to be out in public with Sullivan. One of the other diners even came up to ask for Sam's autograph. "And this is my friend Winslow," Sam said, while signing the back of a wine list.

After an excellent-if-pricey dessert soufflé, they walked side-by- side through the still-warm night, back to Sullivan's room at the Butterfly Inn, and went to bed.

✦

"SAM, you're getting attached to him, aren't you?"

"And what business is that of yours. Levine?"

"Your well-being is my business. You know that."

"And?"

"And I'm afraid he wants something from you, that if he doesn't get it, he'll get you in trouble. And that if he does get it, you'll be in trouble, still."

"Levine, Levine, Levine. Everybody wants something from everybody else. You of all people should know that. But not every boy who'll sleep with me is a Santa Monica Boulevard hustler, and it is, I hate to say it, insulting for you to suggest that. So would you quit being my cynical, caring best friend? It's so Eve Arden."

"All right, Sam. So he's star struck. So he's thirty years younger than you are…"

"Twenty-five."

"Thirty. I'll take your word for it: He's no Eve Harrington. He's no Scott Thorson. And anyway, the show opens tomorrow. Three weeks from now, it'll all be over, so really, how much harm can it do?"

"Well, thank you for that vote of confidence. I guess."

"And Sam?"

"Yes?"

"The kid *does* look good in shorts."

✦

OPENING NIGHT WAS, by any measure, a success. The run had already nearly sold out, thanks to the stars' names and, perhaps, the audience's fatigue with threadbare retreads of *The King and I* and *Mame*. Anne Barksdale had been sober enough to remember nearly all her lines, but it was Sullivan who garnered the lion's share of the critical praise. The *Trenton Times* called his performance "understated, compelling, and wise." ("Who the hell reads the *Trenton Times?*" Sullivan had sneered, but Levine could tell he was pleased.) And they'd finally put the second "L" in "SULLIVAN."

The Monday after opening night, Sam borrowed Levine's Acura, picked up a boxed picnic lunch from The Gourmet Shack, and drove Winslow down the Delaware River to Washington's Crossing State Park, where the famous Christmas Eve boat trip had taken place. It was probably the last time anyone wanted to get to Trenton so badly.

"This whole place is simply lousy with history," Sullivan said, just after they'd launched into the ratatouille.

Winslow thought that Sam looked so handsome sitting there on the grass, wearing worn jeans and a tight T-shirt that was rapidly becoming soaked with sweat. He wanted to kiss him, and so he did, tasting extra-virgin olive oil on the actor's lips. Nobody around them even seemed to notice, so Winslow kissed him again, feeling his unruly dick swelling up inside his shorts.

After they'd killed off the bottle of Chardonnay, they found a shadier spot and lay on their backs, side by side, and talked—about theater, about their lives, about everything but whatever their relationship was becoming.

Sullivan realized, with a smile, that he hadn't felt so contented in years.

✦

"SO DO YOU LOVE HIM?" Matti seemed like she wanted the answer to be "no."

"Yeah, I guess so. Whatever 'love' means." It was meant to sound offhand, but it might as well have been a line from Sullivan's soap opera.

"Have you told him?"

"Matti, I think he knows."

"Um, OK." She had briefly toyed with the idea of telling Sabina Brown, the Playhouse's executive manager, about the affair. But then she got stoned on some excellent weed that a stagehand had sold her, and when she thought about it, she realized that ratting wouldn't be protective of Winslow. It would be melodramatic and destructive and…well, just plain wrong. And anyway, anyone with two eyes in their head could see what was happening between the actor and the boy.

✦

AFTER THE FINAL PERFORMANCE of *Virginia Woolf*, Sam and Winslow got drunk on moderately good champagne, and then wove their way back to the B&B where Sullivan was staying.

They fell into bed, laughing, and within minutes, Winslow was fucking Sam for the first time.

After they'd come, and were cuddling up under the summer-weight duvet, Sullivan said, "Hey, you're not a bad top, you know that?"

"Beginner's luck, Sam." He leant over and kissed Sullivan's weathered cheek. And then there was silence.

"I'm going to miss you," Winslow said.

"Winslow, don't…"

"People think this is wrong, what's happening between us. But I mean, I just don't get their objections. Love is love, right?" It may have been the first time Winslow had used the L-word with Sam.

"Jesus, you're not going to start singing something from *West Side Story*, are you?"

"There's a place for us…"

Sullivan stuck his fingers into Winslow's ribs and tickled him till he was laughing uncontrollably. Then Sam leaned over and kissed the boy's lips, gently, for a long, long time.

Sullivan would have liked to have sex again, but Winslow passed out quickly, the aftermath of the bubbly and the fuck. So Sullivan lay there on his side, staring at the boy's smooth, dimly illuminated face, and jacked off. He came into his own hand, licked it up, and curled up in Winslow's arms. It took a while for him to get to sleep.

It was the first time they spent the night together.

✦

MATTI AND WINSLOW were painting scenery for the summer's final production, which was, thank God, "Send In the Clowns" or no, *A Little Night Music*.

"So do you miss him?"

Matti didn't have to say who.

"Yeah, of course. We've talked on the phone a bunch. He's invited me to go up and stay with him in New York for a while."

"And will you?"

"Jeez, I don't know. I want to, of course. But...do you think it's smart?"

"Fuck, who am I to say what's smart and what not?" Winslow did a double take; Matti had said "fuck."

✦

LEVINE AND SULLIVAN were finishing lunch in a trendy, only moderately overpriced restaurant in Tribeca.

"So you miss the Winslow kid?" It was the first time Levine had mentioned his name since they'd returned to Manhattan.

"What do you think?"

"Uh-huh."

"I mean, when you're getting old, you find happiness where you can."

"Regardless. People do that regardless, however old. Smart people do."

"I invited him to stay with me in New York."

Levine raised an eyebrow.

"For a while. Only for a while."

"OK, *tatelah*. Whatever. It's your life."

"Which I've made a proper mess of."

"Sometimes, Sam. Only sometimes."

"I don't know. I mean, it was what it was, maybe. A summer fling."

"Too hot not to cool down."

Sam Sullivan made a face. "But what if it was more? Or at least could be? How wrong could it be to at least try to find out?"

"Here, Sammy, have a bite of this tiramisu. It's really, really good."

"You know I shouldn't, Levine. Cholesterol."

"Just a bite."

SUMMERS ON THE BAY

JEREMY M. MILLER

THE SUN WAS IN FULL FORCE as I pulled into the small town of Bay St. Louis, Mississippi. The Bank Of The Bay sign on the corner of Main Street told me that it was ninety-eight degrees. I couldn't disagree with that. There was a nice breeze however, so I decided to roll the windows down and soak in the warmth of the day. I pulled into Suber's Market to get some supplies. I quickly went in and got groceries and plenty of Corona and ice. I put the bags in the car and walked to the package store next door and bought a couple of bottles of wine, one white and one red, so that I would have them on hand if the mood struck me. As I pulled onto Beach Boulevard, I remembered how much I loved this place. The warm breezes coming off the bay. The salty smell of the air.

My name is Ron Willis, and as a child, my parents, my sister, and I would come down here from Memphis every summer to visit my Uncle Syd, who owned a small Acadian cottage just across the street from the beach and the bay. We would spend two weeks and had the best time of our lives. I loved the beach and playing in the salt water. Even something as simple as rocking on the cottage's front porch while sipping a sweaty glass of iced tea seemed like heaven. This became my favorite place in the world.

But the main reason I loved our visits so much was Billy Parsons. Billy's family lived in the house next door to Uncle Syd. He was a year younger than me, but that didn't matter. Over the years, we became great friends and I couldn't wait to get to the cottage each year and see him. In fact, Billy Parsons was my first crush and I became almost obsessed with him, even before I knew what it meant to be gay or that *I* was gay.

Billy was very kind for a boy our age. And cute. Skinny little tan body and sandy blond hair. He and I would stay outside all day just enjoying each other's company. We would pitch a tent on the lawn between the two houses and spend most nights out there, where we would play cards and listen to the radio, or just lie on our sleeping bags, talking about whatever was on our minds. His parents didn't get along that well, so he always had that on his mind and liked staying in the tent so that he didn't have to listen to his folks argue. Things went on like this well into our teens, with the two of us growing closer each summer.

As we got older, our campouts became more experimental. When puberty came, we naturally started talking about sex, which led to boners, which led to masturbation. I don't even remember how we learned how to do it, it just happened, and we did it like there was no tomorrow. When I was sixteen, I pretty much figured out my sexuality, since girls never seemed to excite me in the same way that they excited all my friends. When I would jerk-off, my thoughts always seemed to roam to one of my friends, or more often than not, to my campouts with Billy. Then, something happened that would change my life forever.

As always, my family packed up and went down to the bay for our summer break, and as always, Billy met us in the driveway, his tent already set up in the yard. At fifteen, he had filled out some and was playing on the school soccer team. He still retained his boyish charm, though, and was still thoughtful and kind. He helped us unpack the car and, later, our families grilled burgers together.

As the sun went down and everyone else decided to call it a night, Billy and I ran for the tent and closed ourselves into our own little world. It was a hot night so we plopped on top of our sleeping bags wearing just our shorts. Billy was in an unusually giddy mood. We made small talk to catch up on what was going on in our lives.

"How was the school year?" I asked.

"Great. I made the all-star team," he said.

"Awesome. Congratulations."

"Thanks. I broke up with my girlfriend," he said as an odd look came across his face.

I tried to look sympathetic. "That's too bad. What happened?"

"Nothing, really. I just wasn't into it." He stretched back on his sleeping bag and put his hands behind his head.

My eyes began to scan his smooth chest and made their way down to his shorts. "My year was uneventful. I got all A's and B's, though."

It was starting to get dark now, so I reached behind me and flipped on my battery powered lantern.

Billy said, "I've brought something to show you," as he reached into his duffel bag. "I got this cool magazine."

I rolled over onto my side and waited for him to show me what I was sure was a copy of *Playboy* or *Hustler* that he had swiped from his dad's nightstand. When he set it down, it was not what I expected. It was an issue of *Muscle & Fitness*. And a well worn issue, I might add. "You into working out, now?"

"Not really." A look of embarrassment came over his face. "I just like looking at the pictures." He opened the magazine and started flipping through it.

I was at a loss for words. Was Billy into guys? Did he think of them when he was jerking-off like I did? Better yet, did he think of me when he did it? I finally managed to mumble, "Cool. Let's have a look."

I was mostly silent as Billy flipped through his magazine, pausing to tell me which pictures were his favorite. I was starting to get aroused, not only from the magazine, but also from seeing Billy's excitement while looking at the pictures, and as I glanced at his shorts, they were tented up with a small wet spot forming on the front. Now, I was completely hard.

"You've got a boner," I blurted, wondering if I had just said the words out loud.

His face turned red as he moved his hand down over the wet spot.

I rolled back a little to reveal the bulge in my pants. "You're not the only one."

His eyes brightened. "You like looking at pictures of guys, too?"

"Yeah," I said, feeling better finally saying it out loud to another person.

He grinned at me as he reached down and lowered his shorts a little. Now exposed, he wrapped his hand around himself, started rubbing slowly.

I immediately took my shorts off, enjoying the rush as the night air hit my naked body. Billy slid his pants off and the two of us stroked ourselves as we looked at the hard bodies in the pictures before us. He closed the magazine and we both laid back, completely naked, and rubbed ourselves.

He stopped and looked at me. "I got an idea. What if I do yours and you do mine?"

My heart skipped a beat. I'd never touched anyone else, nor had anyone touched me, but indeed, I was willing. "OK."

Billy leaned up, took hold of me and started stroking. I returned the favor and immediately realized that this was the best feeling that I'd ever experienced. We both began to let out little moans as we rubbed each other, our breathing picking up. We finished each other off fairly quickly, rolled over and lay back on our sleeping bags, trying to catch our breath. Exhausted now, we didn't talk much more that night. We just pulled on our shorts and lay there staring at the ceiling of the tent. It was at that moment that I realized I was in love with Billy Parsons, and I replayed the night's events in my mind until I was sound asleep.

We continued our new pastime every night for the next two weeks, getting better at it and enjoying it more each time. When the summer break came to an end, I became depressed. I begged my parents to let me stay with Uncle Syd. I could go to school here just as easily as I could in Memphis. The thought of not seeing Billy again for a year was more than I could take, and I sat in the backseat of the car, crying softly for the entire ride back to Memphis. The worst, however, was yet to come.

The next summer, a couple of weeks before our annual trip, my mother got a phone call from Uncle Syd. As she spoke to him, I could tell that something was wrong.

When she finally hung up the phone, she said, "Ronny, come in here and sit down. I've got some bad news."

I went into the kitchen and sat down at the bar.

"That was Uncle Syd on the phone. He says that, apparently, Sue and Tom Parsons have decided to get a divorce. I'm very sorry, honey, but Billy and his mom have moved to Miami, where Billy's grandparents live. He won't be there when we get to the cottage this year."

I was devastated. I couldn't even speak. I went to my room, where I buried my head in my pillow and cried myself to sleep. I didn't know it at the time, but I wouldn't see Billy at all for the next fifteen years.

Uncle Syd passed away last year, and since my parents are both now deceased, he left his beautiful piece of heaven on the bay to my sister and me. Now, with the August heat blazing, I was nearing the cottage for two weeks to myself, and I had been looking forward to it. I needed a break, some peace and quiet, time to think. I'd been through a long string of failed relationships in the past couple of years, so had sworn off dating for a while. I was starting to get lonely, though.

I turned into the shell driveway, winding through the live oaks draped with moss, and parked in the shade. The cottage looked just as it always had. White clapboard siding with green hurricane shutters. The front porch ran the entire width of the house and the sun gleamed off the tin roof. Another porch ran along the back of the house.

My sister, Lucy, called last night to tell me that she had a surprise waiting for me there, but would offer no more information.

"You'll know it when you see it," she had said.

I looked around, but saw nothing exciting. I guessed that I'd find it soon enough.

I unloaded the car, icing the beer down in a cooler on the front porch and putting the rest of the groceries in their proper place. I turned on the air conditioner and changed clothes, exchanging my khaki's and button down for a pair of cut-offs, a white T-shirt and flip-flops. More comfortable now, I put the rest of my clothes away, opened a beer and made myself a sandwich, settling in one of the front porch rockers to eat it. The warm breeze coming off the bay was comforting and after I finished my sandwich, I fell asleep where I sat.

When I awoke an hour later to the sound of a lawnmower, I grabbed another cold beer from the cooler and went inside to wash my plate. Standing at the sink, I peered out of the kitchen window to the house next door, and saw an extremely handsome man mowing the lawn. He could've been anywhere between twenty-five and thirty, had short blond hair and a mustache. He was wearing jogging shorts and sneakers with white sox. The sweat glistened on his well toned chest and arms. I watched as he went back and forth across the yard and began to feel a slight yearning in my nether regions. Placing the clean plate in the dish rack, I grabbed my Corona and a book that I'd started reading the night before. I turned on the stereo, and as Boston's "More Than a Feeling" came pouring out of the speakers, I went back outside and plopped into the rocker to enjoy the afternoon and the scenery.

"Howdy!" yelled the man next door.

"Hello," I replied.

"Great out here today, ain't it."

"Doesn't get much better," I said.

I opened my book and pretended to read as I watched the man wheel the lawnmower into the tool shed on the side of the house, disappearing inside. I started reading and got through about two pages when the man appeared from around the side of my porch.

"Could I trouble you for one of those cold beers?" he asked.

"No problem," I replied, taking a bottle from the cooler, popping the top, and standing up to hand it to him.

"Much obliged." He took a long swig and then wiped the sweat off his forehead with his arm. "Bill Parsons," he said, extending his hand to me.

My legs nearly gave way underneath me. "You've got to be fucking kidding me!"

"What?" he said, probably assuming that I was some sort of lunatic.

"I don't believe it. Billy? Oh my God!"

"Wait a minute. Ronny? Ronny Willis?"

"It's me." I couldn't believe my eyes. I hadn't recognized him at all. Now that I stood staring at him, I could see that it was Billy, all right. Fifteen years had changed him enough that I didn't see it at first, but the more I looked, the more that I saw the fifteen-year-old that I had thought about for all these years. "I thought I'd never see you again."

"Same here," he said, his face completely lit up. "It's so great to see you." He held up his arms and hugged me tightly. "This is so awesome."

We hugged for what seemed like forever, and the smell of sweat coming off his body was almost intoxicating. I had to break out of the hug as my cock started to stir. "Are you living here?"

"Yeah. Pops passed away a couple of years ago and I was gonna sell the place, but I couldn't bring myself to go through with it. Best times I ever had were here. I couldn't let it go."

"Sorry to hear about your father," I said. "I hadn't heard." We were both still kind of staring at each other in shock.

"Thanks. He went peacefully. What about you?"

"Living in Memphis. Syd left this place to Lucy and me. This is the first time I've been down since he died."

He just shook his head. "Well, your timing couldn't be better. I just moved in last week. How long are you gonna be here?"

"Two weeks. Sit down, please. I'm getting lightheaded." I motioned to the chair next to mine and we both sat.

We spent the next hour quickly telling each other about what we'd been doing for the last fifteen years. Billy had moved to Miami with his mother, where they lived with his grandparents. He had met a girl that he dated through high school, but she had broken it off when they went away to different colleges. He had met another girl while attending LSU School of Dentistry in Baton Rouge and they had become engaged. After graduation, they moved to New Orleans, where he started a practice.

"I broke it off with Laura shortly after moving to New Orleans," he told me. "It just wasn't right. I loved her. I'm sure of that. I just wasn't in love with her. There was still something missing."

I told Billy that I had stayed in Memphis, dropped out of college after just two years and began selling real estate, which I had been doing ever since.

"I came out of the closet as soon as I graduated from high school," I said. "I'd known I was gay for a long time. Luckily, my family and friends all took it well. Never found a relationship that lasted, though. I haven't been involved in anything that I would consider serious."

Billy told me that he was proud of my having the guts to do that. "It couldn't have been easy."

"Surprisingly, it wasn't so bad. I think everyone had known for years. It was a relief actually and I've felt better about myself ever since." Suddenly realizing that my bladder was about to betray me, I got up. "I'll be right back."

As I stood in the bathroom relieving myself, I dialed my sister's number on my cell phone. "Lucy!" I said when she picked up. "I just got to the cottage this afternoon. You'll never guess who's sitting on the front porch."

"Surprise!" she said, amusement in her voice.

"You knew?"

"While I was down there last month, I spoke to the neighbor two doors down. He told me about Mr. Parsons, and that Billy was moving back to live in the house. I wanted to tell you, but when I found out that he would be there by the time your vacation rolled around, I thought it would be more fun this way." It almost seemed as if she was giggling. "Have a nice vacation."

"I'll get you for this one," I said as I ended the call.

I walked out of the bathroom and found Billy in the living room flipping through the CD collection. "Can I get you anything?"

"No thanks. I'm gonna have to run get in the shower and wash off this funk." He joined me in the kitchen.

"I was gonna crank up the grill. Do you have plans?" I asked as I prayed that he didn't.

"Actually, I do. I've got a reception to go to tonight."

Damn, damn, damn!!

I tried to keep the disappointment out of my face. "Too bad. I was really enjoying this."

He smiled and walked closer. "I'm enjoying it, too. Listen. I have this thing tonight, but tomorrow, it's you and me. I'm free all weekend."

"That's great. I'll save the steaks for tomorrow night, then. I have to drive over to Biloxi for a meeting with Uncle Syd's attorney tomorrow afternoon, but then, I'm free."

"It's a date, then." He gave me another huge hug. "It's so good to see you again."

I watched him walk across the lawn to his house and my eyes welled up. Was this really happening? Had I just spent the last two hours drinking beer on the front porch with Billy Parsons?

Please, God. Don't let this be a dream.

I woke up on the sofa the next morning in only my boxers, feeling a little hung over. It seems that I polished off the bottle of red wine all by myself as I reminisced about the night fifteen years ago and fantasized about the night to come. And from the looks of the stiff wad of tissue on the floor beside the sofa, I must have plea-sured myself at some point. Too bad I don't remember it. I hate when that happens.

Driving home from my meeting with the attorney, I decided to stop at the liquor store and pick up a few more bottles of wine. I felt they might come in handy. I tried to call Billy to see if he needed me to pick anything up while I was out. No answer.

Shit!

Was he blowing me off? Was he having second thoughts? He seemed genuinely happy to see me, but maybe he was now freaking out. I couldn't stop thinking about it. I had dreamed about seeing him again for years, and still had a hard time believing that he was actually here. We were both here.

I drove down Beach Boulevard, anxiety raging, hoping that nothing would go wrong tonight. Then, as I turned into the famil-iar shell driveway, my stomach dropped and I felt like I was going to puke. There in the middle of the lawn between his house and mine, a tent had been set up.

Trying to be cool, I got out of the car and headed for the house. I heard a door shut and glanced back to see Billy strolling towards me, grinning from ear to ear.

"What do you think?" he asked.

I didn't know what to think. "What the hell is that?"

"Just seemed appropriate. I can't remember a time that we were both here without there being a tent right in the middle of the lawn." He threw his arm around my shoulder as we walked into my house. "Tonight, it's just you and me. Like old times."

The evening was going great. We drank wine. We talked about our old lives and our new ones. We grilled steaks and ate, all the while cutting up as if we were teenagers again. We were getting drunk, having polished off two bottles of white wine and counting, and at some point, Billy decided that we would sleep out in the tent. Sounded crazy to me and I told him so.

"Listen, Ronny," he said as he scooted his chair closer to mine and took my hand in his. "That last summer we spent together, it changed me. I haven't been the same. My life has been a mess. Then I saw you yesterday. It was like a something went off in my head. Or my heart. After this evening, I'm sure of it."

"Sure of what?" I said, trying not to seem too anxious.

"Sure of what's been missing. It's you. Please, tell me that you feel something, too."

I fought back tears. "If you only knew. I haven't been able to stop thinking about you since we last saw each other."

Billy smiled as he put his hand on my face and, looking into my eyes, he kissed me. Softly, but with more passion than I had felt in my life. We sat there for the longest time, just holding each other in silence, as if the world had stopped around us.

We got up and started tidying up the kitchen. Billy cleared the table while I loaded the dishwasher. I was floating and so was he. He was right. This felt perfect. I was happier than I had ever been and I didn't want the feeling to end. Just being here with him was comforting. I felt safe. I felt like this was where I belonged. I had fallen in love with Billy all those years ago. Now I knew that I was still in love with him. More than ever. And even better, he was in love with me.

I thought about our impending campout. "You really wanna sleep out in that tent?"

"Absolutely. Why, you having second thoughts?"

"No. I've never wanted anything more."

"Good. I've got everything we need out there. The only thing missing is the two of us. And maybe a bottle of wine."

"You've thought of it all, haven't you?" I glanced over my shoulder at him as I was rinsing the last of the dishes and then turned back. I felt Billy coming up to me. He put his arms around me from behind. Then he kissed me softly on my neck, put his cheek against mine, and said, "I've missed you."

"I've missed you, too." I closed the dishwasher and turned toward him. "Alright," I said, putting my arms around his neck. "Let's go camping."

THE DAY THE GOVERNOR CAME OUT

JOEL A. NICHOLS

THE PLANKS RATTLED as the roller coaster fell down one of its parabolas, and the riders shrieked and threw up their arms. Cooking grease hung in the heavy salt air blowing around the pier. The game that Anthony manned was six black water pistols mounted on a high wooden counter and pointed at Martians. Muted green and red stage lights lined the ceiling of the stall. A Christina Aguilera song boomed from the Matterhorn ride across the boardwalk.

"Shoot the Martians in the mouth, win a prize," he called. Anthony wore cargo shorts with a half apron stuffed full of yellow tickets and one dollar bills. Kids darted past the booth, cutting off the slow moving couples. A skinny guy in a white tank top with his arm hooked on a girl's round hip loped close to the game, and Anthony gestured to the tall, lanky blond working the stand with him. "Come on," he mouthed.

"Pop the balloon, win a prize. Pop the balloon, win a bear," said Mat. The end of the words disappeared in crisp, unselfconscious gulps. The guy shook his head no and pulled his girlfriend closer. Mat turned to look at Anthony and shrugged. "He didn't want to play." Mat had crooked teeth inside a serious grin. His eyes were watery blue and he had short, sandy sideburns.

"Nope," said Anthony. "But you've got to get in there quicker. Like I showed you." He'd showed him every day since Mat had arrived from Lithuania to work the season and ended up staffing "Invasion: Mars," with Anthony. It was Mat's second summer at the shore; he had spent the year before in Ventnor, working at a grocery store, but wanted to be on the beach for his second summer in America.

Another couple was strolling past. They were holding hands with their fingers laced. The guy had a deep tan, with a tight T-shirt stretched over his pumped up chest. The girlfriend's skin was even more tanned and she had blond streaks tied back in a ponytail. Anthony leaned over the edge. "Win a prize for her," he said. "Shoot the Martians, win one of these—any one, your choice." He pointed at the colorful stuffed animals strung on chains the length of the booth. The girl's eyes flicked at Anthony, then at the prizes. Anthony had wide shoulders, a short torso and thick calves covered in curly hair. He wore a sleeveless T-shirt, and one stray mark of his tattoo trailed down his sweaty shoulder. When girls looked at his arms, he looked at their boyfriends.

"Which one you like, doll?" That made the guy look over and size up the game. "Come on. Four bucks. Fill up the Martian's head and you can have any of these," he said as he reached up with the hook and shook the first row. Foot-long plush tropical fish Disney knockoffs and SpongeBob imposters swayed. The boy and girl looked at each other, and the guy slapped four dollars down on the counter. Mat scooped it up and put it in his apron pocket. He activated one of the water guns and then moved to stand next to Anthony. Shoulder to shoulder in the small game booth, they watched the guy grind one elbow into the counter as he hunched over the water gun. A strong jet of water started, splashing the Martian's cheek and chin before the guy finally pointed it in the mouth and the pale balloon bulging from its forehead began to fill. The red and green Christmas lights decorating the UFOs painted on the back wall blinked as the balloon stretched and stretched, bursting finally just as the water shut off. He dropped the water pistol and water trickled out the plastic barrel. He turned around to the girlfriend.

"Which one you want?" She pointed to a green and pink striped clownfish. Anthony nudged Mat and handed him the hook. As he reached up to knock down the stuffed animal, his blue T-shirt pulled itself from his faded, slim fit camouflage cutoffs. He caught the falling fish in one of his big hands. The girl took it and tucked it under her arm as she lit a cigarette. Mat slid his fingers down his belly and tucked his shirt back in.

"See," said Anthony, "it's not that hard. You try the next one."

"They always don't want to talk to me. Don't you see their faces when they hear that I'm Lithuanian." His intonation on that word combed the "th" and "u" in one syllable instead of making the natural English break between them. Anthony smiled whenever he mentioned where he was from. "See—you stop snickering at that." Mat shadow lunged toward Anthony, and feigned a punch. "How do you think you'd do in Lithuania, working at a carnival?"

"Well you remembered to say snickering...I thought you wouldn't remember that word. You know I'd suck in Lithuania. It'd be nice to visit, though. Nice to go somewhere for once."

"I remember what I hear," said Mat. "Everyone there just wants to visit America...you don't know how lucky you have it." Anthony saw two kids over Mat's shoulder and pointed. He turned around and leaned his skinny frame over the edge of the counter.

"How much to win one of those fish?" said one. The other picked his nose.

"Four bucks to play," said Mat. "And if you blow up the balloon, you can win the fish."

The kid squinted. "Any one of 'em? Even that green one?"

Mat shook his head up and down. "Any one in the first row, here." The kid looked at his friend, shrugged and walked away. The friend flicked something off his finger.

"Don't sweat it," said Anthony, clasping Mat's shoulder and squeezing. "Kid that young would never spend four bucks for a stuffed fish, even if he's trying to impress a girl."

"It's always worth a try."

"I guess so." Anthony let go of his shoulder and walked back to lean on the edge of the stall. He pulled a fold of bills from his apron pocket and thumbed through, counting. "We've had a good night, though. Let's get a beer to celebrate it. Or should I put this in my 'flight to Lithuania' account?"

Mat shook his head. He slid his hands in his pants pocket. "We should go to my house. Agniya and Cody have to work tonight and my apartment will be empty."

Anthony smiled, running his hand through his thick black hair.

"That'd be great," he said as another couple tethered at their sweaty palms floated past.

Mat leaned in. "You will have to wait. And don't snicker at me like that. I know what it is you are thinking." Anthony blushed.

✦

WHEN THE PIER CLOSED DOWN at midnight, Anthony shuttered the stall and fit the thick padlock together with a click. People still strolled, trotted, and tottered down the boardwalk. The ones stumbling smelled of beer. Pairs of cops moved slowly through the clumps of people.

Anthony and Mat walked fast up Bluebird Avenue and took a left on Sunset Drive. Mat sang almost under his breath, walking a few paces ahead of Anthony. It was a Lithuanian parade song, he'd said, whatever a parade song was. He was always humming or singing something.

"Slow up," Anthony said, taking overlong strides. "Let's enjoy this walk."

"It's hot. I am feeling damp all over," he said, pinching the fabric of his striped polo shirt and waving it against his skin. The collar lay open to the lowest button, at the bottom of his throat, where sparse brown hairs curled. But he slowed down.

"I can't believe the governor came out today," Anthony said.

"I know. In Lithuania, that would never happen. He will never win an election again, will he?"

"Doesn't sound like he cares about that very much."

"There must be another story. Otherwise, why would he do it?"

Anthony looked sideways at Mat. "He might have just been ready...you know. Sometimes people feel ready."

They crossed the street and walked toward the cottage Mat rented with Agniya, his cousin who had come from Lithuania with him and Cody, a bartender from Texas who had taken up with Agniya at the beginning of the summer. They both worked at the Crab Saloon. Their uniforms—ten-gallon hats with crabs glued around the brim and pleather vests with stringy fringe—lay on the floor next to the door.

Mat kicked off his shoes and lined them up, toe to the wall. He slipped on a pair of black rubber flip-flops and padded across the living room toward the kitchen. Anthony pulled off his black sneakers and left them where they fell. He sat on the couch and leaned back into the scratchy plaid cushion that smelled like dog. Anthony brushed grains of sand from the couch to the floor.

"Are you hungry?" Mat yelled from the kitchen.

"No. Just a beer."

"You don't want me to make sausages? Hot dogs, you know?"

"Beer's fine." Anthony clicked on the TV and thumbed through the channels. Mat came in, walked through Anthony's line of sight and yanked closed the metal blinds. The blades screeched and blocked out the streetlight. Anthony lingered on a music video. It was one of the songs they heard blaring from the Matterhorn ride every twenty minutes during their shifts at "Invasion: Mars." He clicked on the ceiling fan and it thrummed.

"No! Turn that junk off," Mat said. He set two sweaty cans of beer on the coffee table and sat down next to Anthony. He eased into the cushions, and rutched himself closer to Anthony until their knees touched. The TV blinked onto a Western with a lonely white hat walking through a sparse desert. "Hold on!" said Mat. "Leave it here please. That actor...he is Lithuanian. What is his name? Charl, Charles..."

"Charles Bronson?" Anthony leaned forward and put his hands on his knees. "Charles Bronson isn't Lithuanian."

Mat shook his head up and down. "He doesn't have an accent," Anthony said. "And he's short and dark."

"Not all Lithuanians are like me," he said. "His father is, I think. A different type than me."

"I think I like my Lithuanians tall and blond, like you." Anthony leaned back and put his hand on Mat's knee. "But please let's find something else to watch." Mat rested his weight against Anthony and his skin prickled goose bumps all over.

"I wish Agniya would go somewhere—for a whole night," he said.

Anthony shared a room with another guy, Bobby, who played video games from his bottom bunk all night long, every night.

He massaged Mat's hairy kneecap with his thumb. His skin was warm. "You know...it's not that crazy that I wouldn't want to walk all the way to my house so late."

Mat's leg tensed. "She would find out. She acts empty-headed, but she is more clever than that."

Anthony sipped his beer, and leaned in closer. He felt the burning seam where their bodies touched: at the ankle, the knee, and thigh. Mat's ruddy leg looked long and thin next to Anthony's tanned muscles, but it was strong.

"I'm sorry you cannot," he said. "But it would be big trouble for me at home." Anthony handed Mat the remote control. It wasn't a fight Anthony wanted to have, or thought he would win. He cycled through the channels and landed on the Western. Anthony leaned over and kissed Mat. They pushed at each other hard for a few seconds. Anthony slowed down and sucked on his lip, biting and licking softly. Mat threw back his head and Anthony kissed his jaw line and neck. Mat swung his arm around Anthony, pulling him against his chest. Light flickered from the desert sunset on the TV screen as the two of them held each other tight.

✦

"WAKE UP!" Mat shook Anthony off and stood up. Anthony blinked slowly. An infomercial for a dehydrator played, casting a blue and white halo on the ceiling above the TV. There was scratching at the door, then the metal grind of a twisting key. Agniya stumbled over the threshold. Her blond hair was limp and her eyes bloodshot. Mat stood nervously, watching Cody follow her in. The acrid smell of vodka and cigarettes tracked them through the room.

She went straight to the bathroom and sat on the pot without closing the door. On the couch, Anthony yawned. Cody scratched his patchy goatee. He was leaning against the wall, fiddling with the bandana he'd tied on his dirty hair. "Crazy party, you guys. At the bar then at Miriam's. You know Miriam?"

Mat and Anthony didn't say anything. Cody stared for a second, then said, looking at the floor, "Did you hear about the governor? That shit is crazy."

"Yup," said Anthony.

"There must be a story behind that. Don't you think man?"

Agniya came out of the bathroom with her pants undone. She slurred something in Lithuanian to Mat.

"She's been doing that all night." Cody took a few tentative steps toward his girlfriend. "Keeps telling me I need to learn."

"It's because she can't remember English when she's this drunk," Mat said. Agniya turned on her heel sloppily to face her cousin.

"Yes I can," she said slowly. With unfocused eyes, she looked down at Anthony on the couch. "Hello. What are you doing here in my house?"

"Hi," he said and stood up. Agniya grabbed Cody's arm and pulled him down the hallway to their room. When they were gone, Anthony sighed. "I've never seen her quite that drunk," he said.

"She's that drunk every night after work. Such a bitch when she's like that."

"Don't sweat it. She won't remember anything."

"I don't care," Mat said. He reached out and pulled Anthony to his chest. His head came up only to Mat's shoulder. With his ear pressed against Mat's heart, the beats thundered. They held on to each other and Anthony started to drop off again. He jerked himself awake. "Come on," Anthony said. "Let's go to sleep."

"We better not," he said. "Agniya."

Anthony put his hands up, and stepped back. He walked around the couch and reached for his shoes. Mat followed him and put his hand on Anthony's shoulder. He shrugged it away. "Come on. Don't do that. You can sleep here, on the couch at least. It's so late."

Anthony paused, and stood up straight. "That's not what I want, Mat." He lowered his voice, and said, "I'd like to stay in your bed. But whatever...it's late and I'm tired. I'll see you tomorrow."

He slipped on his sneakers without untying them, and walked out the front door. The street was quiet, and damp with coming dew. Cars filled every parking spot. The windows were dark but for blue TV glow and a few porch lights. Anthony was walking too fast, and his feet thudded and his legs began to stiffen. He took a deep breath and slowed down, cursing a string of fuckity fuck fucks under his breath. He heard a screen door hydraulic joint and the door's metal slap down the street, and feet pounding. He turned around and saw Mat rushing down the middle of the dark street.

"Come back," Mat yelled, waving his arms. "I am a gay Lithuanian!" Anthony grinned, and opened up his arms to hug Mat. Their chests crashed together and they kissed, standing in the street on that dark, humid night.

A THIEF AND A KILLER

MATTHEW HALDEMAN-TIME

SPRAWLED BACKWARDS across the floor just inside his own front door, Rick groaned at the slick slide of the mouth over his dick. Still not used to living alone, he clapped his hand over his mouth to stifle the loud, appreciative moans as his hips pushed up eagerly. The rhythm of suction on his erection reverberated up his spine in rolling pulses that were forcing him over the fucking *edge*, and he just couldn't stay quiet, and...his fingers tasted like molasses, ketchup, and bourbon.

His fingers tasted like barbecue, but he wanted to taste *summer*. "Here, come here," he panted, pulling and tugging and rolling. One possessive, dirty kiss and he buried his face against a slender neck, inhaling, kissing across one broad, freckled shoulder. More than bright sunlight and green grass and the incessant buzzing of flies, this was summer, here, reclaimed.

✦

RICK HAD MOVED to Wilmont late last year. After graduating college, he'd spent a few years working interchangeable desk jobs, but he'd known all of his life that he'd never get anywhere in the one-horse town of his youth. When his aunt had invited him to work for his uncle's agency, he'd had his suitcase packed before the phone call ended.

Each summer of his childhood, his parents had sent him down south to Wilmont, where he spent a weekend with his aunt, followed by three weeks at Camp Poplar.

Those weeks had been the best of each year. The sadistic counselors, the sweltering heat, and the mosquitoes large enough to carry off a cat, meant nothing in the face of Thief.

Rick had met Thief, known to adults as Frank, the first summer of camp. His age but taller, Thief had been demanding and energetic, with tousled blond hair, freckled shoulders, and scabbed knees. Rick had spent the entire three weeks by Thief's side that first summer, tagging along after him, absolutely captivated by his constant energy and the arrogance in his blue eyes.

In Rick's second summer at Camp Poplar, he unknowingly passed some kind of test, and instead of shadowing Thief, he was included. Over all of the other boys, Thief sought him out; their free time was spent together, wandering down the creek and testing how far away they could get before the counselors noticed they'd gone.

That summer, he learned the naming system. Franklin Henry Taylor had named himself Thief, by taking his initials and flipping them, THF, then inserting vowels. Thief declared that Rick, formerly Richard Lawrence Keyes, would now go by Killer. Rick didn't dare try to make anyone back home call him that, since the kids at school would laugh at him, but Thief got everyone at camp to use the new name, and that's what mattered.

Over the years, Rick's initial impression of Thief didn't change. No matter what age they were, Thief was always at least two inches taller. The scabs appeared in different places—on his elbows, maybe, instead of his knees, and once he had a huge gash across the back of his hand—but they were always there, somewhere. Thief, always the first to climb a tree, always the first one in the creek, and always the first to break into a run, had a fearlessness that made him reckless. Rick, in his summer life as Killer, Thief's best friend, found himself the second one up the tree, the second one in the creek, the one hot on Thief's heels, bold and brave. At home, his mother would've yanked him back and told him to sit down before he broke something, but here, at Thief's side, there was only freedom.

One summer, Rick showed up, and Thief wasn't there. Camp that year was a droning, endless hell. The counselors were sadistic. The heat was murderous. The mosquitoes ate him alive. Two weeks in, he called his aunt and begged her to come for him. He never went back.

He wanted to hate Thief for abandoning him, but then he'd

think about that tall, skinny body shimmying up a tree; all of those hours exploring the creek together, the two of them alone in the wilderness; the careless arrogance in blue eyes that faded when Thief looked at him and only him.

Once, he signed his homework, "Killer," but it got him sent to the guidance office. While he sat there, explaining that no, he didn't "harbor antisocial tendencies," he wondered if Thief had ever sat in a counselor's office to explain that he didn't actually steal, which made him burst into "inappropriate laughter," which only got him into more trouble.

Whenever Rick thought about summer, he thought about Thief. Blue eyes, messy blond hair, long limbs, freckled shoulders, a sense of adventure. That's what summer meant to Rick: splashing through the creek with Thief, skinning his knee and knowing that Thief's knee already looked worse, climbing a tree with Thief waiting for him up in the branches; that sense of inclusion, of having someone who'd chosen him and only him, someone who wanted him enough to rename him.

He found other ways to spend the summer months. The pool, the beach, greasy jobs, hot guys. But it wasn't summer without Thief.

When he moved to Wilmont, he thought of looking Thief up, tracking him down somewhere. But there were too many Taylors in the phone book, and he couldn't remember which town Thief had lived in. This most likely meant that Thief had never named a town, because Rick's memory had latched onto everything that Thief had ever said.

Wilmont was a welcoming place. He'd moved there in October and, two months later, he'd received Christmas cards from every neighbor he'd met and a few he hadn't. When summer rolled around, with its monstrous mosquitoes and blistering heat, the man next door, Kent, had invited him to the neighborhood barbecue held every Sunday afternoon. The food and fun were free, but everyone had to bring his own lawn chair.

Not one to harbor antisocial tendencies, and finding it hard to ignore a block party happening right up against his own backyard, Rick bought a chair and went to the first barbecue of the summer. The food was so good, he showed up for the next two, quickly learning that some of his neighbors could gossip for thirty minutes straight without pausing for breath, Lisa from three houses down had a two-drink limit before she forgot to keep her hands to herself, and Kent tinkered with the sauce recipe every week.

Standing outside, talking to his neighbors, shouting to be heard over a blaring radio, gnawing on an ear of corn, swatting flies and ducking mosquitoes, Rick decided that a friendly outdoor barbecue made a great summer memory. He only wished that Thief could be there.

At work one day, he searched the web for anyone named Frank Taylor living in the county. He came up with several, including a reporter, a librarian, an engineer, and a historian. None of them struck him as the right guy, and since he wasn't willing to call someone out of the blue and ask, "Is this Thief?" he told himself to forget about it.

He couldn't forget his own personal embodiment of summer, as temperatures rose, sweat trickled, and the glub-glub of the office water cooler made him wonder if he could go back to camp and walk in the creek again.

During the fourth barbecue of the summer, on a slow Sunday when even the flies were particularly lethargic, Rick wanted to try out Kent's latest sauce variation without fending off Lisa's quick, grabby hands, so he joined a circle of older folks in lawn chairs in the shade. After they sent him to fetch lemonade, and napkins, he eventually was allowed to sit and eat.

The bulk of their conversation, he tuned out, since they talked mostly about church and physical ailments. As long as he made agreeable-sounding noises at the right moments, they left him alone. He did notice, however, when the woman on his left asked the woman on his right, "How's Frank? We haven't seen much of him at church, lately."

Rick tried to picture his own Frank sitting still through a church service, and smiled. All he could imagine was Thief at about eleven or twelve years old, blond hair tousled despite anyone's efforts to tame it, wrists and ankles exposed due to another growth spurt, long fingers tapping impatiently as he shifted around waiting for the sermon to be over. Thief, inside a quiet, peaceful place like a church? In the summer?

The rich, tangy flavor of the sauce distracted him, and then someone sent him to fetch iced tea. When he returned, the chair to his right was empty. A while later, as everyone began to drift home again, he helped to clean up; since no one claimed that particular chair, he asked, "Whose is this?"

"Oh, that's Betsy Taylor's," Kent's wife said, gathering used napkins. "The little yellow house. Jack usually carries it for her, but he left early."

Betsy Taylor, the woman who'd been asked about Frank. As hope coiled nervously in Rick's stomach, he strained to keep his tone nonchalant. "I'll take it over to her. The yellow house?"

"Two back from the corner," she said, distracted from his eager anxiety as she leaned down to pluck a fork from the grass.

Snatching up the chair, Rick hurried down the street. Frank and Taylor were both common names, and he couldn't track down a childhood summer friend by knocking on a neighbor's door. That didn't explain away his nervous, fluttering anticipation as he rapped on the frame of the screen door of the small, yellow house.

"Yes? Who is it?" Betsy Taylor appeared on the other side of the screen, peering at him with vague distrust.

"Your chair, ma'am," Rick said, holding it up. "Is this yours?"

"Oh, yes! Thank you." Opening the door, she took the chair from him.

As the screen door fell shut again, he said, "Mrs. Taylor." Now that he had her attention, he didn't know what to say. "Do you know a Frank Taylor?"

Eyes lighting up, she hurriedly set the chair aside and smiled at him through the screen. "Yes, of course I know him, I used to spend every summer bandaging up his knees. He's my grandson!" she explained proudly.

Bandaging up his knees. Rick grinned as impossible hope flooded him with quick warmth. "I think that we used to go to summer camp together. Camp Poplar?"

Beaming at him, she said "You must be that friend of his, the one he was always going on about! What did he call you? Some dreadful nickname, even worse than his own. What was it? Murderer? Assassin?"

"Killer," he admitted, as happy to claim the name as he'd been

on the day that Thief had given it to him. Thief had talked about
him!

The phone rang. "Dreadful name," she scolded him. "That's my
sister calling, I have to get that, if I don't answer right away she
thinks I've fallen and hurt myself. Thank you for the chair, good-
bye," she said, scurrying off into the house.

Abruptly cut off from his first link to Thief in years, Rick stared
through the screen, willing her back. She didn't return.

He'd found Thief's grandmother. More than just a summer fantasy, Thief was a person, someone's grandson. He hadn't disappeared with the carefree sunlit days of Rick's youth; he was out
there, somewhere, skipping church.

Rick had to find him. Reluctantly heading home, he pledged to
return the next day.

Monday, dinner with his aunt became a night of assembling
shelves.

Tuesday evening, his uncle made him stay late at work, fixing
other people's mistakes.

Wednesday, when he knocked at Betsy's door, there was no reply.

Driving home on Thursday, he edged past Betsy's house. Parking in his own driveway, he looked down the street, but he couldn't
make himself go. What could he say? She'd probably give him
Thief's address if he asked, but then what? It had been years since
they'd seen each other. Thief had probably forgotten all about
him. Probably had a wife and kids. Wouldn't understand how
much a reunion meant.

It meant everything to Rick. Thief had been summer to him,
had been hot sunshine and days that lasted forever and the scratch
of grass under his feet. Thief had been freedom to him, and confidence, and courage, not caring what anyone thought, not seeking
permission, doing what he wanted to do and refusing to be held
back by worry and what-if. Thief had been life to him, had shown
him what it meant to live, the first one up the tree, heedless of the
cuts and bruises along the way because the view from up in those
branches was always worth it. And even if the view wasn't that great,
it was still an adventure climbing up there for it.

Before he knew it, Rick was across the street and down the
block, knocking on Betsy's door and ringing her doorbell.

No answer. No one home.

Friday, he went over there before work, needing to catch her, needing to interrogate her. She had information that he required; Thief was out there, somewhere, close enough to be expected to attend a local church, close enough for Rick to see him if he only knew where to look.

She didn't answer his knock. The old man watering flowers next door waved and said, "She isn't home, son! Fridays, she goes out to breakfast with her friends. They came by to pick her up ten, fifteen minutes ago."

How did someone's grandmother have a busier social life than he did?

Rick thanked the man and went to work, where he spent all day plotting how to catch an old lady. He'd stake out her house. He'd go to her church. He'd break into her house and steal her address book.

His uncle invited him home for dinner, with a tone that warned him to accept. Once he was there, his aunt explained that she needed him to help her with a few things around the house, minor tasks like hanging wallpaper in the bathroom, laying down new tile, caulking the tub, and painting the hallway. Rick found himself spending the night in their spare room, sleepless and agitated, wondering why the universe hated him. Maybe he wasn't supposed to see Thief again. Maybe summer couldn't be recaptured.

Maybe Thief had grown up into someone dull and plain. That magic couldn't last forever. Maybe he was a prematurely balding accountant with a wife, kids, and a pot belly.

Maybe Thief was still fearless and full of life. Maybe he was still capable of looking at Rick like the two of them were the only people who mattered. Maybe he was gay. Maybe he'd be happy to see Rick.

That old fantasy of making out with him in the grass still got Rick off faster than anything else.

After a long, busy Saturday, Rick went home and collapsed. When he wakened, it was late Sunday morning. By the time he got out of the shower, he could smell Kent's barbecue from next door. Throwing on shorts and a T-shirt, he went down to Betsy's house. No one home; she was still at church. Restless, he decided to busy himself, so he offered to help set up for the barbecue.

He put up a table. Checked on Betsy's house. Stirred lemonade. Plotted how to ask for Thief's phone number. Kept flies away from the potato salad. Wondered if Thief would recognize him anymore.

The whole damned neighborhood showed up, and Betsy was nowhere in sight. The other neighbors were enjoying themselves, eating and gossiping, and complimenting Kent on adding booze to the recipe. Rick's back ached from yesterday's unpaid manual labor, he'd proven unable to track down a seventy-year-old woman who lived down the street, and his own personal summer remained out of reach.

Kent handed him a plateful of food and told him to stop scowling down at his feet before he killed the grass.

Leaving everyone else in the back and strolling toward the front lawn, morosely picking at his food, Rick glared at Betsy's house. Thief would never let an old lady thwart him like this. Thief would have found a way past her disappearing act. Thief would have—

Rick's attention was distracted as a sleek, red car eased around the corner and onto the street.

It rolled to a stop right in front of Betsy's house.

His fingers tightened on the rim of his plate, thumb slipping through a puddle of barbecue sauce.

A door opened, and someone rose from the driver's seat. Someone male, Rick's age, tall. Tall and blond. Lean, in jeans and a T-shirt, stepping around the front of the car to help out Betsy Taylor.

Heart pounding, Rick dropped his plate right there in the grass. Thief. Thief was back.

After taking some things from Betsy's hands, a purse and maybe a Bible, Thief turned away, loping toward the house; Rick's stomach twisted, and he wanted to go after him, still felt that irresistible urge to follow him everywhere, up a tree, down the creek, anywhere. But the door had barely closed after him before it opened again and he returned, tall and energetic, meeting his grandmother at the car and starting across the street.

They were coming to the barbecue.

Blood pumping furiously, sweat beading on his upper lip, and trickling down his back, Rick stared, taking in everything. Thief was as confident in his body as ever, his stride slow and relaxed to accommodate Betsy's shorter legs. He was a man, more filled out, his shoulders broader; his tousled hair was a deliberate style choice now. He didn't have any visible scrapes anymore—no, there was a Band-Aid on his left thumb. His eyes were, god, looking right at Rick.

A flicker of shock in those blue eyes, then eager happiness that Rick could *feel*, and Thief lit up like the sun, hurrying forward the last few feet toward him. "Killer?!"

"Thief," Rick said, but the words were muffled against Thief's shoulder, because he'd just been swept into the tightest hug of his life. It felt so good, he closed his eyes and held on, wrapping his arms around Thief's slender body and letting his heart hammer away. He'd never hugged Thief once in all of their time together before, but he immediately recognized this embrace, knew it as if he'd been born to it.

"Grandma said that it was you, but I couldn't believe it." Quick hands slid up his back to cup his nape, and then Thief stepped away, about an inch or so, to stare down into his eyes. "I can't believe you're here." He looked dazed, but behind the amazement was an eager excitement, an energy, as if he were about to challenge Rick to a race. "You live here now?"

"Since October." He wanted to put a hand on Thief, to tether him so he couldn't ever leave again.

"October," Thief repeated, with a shake of his head. "You lived right across the goddamned street and I never—but you're here, you live here, you're staying," he said, looking into Rick's eyes. They were the only two people in the world, the only two who really mattered, just the two of them; it was all there in his gaze.

"Yes. I moved down here to work for my uncle."

"The one with the modeling agency?" There was that grin, that clever, knowing, wicked grin, so bright, so mischievous. "You work with hot guys all day, every day?"

Rick grinned back. There went his fears about a wife and kids. "You want me to introduce you to some of them?" Thief had remembered what his uncle did for a living. He and Thief were *flirting*.

"I want you to tell me about you," Thief said, gazing into his eyes. "Which house is yours?"

He couldn't believe that Thief was back. He'd never expected to have this again, this strong and intimate bond, this man at his side. "It's right over there," he said, gesturing without looking away from Thief's bold, blue eyes. "The white one."

"Come on," Thief said, and started off. Obeying instinct, Rick followed him, right behind. Thief walked right in through the front door; it was so familiar to see him take ownership of something, the way he'd taken ownership of bunks at camp, of cabins, of trees, of lunch tables, of Rick himself, that Rick didn't question Thief's right to his home.

"You cut yourself?" he asked, closing the door.

"Paper cut," Thief said, turning to him there in the foyer with a new grin, an abashed one, something Rick hadn't seen before. Blue eyes sparkled. "How the mighty have fallen."

"Paper cut?" He laughed, surprised. "You used to try to climb trees feet-first, and now you're victimized by office supplies?"

Grin bright, eyes brighter, Thief said, "You were the best tree-climber I ever knew."

Feeling warmth in his cheeks, Rick shoved his hands in his pockets. "I just managed to fall less than you did."

"You with that look on your face and your hands in your pockets," Thief said, and Rick found himself caught up in another tight, hard hug. "I can't believe you're really here, and I can't believe it's been this long. Tell me what I've missed. Tell me what you did when you were sixteen."

Rick was in an embrace so tight he couldn't breathe, and he never wanted to leave it. "I got a C in geometry because I sat through class fantasizing about kissing your freckles."

"I don't—the ones on my shoulders?"

"Yeah." He didn't regret saying it; Thief had shown him how to be fearless.

"I tried to sneak on a bus to see you, but I got caught and my dad had to come get me." Before Rick could respond to that, he heard, "The paper cut was from a book. I'm a librarian."

Rick's eyes opened as his brain contorted itself trying to assimilate that information. He raised his head to see a lean cheek turn pink with embarrassment. "What?"

"I'm a librarian," Thief said, ducking his head and mumbling it against Rick's shoulder. He turned his face and kissed Rick's neck, which shot a sudden flare of heat straight through his body. Soft, tempting, seductive kisses brushed a crisscrossing pattern up the side of Rick's neck. "I know that's not what you expected—"

"You told me that you were going to be a fighter pilot," Rick said, curling his fingers in Thief's T-shirt as he twisted to give Thief more of his neck, grinding his suddenly aching dick against one firm, slender thigh. He'd enthusiastically followed everywhere Thief had led him, all of those summers ago; he was impatient to travel down this path, too.

"Do you forgive me?" Thief asked, thigh pushing up in between Rick's legs, kisses crossing his cheek toward his mouth.

Did he forgive Thief for turning into a librarian? Did he forgive Thief for abandoning him? Did he forgive Thief for showing him that it was possible not only to live but to seize life and claim it for his own? All of this time, he'd needed Thief, all of these years, had needed Thief's example and spirit to remind him that he wasn't just quiet and cooperative Rick, he was also Killer, he mattered, and if he'd rather stalk an old lady than paint his aunt's hallway, that's what he'd do.

It wasn't about forgiveness, but, "I missed you," he said. "A librarian," he muttered, in disbelief; then, because he wanted to, because this was his life and summer was back, he kissed Thief, right on the mouth, just the way Killer would.

HOT TIME, SUMMER IN THE CITY

ROB ROSEN

I'D BEEN LOUNGING on my sofa, reading the latest Danielle Steele epic, sipping an oh-so-sweet, frigid-cold iced tea, when, suddenly, chillingly (no pun intended), I heard the dreaded sound: clunk, clunk, clunk-a-dee-clunk, and then an ominous hisssssss— like a herd of buffalo coming to a screeching, surprised halt.

My air-conditioning unit, that great, big monstrosity that hung precariously ten stories above the teaming masses, had, without warning, up and died.

My heart, when it realized what had just happened, went clunk-a-dee-clunk, as well.

"No, no. Not now," I shouted at the cold, lifeless beast. "It's August in New York. Are you insane, dying now? Are you trying to take me with you? I'm sorry I didn't pay more attention to you these past ten years, but I've been busy." Those Danielle Steele novels didn't read themselves, obviously.

It was then I noticed it: the silence in my too small, overpriced walk-up. It was deafening. And the heat, the dreaded heat that had been kept at bay by a mere few centimeters of cracked, rattling glass, plus the unappreciated efforts of my overworked, now-dead unit, was slowly, menacingly creeping in.

A certain prophetic last few, terrifying words seeped into my already addled brain: *I'm melting, meeeltiiing.*

I slipped on my slippers and ran, as fast as my legs could carry me, down, down, down the endless, narrow, paint-chipped flights of stairs to the one person who could save me from certain disaster. I dreaded knocking on his door, though. The building superintendent, a crotchety old man that hated everyone and everything accept for the Mets and the occasional Nathan's hotdog, would not be thrilled at my uninvited, though obviously quite necessary, interruption.

Gingerly, I rapped on his door.

Nothing. Not a peep from within.

I knocked again. Louder this time. "Mister Wordlow, it's Sean O'Malley from apartment 1015," I spoke into the door, sweating profusely in the sweltering, airless corridor.

Still nothing.

I tried again, fearless now in my desperation. "Please, Mister Wordlow, it's life or death." My life. My air-conditioning unit's death.

And then I heard the faintest of sounds. Feet shuffling from behind the door. Then the familiar click-click-click of several locks being unlocked. Then the door creaking slowly open. And then…KAPOW! This was the sound of my heart nearly exploding out of my chest.

For there, in Mister Wordlow's very entryway, stood a be-toweled behemoth, dripping tiny drops of water on the buckled, worn hardwood floor. "Sorry," he said. "I was in the shower."

The sun from the living room window rocketed through the tiny apartment and bathed the near-naked angel as if he had emerged from a Botticelli painting. I gasped and gaped and gawked at the site of him—at his wheat colored, wet hair, sparkling blue eyes, full lips, chiseled jaw, chiseled chest, chiseled, well, chiseled *everything*.

"You're not Mister Wordlow," I managed. A gross understatement if ever I'd heard one.

He smiled, a big, toothy, glimmering, white smile. "The guy retired. Moved to Fort Lauderdale. Name's Dillon. Dillon O'Leary." He reached out his mitt of a hand to me. "I'm the new super."

The word didn't do him justice, I thought. I'd heard of the luck of the Irish, of course, but this took the cake. The cake, the icing, and all the candles. Hell, the whole damn bakery, for that matter.

I grasped his hand in my own. A tiny shock, a spark, ricocheted up my arm, through my aching heart, and, *boing*, landed smack-dab in my groin.

"Sean O'Malley. Pleased to meet you," I said, breathlessly. The heat had suddenly jumped another ten furious degrees in those briefest of moments. "Sorry to disturb you, but my air-conditioning unit decided to quit on me a few minutes ago." This, under the circumstances, now seemed like a godsend.

His radiant smile widened. He released his grip on my sweat-soaked palm. "Well now," he said. "That was awfully inconsiderate, what with it being summer and all." His slight Irish brogue harkened me back to my childhood—to parades, to corned beef and cabbage, to Lucky Charms. Then he laughed, which, to my ears, sounded like a heavenly chorus. "Guess I'll get dressed and see what I can do for you then."

"Don't!" I shouted. Quickly, I amended with, "I mean, sure, get dressed, but don't hurry on my account." I blushed, feeling the crimson creep up my neck and spread across my cheeks. "I mean, take your time." Which meant: take your time so I can run upstairs, clean my dumpy apartment, towel off the sweat that had accumulated in every nook and cranny of my body, throw on some mood music, and lounge seductively on my sofa for you.

"Okay," he said, with a hearty chuckle. "I'll be up in a few minutes then."

He smiled, nodded, and slowly closed the door behind him. And in the briefest of seconds before the door met the frame—oh joy, oh joy—I saw the towel drop, and caught a glimpse of what will forever be etched in my memory of the most perfect, alabaster ass in the history of all mankind. Forget Botticelli, we're talking Michelangelo's David now.

I froze, relishing the moment, then turned and hightailed up the stairs, taking two then three at a time. I reentered my apartment, which, in the short while I'd been downstairs, had become a veritable oven, and quickly began putting my plan into action. Hurriedly, I tidied up, toweled off, put on some clean clothes, popped in some Barbra, circa 1971, poured two glasses of cold iced tea, and then flung myself suggestively on the sofa, just as there came a knocking on my door.

"Come in," I said, encouragingly, then gulped for air. "It's open."

In he came, newly dressed, with the same smile and a rusty metal toolbox in his grip. "You okay? Did you throw your back out or something?" he asked, setting the box down and closing the door behind him.

Guess my pose wasn't as wanton as I would have hoped for.

"Oh, no, I was just stretching," I lied. "It's all those stairs. Murder on your back."

I hopped up and went for the cold drinks. Then I ran back and handed him one. Well, I ran and tripped, really, sending the glass, the tea, and the small lemon wedge flying up, and on and over my would-be rescuer, my Irish Adonis.

"Oh my God, I'm so sorry," I cried. "It's the heat. It's the sweat. It slipped." It was him. In my apartment. Looking like he did.

He laughed, yet again. "Actually, it felt kind of nice. A guy could melt up here." Then the silver lining ran circles around my cloud. He reached down, lifted his T-shirt up, raised it over his head, and dried himself off with it. "All better," he added. "Now, let's get this baby fixed."

He could fix my air-conditioning, hopefully, but what about my heart?

"Great," I said, quelling my stomach butterflies as I led him to the defunct window unit. "Here you, um, go." I pointed at it with a wave of my hand, like one of Bob Barker's beauties.

He paused and looked instead to the left of the dead machine, towards my low-rise bookcase. Lifting a framed photo off the top, he asked, "Your family?"

I smiled as I looked at the familiar picture. "All ten of us. Family trip last year, to the old homeland."

"Mother Ireland," he said, with a heavy sigh. "I haven't been back since I was a wee lad." The brogue deepened. "New York is a nice place, but, well, you know…"

Indeed I did. "It was my first time there, but almost immediately it felt like home. I was actually planning a trip back as soon as I can afford it."

He looked at me, his stunning blue eyes locking on to mine, and his frown turned upside down. Then he handed me back the picture. His finger slid over my own, sending that lovely spark once again through my body. "Aye, small world, I was doing the same thing," he said. "Working two jobs even." He looked over at my other pictures, lifting each one up in turn and smiling as he did so. "Nice looking family," he commented. "But no one special on your arm, I see."

The blush crept back up my neck. I diverted him towards the topic at hand. "Who'd want a guy who lives in a ten story walk-up with no air conditioning?" I laughed, weakly.

He took the hint, set the picture he was holding back down, and started unscrewing the rear side of my lowly air-conditioner. I watched intently (lustfully) from my sofa as he began his work.

First thing he did was to remove the outer casing. His sleek back muscles rippled and flexed as he set the heavy metal object gently on my floor. I stared in awe as his biceps and triceps, and all the other ceps, quivered and quaked and then relaxed.

But that was just the warm up, the pre-show.

He opened his toolbox, removed a long, thin screwdriver, and sat cross-legged beneath the unit. He worked that way for a while, his head tilted upwards, and his hand now buried inside the bottom of the silent machine, offering me a full-on view of his magnificent body.

Thank goodness I was so poor and my apartment was so tiny, because my sofa and the rear wall were only about five feet apart. I could see every bead of sweat that cascaded down his broad chest. Could follow the path of dirty blond chest hairs as they worked their way along his torso and gradually became a thin line down his rock-solid, six-pack abs, ending, sadly, out of sight inside his tight denim shorts, only to reemerge darker and thicker around his tree-trunk thighs and prominent calves. And the pouch in the center of those shorts, well now, let me tell you...

"Um, Sean, could you lend me a hand here?" I was jolted out of my reverie.

"Sure, no problem," I said, jumping up and over to his side.

"Down here," he said. "Like I'm sitting."

I got down on the ground and sat like he sat.

"Put your hand here," he said, taking my hand in his own and placing two of my fingers against a hot, metal disk. I was worried that all the electricity he was causing every time he touched me would cause a circuit to blow (or something to blow, anyway), but I kept this thought to myself. "Now," he said. "Hold on to that and don't let go until I tell you to. If it drops, we're out of business."

I did as was told, which wasn't easy. We were now mere inches apart, with our hairy legs rubbing up against each another and our arms and elbows bumping and sliding, covered as they were in slick sweat.

"Okay," he said. "Just a quick twist of the screwdriver, and…presto."

He turned to me, our faces so close that I could smell his after-shave and the fresh, minty scent of Listerine. Our arms were still embedded in the machine above, but our eyes were once again locked, blue on blue. He didn't say anything yet, just sat and stared into my eyes as if he knew exactly what I was thinking.

"Sorry about that comment earlier," he said, almost in a whisper. "None of my business, really, if you're single or not."

"Oh, it's no, um, *sweat*," I replied, glancing at the river of perspiration that ran down our necks. We both laughed and moved in a few centimeters closer. "And you? Single, I mean?"

Closer now. Even closer.

"Guess I haven't met the right…"—he paused, looking for the right word— "*man*, yet."

Well, that did it. There was nowhere else to go. Our lips, at once, joined, merged, meshed, then parted, to allow tongues to swirl and slide and careen. The eyes stayed opened, locked, as always. He brought his hand down from the air-conditioner. I did the same. His arms encircled my shoulders, mine his waist. We turned ourselves into each other, pressed our sweat-covered bodies up tight, until I could feel his thumping heart against my chest. We stayed that way for countless magical minutes.

And then, "Damn, it's hot in here," he said into my ear, just before nibbling my lobe, then my neck.

"Well, it could be that the air-conditioner isn't on, but, honestly, I think it's you."

He laughed. "Only one way to tell," he said, jumping up and putting the casing back on. "Now, if you'd be so kind as to flick the switch."

I too stood up, and, with a flourish, did as he asked. The beast sputtered and coughed and clunked and clicked, and then, like music to our ears, whirred and purred like a kitten, sending a blast of cool, sensuous air against our over-heated bodies.

I reached out and pulled him towards me, grinding my chest, hips, and mouth into his, and holding on for dear life. When I'd at last came up for air, I leaned into his ear and said. "Nope, still hot in here, must be you."

"And you, Sean. Most definitely you."

We walked away from the living room and into my, thankfully, now cooler bedroom. He sat on my bed and looked at another picture that sat on my nightstand. It was of me, alone, on an emerald green hill overlooking the dark ocean below.

"You look lonely," he said, taking my hand.

I winked at him. "Maybe next time I go I'll have someone who'll hold my hand and enjoy the scenery with me."

He looked down at my hand in his, then looked back up into my eyes. He smiled and kissed me tenderly on the lips. "I've got a hand right here, Sean," he said.

"I've got one too, Dillon. And it's all yours."

What a great summer we had.

The next one in Ireland was even better.

WATER TAXI

LAWRENCE SCHIMEL

THE ROUGH ORANGE FABRIC of the life jacket was rubbing my nipples raw. At times like this I'm glad I didn't let Jaume talk me into getting my nipple pierced when he had his done. I like the way it looks, the small silver loop, especially since he only had one side pierced; I don't know, when men have both sides done it makes me think of door knockers, and the whole aesthetic changes and loses something. But I thought, he must be suffering more from the life preserver than I was right now, since the pierced tit is supposed to be more sensitive than before.

Jaume, though, didn't seem about to complain. He sat at the prow of the double kayak, his powerful arms dipping to one side and then the other as he paddled. His shoulders were hidden under the life preserver, but I could watch the musculature of his back flex as he twisted left and right with each stroke, and I wondered once again what I'd done to be so lucky to have such a beautiful man as my boyfriend. I felt lucky about everything right then—Jaume, the crystal-clear blue sky, the afternoon sun, the warm surf, the party on the beach, life in general. I forgot about my sore nipples and matched Jaume's strokes, and we just glided across the waves for a while.

My mind was wandering as my body worked through the simple repetitive task of kayaking, but I was awakened from these musings by a call from a pleasure boat that had anchored in front of the beach, neither especially near to nor all that far out from the shore, as if undecided whether they wanted to simply watch the festivities or be included. Apart from the all-male crew on the deck, it was obvious from even a cursory glance at their postures as they stood about drinking afternoon cocktails and watching the shore that they were not here by mistake but had come for the Gay Pride party.

One of the men, blond and shirtless, was leaning over the side and hailing us. I was sure it was us, because when he saw us glance up he waved in our direction, but I looked over my shoulder anyway. I had that feeling like when you're in a crowded bar and a guy you think is cute smiles at you, and you can't believe he's really smiling at you, certain that one of his friends or some hot number must be standing just behind your shoulder and is in fact the intended recipient of the smile.

"What do you think?" Jaume asked, not breaking his stroke. We were angling parallel to the beach, and if their boat had been in motion our paths would've crossed in a hundred meters or so.

"Why not see what he wants?" I answered, using my paddle to change our course. "Maybe they want to offer us a drink?" I laughed and our little shared kayak spun around toward the boat, and in a moment I again matched Jaume's even strokes.

As we drew up to the boat, the shirtless blond moved to stand at the deck's ladder. It turns out he was dressed in a skimpy bright orange Speedo. "Can you take me to shore?" he asked, in Castillian rather than in Catalan as Jaume and I had been speaking. "The water's full of jellyfish."

I looked him over, and from my angle I got a good look at certain parts. Which, I had to admit, looked quite nice from here.

Jaume and I have been together nearly two years, during which time we've tried a number of different relationship options, from complete monogamy to a period when we were hardly having sex with each other we were slutting around so much. This led to a trial separation and eventual reunion under our current agreement: whenever we want something outside our relationship, we do it together. This doesn't mean that we always wind up in threesomes, although that is usually the case. Sometimes we might go to a sauna together, and maybe each of us pick up someone; the cabinas aren't really big enough for all four of us to go into one and have our two separate pairings, but the one time we tried it was pretty exciting watching Jaume get fucked by someone else while he watched me fuck the trick I'd picked up. I still felt some jealousy, but at the same time I felt Jaume was including me in his pleasure and vice versa.

Most of the time, we were happiest with the more traditional threesome, and our taste was similar enough that we didn't have too many disagreements—at least among ourselves. It was not always the easiest thing convincing our prospective third, but actually many guys have a fantasy about doing threesomes. They're not always so easy to come by in the typical bar or dance club scenario (as opposed to, say, a sauna, where they're easier to arrange), so many men were willing to give it a shot when we asked them. I always think they took one look at Jaume and decided they'd put up with sharing him for a chance at sex with him, half a cake being better than no cake. I'm just glad I'm a deciding voice in who I share him with.

Since both Jaume and I have active libidos, we're usually up for anything attractive the other proposes. So I boldly asked our blond boatman, "And what's our fee for the taxi service?" in Castillian while rubbing my crotch with one hand in an unmistakable gesture. Jaume, looking over his shoulder at me, glanced down into my lap and smiled, his silent agreement to what I'd proposed, then looked up at the guy on the deck as we waited for an answer. He looked down at the bulge growing in my skimpy blue swim trunks, glanced out at the shore for a moment, then back at Jaume and me.

"OK," he nodded, "come on up," and he stepped away from the side of the boat.

I, too, looked back at the shore, my mind crowding with thoughts: I wondered what people could see from the beach. I wondered if anyone would see us board the boat and especially if the kayak crew would get mad at us for abandoning ship. I wondered if our stuff, still on the beach, was safe. I wondered about the wisdom of climbing onto a boat full of strange men; what if they were the proverbial axe-murderers, who dumped the body bits overboard where the fishes ate up the evidence? I wondered what our prospective passenger looked like without his bathing suit, and I nudged Jaume in the back with my paddle. "Let's go," I said.

We tied the kayak to the bottom rung of the ladder and then climbed up it, taking the paddles with us. The last thing we needed was for a wave to knock them into the water while we were up on the boat, leaving us *all* stranded. Besides, I figured if we had them with us, it would be more trouble for one of the guys on the boat to steal the kayak. I was still feeling a little suspicious. But I've always been cautious: Even with tricks on land, I was wary if I brought them home, making sure there were no easily-pocketed valuables lying about and guarding my wallet someplace unexpected. I'd never had any problems, but it didn't hurt to be on the safe side, I thought, even when walking on the wild side.

I followed Jaume onto the deck. We were surrounded by a group of maybe seven men—some in swimsuits, like we were, others in more ordinary summer clothes. They were all eyeing us, as if they were feeling suspicious, too. And who could blame them? Or was there something more than curiosity in their gaze? How much of our interchange had they overheard?. And what did they think of it, those who'd heard and understood?

The guy who wanted a ride stood with the rest of them, but he didn't really blend into the crowd. Maybe it was because he was the only one I recognized—he had an identity separate from that of the group because I'd first seen him alone, leaning over the side of the boat as he called out to us. Also, he stood a step apart from them physically, as if to underscore the fact that he was leaving, and they would stay. As I took in the other men—who were as varied a lot of homosexual types as one could imagine, from an over-dressed, highly coifed queen to a quiet butch number who looked like an ultra-straight soccer player—I wondered if he'd always been part of this mixed crew or if he'd swum out here. I glanced at his crotch, but his swimsuit was dry. All that meant was that he'd been onboard long enough to dry out. As I watched, I thought his basket gave a small jump, as if in anticipation of what we planned, and I smiled, as much at the thought of our imminent sex as the idea of how I imagined this was making him feel. I glanced at the other men as I idly rubbed my crotch, but got no sexual connection from any of them. Suddenly, I wondered less why he wanted to go ashore.

Our blond made no move to introduce us, or himself, and I wondered if we were planning to do whatever it was we would do there in front of everyone. It would hardly be the first time we had an audience, so it didn't really faze me, and I was sure it wouldn't be much of a problem for Jaume either. I reached over and helped him unbuckle the life jacket, letting it fall to the deck. It made a small clatter as the buckles hit the wood, and the noise seemed startling in the absence of any social chatter. Jaume hadn't moved and was still straddling the strap that had gone between his legs, which now made two separate circles connecting to the life jacket. As I looked at Jaume's muscular thighs I imagined him as the famed Colossus of Rhodes straddling the strait. What a sight it must have been to sail between those massive thighs and gaze upwards!

I reached down and fondled Jaume's cock through the fabric of his green swimsuit, staring defiantly at the men around us. Like me, Jaume was half-hard already and I could feel his dick respond to my fingers. The men said nothing—content, it seemed, to be voyeurs and nothing more. Even the blond in the orange bathing suit was silent, although he watched my hand as it moved, looking up every now and then to meet my stare and then letting his gaze drop once more. Finally, he moved closer to us and dropped to his knees before Jaume. I pulled the green nylon down over Jaume's hips and his cock sprang free of the confining fabric. The blond reached out to hold it, and I looked up at the crowd around us, expecting them to respond in some way, but they were all as still as statues. It would've been much more normal for them to try and be involved, or to comment in some way, to somehow indicate that they were, if not exactly participating, at least present and aware. Even pointedly ignoring us, carrying on their conversation as if we were not fornicating in their midst, would be a more direct acknowledgment.

I put them out of mind and looked down at Jaume's ass clenching and unclenching as he thrust his cock into the blond's mouth. My cock grew longer at the sight of my lover's cock being worshipped by this stranger's mouth, and it poked out from the side of my swimsuit. I still had my life jacket on, so I couldn't actually pull the trunks down the way I'd done with Jaume, since the strap that ran between my legs prevented this. But I pulled my cock and balls free through one of the leg holes and started pulling at my dick; I didn't want to bother with the hassle of untangling the jacket, and the tight fabric of the swimsuit's leg hole against the base of my cock was a pleasurable pressure.

The blond still wore his orange swim trunks as he sucked off my boyfriend. As if my glancing at his cock awakened some sixth sense in him, he seemed to realize that my cock was also loose and seeking attention, and without either looking up or breaking his rhythmic motions along Jaume's cock, he reached out and grabbed hold of mine with unerring precision, as if he'd all this time been completely aware of where it was in relation to him. This was a skill I often admired in men who had it, like the ability to locate another man's nipples through his shirt without groping around.

I looked up again at the men around us as the blond jerked on my dick, but it was as if time had stopped as far as they were concerned, for all the life they showed. I glanced at their crotches to see if at least we were providing them with a good spectacle, but it was hard to tell if they were aroused or not. As if he could tell that my attention had wandered away, the blond's tugging at my dick changed, and suddenly he pulled me forward by my cock until I had to shift my stance; I stumbled forward and suddenly I was sliding into the wet of his mouth. I watched his lips work their way up and down my shaft, and looking past his face I could see the outline of his own dick, obviously hard, within his orange swimsuit. But he made no move to take it out or even touch himself through the fabric. I was glad, judging from his arousal, that he was obviously enjoying some aspect of this scene. And then I closed my eyes and stopped worrying, and let myself enjoy the slippery magic of his tongue on my cock. With my eyes still closed I reached out and found Jaume's pierced tit, as if I'd suddenly acquired that skill that had always amazed me, although I think it was simply because the piercing made for a much larger area for my fingers to find. I tugged at the silver loop gently, and smiled and opened my eyes and found my lover smiling back. I grabbed him by the neck and pulled him toward me for a kiss.

Below us, the blond had grabbed both of our dicks and was jerking us off as he caught his breath. Or perhaps he was simply considering, weighing our cocks in his fists as he contemplated his next move. He tugged our cocks until we were standing close to one another, then put both of us in his mouth at once. It's a strange feeling, because it's not as wonderful as having a pair of lips clamped tightly around the shaft of your cock, but sharing something so intimate with my lover made the experience even more intense. Jaume's and my own tongues locked as the blond ran his back and forth over the sensitive crowns, pulled free from their foreskin by the state of our arousal. I could feel my breath quicken in those moments leading up to orgasm, and I grabbed my own dick with one hand and began to jerk myself off. Jaume followed suit, and I looked down at the blond to see how he was responding, thinking that he might be touching himself, but he seemed to be just watching us jerk off and enjoying the sight from his crotch-level view. But then he leaned forward and began to suck on my balls, and after a few more moments I was sending short white arcs of cum onto the wooden deck. I made a sort of grunt into Jaume's throat with each spasm that went through my cock, and even with my eyes closed in ecstasy I could tell that Jaume had quickened the pace of his hand's motion. Soon his tongue was pressing deeply into my mouth as he, too, came.

The blond was still kneeling before us, smiling widely. And suddenly, now that the sex was over, the other passengers suddenly came to life. I didn't quite understand the noise at first, lost in the afterglow of orgasm, but I soon made out words and realized they were talking to each other again, going about things as usual, although still keeping an eye turned toward us every now and then. Maybe it was because Jaume's and my cock were still bare for all to see, mine already shrinking now that I'd cum but Jaume's still a rigid pole; he always took a while for it to go down. "Well, that was certainly worth a first-class trip to the shore," I announced. The blond smiled again and climbed to his feet. I wondered for a moment if he were planning to kiss us, and half-hoped he would, since it would make the encounter feel suddenly more...personable. But the moment passed and he turned toward the others.

Jaume bent forward and pulled his swimsuit up. He stepped into the loops of the life jacket and I helped him into it, as the blond said goodbye to his friends. I watched him kiss them farewell, some on either cheek, and some directly on the lips, and wondered what each man must feel, knowing where his mouth had been just moments before. Were they disgusted? Jealous? As indifferent, as they'd been while watching us? I wasn't sure. And it didn't really matter.

Jaume and I descended first to resume our places with the paddles. I wondered for a moment what would happen if we simply took off before the blond descended. It was not as if there were anything truly binding us to wait for him, other than our word. What could he do, complain to the police that he had given us each blow jobs and we wouldn't take him to shore in return? It wasn't as if he'd dive in after us, since he was afraid of the jellyfish. And with reason, I noticed, watching a ghostly white shadow bloom in the water next to our kayak.

We waited for him, an honorable exchange as we'd agreed, and once he'd settled himself on the little ridge between the seats we began paddling and pulled away from the boat. His friends called out after him, and there were other shouts and noises, and sounds of frivolity from the men we couldn't see from our lower vantage. Suddenly the boat seemed like a lively and fun place, quite the opposite of how it had been when we were aboard. Had we been the inhibiting force? Maybe it was our passenger. It didn't really matter. My lover and I had enjoyed our private encounter there amidst the crowd, and I at least had no regrets.

Our strokes had pulled us nearly to the shore. "Thanks," our passenger said as he leaped off the kayak into the shallow water and waded the last few feet onto the sandy beach. He turned around and waved at us, and back at the pleasure boat, and then walked up the sand. I wondered briefly what plans he had here, if maybe we'd see him again later at the dance. Or any of those men from the boat....

One of the kayak crewmen came jogging over and yelled at us for coming this close to the beach. He told us we had to head out to deeper waters or bring the kayak back to the launch. We pushed off, Jaume and I, paddling back out among the higher waves and the ghostly jellyfish. The sky was crystal blue, the sea was warm, my boyfriend was with me, and we'd just had a threesome with a sexy blond. On the beach behind us was a party celebrating being gay: it was one of those perfect moments.

We weren't paddling in any direction, just sort of enjoying being out on the surf. After a while, Jaume looked over his shoulder at me and asked in Catalan, "Think we should go back to the boat and see if anyone else needs a lift?"

I smiled at Jaume, and without a word I stuck my paddle into the water like a rudder again, turning our course back toward that boat at my lover's request.

COUNTRY CLERK MORE THAN JUST A HOT ASS

JAY STARRE

I TURNED THIRTY-NINE last summer. A little frightening, that age with the prospect of the forties looming ahead. The fear that no one would ever call me "hot" again, left me with the uneasy sense that sexual famine lay ahead.

Maybe it was time to stop fooling around. Dare I contemplate actually getting a boyfriend, or at least a steady fuck bud? Would someone even want an old geezer like me? Huge questions.

A summer vacation would have been nice, reclining on a beach after a morning in the gym sculpting my body into the best possible state of physical allure. But before that was possible, I accepted one more July contract from my boss. I had no idea then how life altering that summer job would turn out to be.

Weeks later, I was hot and tired and nearly fed up with my painting contract in rural Idaho. The riding arena I was painting was enormous. The project was stretching out to several months instead of the planned three weeks. I cursed my luck, afraid of a missed summer cruising when it could be my last as a younger-than-forty gay stud.

I needed more paint, and gratefully took the opportunity for a break to drive down the road to the nearby country store, which sold just about everything the locals needed. Inside, although there was no air conditioning, huge ceiling fans blew cooler air down over me. I let out a big sigh of relief as I entered.

"Hot out there. What can I do for you, bud? More paint?"

The clerk was alone, and the store was actually empty at two o'-clock on that blistering summer afternoon. I met his eyes and nodded, managing an exhausted smile. He'd served me twice before, and both times I'd noticed how damn cute he was.

Somewhere in his early twenties, stocky with nicely muscled forearms and biceps, he definitely turned my crank in the right direction. Soft-spoken to the point of diffidence, I was intrigued, but fairly certain he had no interest in a sweaty, dirty painter. An old one at that.

His blue eyes met mine, and a hint of a smile curled his bowed lips. "Cooler down in the basement. We got a load of ice delivered and I left some out in a big tub. Real nice down there."

Was that an invitation? I hadn't given a moment's thought to seeking out sex on the gruelling work junket, merely anxious to finish the job and return to Seattle. Yet those blue eyes seemed to promise more than a mere cooling off in the basement.

"Uh, wanna show it to me? How about a cold soda at the same time?"

His smile broadened, but his placid face didn't exactly light up. He was a cool one. I liked that. He nodded slowly, and moved around the counter to amble over to the front door and turn the open sign around to closed. He locked the door while he was at it.

Promising!

I checked out his ass, jutting with more promise, and nicely rounded in a pair of clean but well-worn jeans. It rolled rhythmically as he led the way to the rear of the store. I followed with a growing boner under my paint-stained work shorts.

When I could tear my eyes from that sturdy can, I noticed something I'd missed before. He wore a red baseball cap turned backwards, and just under the visor I noticed his platinum hair tied in a small ponytail. Unusual. I liked that too. He didn't fit my preconceived notion of the typical rural hick.

Broad shoulders indicated muscles beneath his grey T-shirt. Nothing wrong with that either. Without saying another word, he led me down stairs hidden behind a wall of dry goods.

Cool air wafted upwards. A pair of bare light bulbs illuminated a large storage room neatly lined with ceiling-high merchandise. Another ceiling fan beat a refreshing rhythm. I breathed in the cool air as I felt the sweat finally beginning to dry on my arms and back.

"Soda in the cooler. Your choice."

That quiet voice, a languid wave of his arm, and I wondered if he ever got excited or flustered. Would he pant and groan with a cock up the ass? Or would he just sigh and moan?

I fished out a soda with my back to him, fantasizing all kinds of nasty games. Wracking my brains for a suitable come-on, I turned back to him with that cold can of pop in my hand. He was standing beside the tub of melting ice.

His pants were in his hands!

His underwear were on the low counter against the wall behind him. That placid smile in place, he spoke quietly, just barely audible above the beating of the fan.

"Care to fuck my ass?"

All of the sudden, I no longer felt like an old fuck on the brink of turning forty and becoming a toothless derelict no one would ever desire again. This young hottie wanted me! My heat-depleted energy skyrocketed, just like my cock under my paint-stained shorts.

Thick, white thighs planted him solidly on the floor. Worn jogging shoes and short white socks, his grey T-shirt and that red baseball cap were all that remained of his clothing. He slowly backed up and raised his hips to sit on the counter behind him, his pale blue eyes on mine. He leaned back and spread his hairless thighs while placing his feet on the counter in front of him.

The cold soda chilled my paralysed vocal chords. The tent in my shorts was evident, while my open-mouthed stare had me looking like an idiot. I stumbled forward, emitting a choked gasp, one hand clutching that soda, the other tearing at my fly.

"No rush. You can fuck me as long as you want."

His quiet promise sent shivers down my spine. His next move had my cock leaping out of my shorts as I released it with a trembling hand. The big country clerk placed both hands under his husky thighs and lifted them up, scooting a little forward on the counter. His alabaster ass gaped wide open at crotch level, totally accessible.

"I'm Danny by the way. I think I caught your name last time you were in. Jay?"

"Uh, yeah. Nice to meet you," I managed to mutter as I moved in between those raised thighs. "Oh my god, what an awesome ass," I added just under my breath.

My shorts and underwear slipped to the floor and I stepped out of them in a fog of lust. My bobbing dick banged against one cheek of his ass, silky-smooth flesh searing it as I finally thought to get rid of the can of pop in my hand by placing it on the counter top beside him.

He chuckled lightly, his knees back against his chest. One hand slid down from under his thigh and reached out to capture my cock. With unrushed ease, he aimed it at his asshole, the rosebud pouting between his ample butt cheeks.

I stared down at that hole. It twitched and then gaped apart. Goddamn! He placed the crown of my cock against it, rubbing slowly back and forth over the slick ass entrance. I shuddered and leaned into him.

I was suddenly and acutely aware of how sweaty and dirty I was. I'd been working out in the hot sun all day. Paint spattered my tank top and my arms. In contrast, he was cool and refreshingly clean.

He read my hesitation accurately. That languid smile remained unchanged as he quietly eased my fears. "You're my kind of guy. All man. A little hard-earned sweat and dirt turns me on. Fuck me, baby."

His fingers around my shank were firm but undemanding. He continued to rub my oozing cock-head against his hot ass lips. It was so damn arousing, I suddenly calmed down, no longer in a crazed rush to get my rocks off.

"You're my kind of guy, too," I muttered through a constricted throat.

His smile widened and became a real grin. "This is nice. I like your dick rubbing against my asshole."

I smiled back, placing both hands on his smooth ass cheeks and feeling all that big muscle for the first time. I absolutely loved a big, powerful butt.

Danny kept on rubbing my gooey helmet over his asshole, pressing into the gaping center and slightly inside, then, pulling out to move it in slow circles to tease the slick lips. It was incredible. Under blond brows, his blue eyes closed halfway as he let out a big sigh and raised his other hand to his mouth to lick and spit on a pair of thick fingers.

I knew what was coming, but it still enthralled me as he dropped his slick fingers down into his crack and rubbed his own spit all over my cock-head and his asshole. Deliberately, slowly and with half-closed eyes on mine, he repeated that nasty action. Red lips swallowed his fingers and licked, then opened to release them as he placed the spit-soaked pair down between his raised ass cheeks again.

This time he dug into his own asshole. A deeper sigh escaped his open mouth as he probed his slot with spit-wet fingers and rubbed my cock against his knuckles. My knees threatened to buckle. It was the hottest preliminary to a fuck I'd ever experienced.

"Go inside me, baby. I want your cock."

His words were a whisper now. The beat of the fan above us seemed loud and strangely erotic. I shook all over as I thrust forward with my hips, his hand on my shank guiding me into him

Danny's fingers slid out as my cock slid in. I was expecting a clamping slot, and instead got a yawing tunnel that enveloped and sucked in half my cock in one easy gulp.

"Fuck! So damn good," I groaned, biting my lip and staring down into his placid face.

"Yeah. So damn good. Slide it on in. I want all of you, baby."

That gentle voice and another deep sigh was followed by a slight roll of his beefy ass. He swallowed cock with his welcoming butt hole. I leaned over him, my hands sliding up over satin ass mounds to his hefty thighs. I pressed him against the wall as I probed deeper into slippery ass.

His fingers on my shaft slid down to cup my balls, gently tugging them forward. His other hand slipped under my tank top and roamed over my rippled belly, tensed from trembling excitement. He explored my torso with slithering fingers, discovering and tweaking my nipples gently. His asshole swallowed my dick to the root.

Once I was buried to the balls, that welcoming hole began to close around my shank with gentle but steady palpitations. I gasped. He was milking my dick!

"Fuck! That's so hot. Keep doing it," I grunted out, my own hand now under his T-shirt. I was greedy for his hairless chest, seizing the taut little nipples and squeezing, while he was all ease and relaxed. A surging need to ram into that spit-slick hole slipped away as his tranquil mood settled over me like a breath of cool air.

I relaxed too, beginning to slowly pump in and out as his anal muscles rhythmically closed and opened in a gentle massage. I pulled all the way out, hovering at the slippery entrance to rub the lips in a teasing circle. Danny smiled up at me and nodded.

"Nice, baby. Take your time and fuck me right."

The whispered words sent another shiver through me. I pushed into him again, slowly penetrating his slick fuck tunnel inch by hard inch. He took it with a low moan and another gentle roll of his big ass cheeks. I buried it to the root again, feeling his insides throbbing around my entire shank. He held me inside him with massaging muscles and sighed against my neck as I leaned in over him. I inhaled his smell, fresh and clean but now redolent with sex stink. He pulled me even closer with his hands around my back under my T-shirt.

My hands moved around his back too, and we were in a tight embrace. I fucked in and out with lengthy strokes, feeling his asshole tighten and relax in perfect, rhythmic timing. My mouth slid over his and we kissed.

That kiss was surprising. His mouth opened to me gently, but once my tongue was inside, he sucked on it with sloppy greed. His asshole began to twitch more wildly and he let out a loud moan around my tongue. I pumped a little faster and harder.

I had his hefty body wrapped tightly in my arms, while he did the same, his hands locked on his elbows around my back. His asshole wrapped around my cock while his lips sucked on my stabbing tongue.

My balls roiled and I feared an imminent orgasm. His asshole was so steamy, his body so totally open to me, his mood so relaxed but so hungry for me at the same time, I wanted it to last forever. I slowed my pace, pulling out for a moment to hold my throbbing cock up against his sweaty, smooth crack between us while I caught my breath and willed my orgasm to subside.

It worked. He waited patiently, his sucking lips smacking around my tongue, his asshole a slippery pit against my shank, ready but undemanding. I found the hole with my cock again, and pushed inside, all the way home in one smooth glide.

His mouth released mine and he moaned out loud. "You're going to make me shoot. I love your cock up my ass, Jay."

It was gratifying to know I wasn't the only one nearly out of control. I clamped my lips over his and stabbed my tongue deep as I began to thrust in and out. My balls slapped against his hairless ass cheeks. The slurp of cock sliding in and out of spit-wet hole beat in time to the fan above.

His dick had been stiff and drooling between us throughout the languid fuck. I felt it swell and throb as my steady stuffing began to take its toll. Our arms around each other, our bodies moved together like one sweaty beast, our emotions now in perfect tune.

The rising need for release altered our steady rhythm. I pumped faster. He squirmed around my cock, his large ass slippery against my belly and balls. He sucked on me with his mouth and with his talented asshole. He groaned deep in his chest. His arms around my back gripped me with a tightening need.

I felt the surge of orgasm hit him. His cock pulsed against my torso. His asshole went into erratic convulsions. His explosive moan rumbled into my clamping mouth. Come suddenly spewed out of him to cream our mashed bodies.

I rode his orgasm with a rapturous glee. I pumped faster, deeper, harder, fucking the jizz out of him as his squishy asshole went into spasms around my ramming dick. I wanted to fuck him like that, his body writhing under mine out of control, for as long as possible.

But I couldn't hold back. I pulled out and backed out of his embrace. Our mouths came apart as my rearing cock erupted. Come flew in a wild arc to spatter his belly, his clean T-shirt, and even up to his neck and chin.

"Oh yeah. So nice," he moaned.

"No kidding," I gasped, my body jerking as I coated him with my load.

He lay back and took it, his smile broad, come bathing him in a sticky rain. His hands were on my naked hips and he held me there, wanting my load, his ass still wide open, his hole gaping and well fucked.

He was in no rush to clean up. We remained like that until every last drop of jizz oozed out of our cocks. Our breathing eased finally. His hands gently stroked my naked butt as he held me close against him.

"I hope you come back for more paint before too long," he finally said, a quirky smile promising more of the same.

"I'll be back for more ass, whether I need some paint or not," I promised with a grin of my own.

I left the store elated. The blistering heat of the Idaho afternoon no longer felt oppressive. A good fuck can do that to you. My ego had been stroked along with my cock. I was still a hot dude!

I returned to the country store before the week was out, actually feeling a few flutters in my belly at the prospect of seeing Danny again. That was weird. Normally, my cock would be fluttering up into a boner, rather than the pit of my stomach churning nervously.

"I'm off tomorrow. Can you meet me by the river for a few hours? The water's always cold, but we can get warm afterwards," Danny said in that languid voice of his. His blue eyes stared into mine, his muscular forearms stretched out over the counter in front of me. He smiled, and my stomach turned over again.

"Absolutely," I replied a little too quickly. I cursed myself for being too eager, then for worrying about it. Another hot fuck, probably, and what was there to worry about?

Danny, for his part, was perfectly composed as he gave me directions to a spot on the nearby river he promised would be beautiful, and private.

I left the store in a daze. Again, I worked through the cloudless summer afternoon in a state of elation. I was looking forward to the next day, and whatever came about.

I parked under the thick branches of a massive fir tree beside the country road. The path Danny promised was exactly where he'd said it would be. Through deep woods smelling of heated pine needles, I traipsed down to the nearby river.

There he was, sprawled out on a towel on his belly in a pair of colourful trunks.

I was suddenly out of breath as I stared at him. His large butt, encased in those bright trunks, the deep crack outlined, the swell of rounded cheeks captured perfectly. His muscular, smooth thighs, slightly tanned, his broad back pink from the sun, his platinum hair tied back in a small tail, the hat missing. How fucking hot he was!

I wanted to leap on top of him, tear off those trunks, and fuck his brains out.

He rolled over just then and caught me staring, my hand at my crotch and cupping a stiffening boner under my shorts. His slow smile and direct gaze sent a wave of heat rushing up and down my spine.

Danny waved me over and began chattering in that quiet tone of his. I sat beside him on his towel, our bare thighs pressing together. Rather than a quick, nasty fuck, we talked. And talked. I found myself spellbound by his easy-going, unrushed attitude.

Yet a growing uneasiness began to grip me. Questions I rarely asked myself reared their ugly heads. Was I falling for him? Or was I just desperate for anyone who would have me? I cursed my own onslaught of insecurity. I'd never worried about any of that crap before. Maybe, just maybe, it was more than my age that fuddled my brain.

Maybe I was falling for this quiet country stud. That was even more frightening than turning thirty-nine.

"You've got something on your mind, Jay."

The soft-spoken question rattled me. My knee was slippery with sweat as it pressed into his inner thigh. We'd somehow slipped closer, half entwined in the shade of the woods with the burbling river below us.

I confessed.

I said things perhaps unwise on a second date, especially when the first was merely a wild fuck, as good a fuck as it had been. "So I'm getting old, and worrying about that, and maybe worrying about settling down too," I admitted at the end of a lengthy spiel.

He laughed quietly, one big hand sliding over my chest and arm as I sat over him and stared down into his amazing blue eyes. "Too much information?" I added with a worried frown.

"Not at all. Not at all."

He rose, pulling me up with him. "We can swim naked here. No one will be likely to come along, and if they do, they won't arrest us for public nudity."

He discarded his trunks, his thick cock rising up and jerking between us. I gasped, wanting him more than anything. He winked as he reached down to pull my shorts off. My stiff dick banged against his. He turned and I followed his white ass down to the water.

It was icy cold, as he'd promised. I let out a shriek as he pulled me into the rushing stream.

The day was so perfect, blue sky above, the heat of a summer sun dispelled by that freezing dip, the soft sand under us as we returned to his towel in the shade. My entire body tingled as we slid into an embrace.

"I like you a lot, Jay," Danny whispered in my ear as my cock thrust up between the cool flesh of his spread ass crack.

"The feeling is mutual," I replied, a catch in my voice.

We fucked for the second time, in no rush to end the perfect afternoon. Danny didn't seem capable of being in a rush anyway, and I found myself wanting his smooth, hot body in my arms forever.

I had him on his stomach, my cock riding his plump white can, his groans just audible over the rush of the stream below. I gasped for air, lunging, thrusting, and finally achieving orgasm. Danny sprayed the towel under us.

We talked afterwards as we ate from a cooler full of food he'd brought. It's funny how mere conversation can be so enjoyable when you're actually saying something meaningful. I told Danny things I'd never told anyone. I found out he was a musician in his spare time and he hardly ever fucked a guy unless he really liked them. Two interesting and important bits of information.

As the sun began to set behind the wall of fir and pine, we found ourselves kissing. Lying together, and kissing. And kissing.

I took my time on the paint job after that, suddenly in no rush to leave the area. With that country clerk ass to look forward to, I could have stayed forever. Danny was the brave one in the end, asking me if I wanted him to come back to Seattle with me.

"Yes. Please."

Our endless summer ended and Danny came home with me. With him around, my previous worries and insecurities seemed a little stupid.

He agreed they were.

1979

MARCUS JAMES

THE CAR TURNED UP THE DRIVE, winding along the cliff-side, seeing the brilliant July sun glisten on the blue waters of Bellingham Bay, the conclave of evergreens illuminating in their gorgeous green, and the mammoth mansions that filled the neighborhood of Edgemoore had their drives littered with luxury town cars and sports cars. This was all new to me—this excessive wealth—and I never thought that in my seventeenth summer of 1979 I would ever begin to enter this world of privilege, and seemingly upper crust seclusion.

I was sent to stay with my religious uncle and his second wife, Patrice, along with her two sons, Jeffery, who was now ten, and Elias, who was nineteen and had apparently decided to come home for the summer from college—he hadn't come home last summer and stayed on campus for all of his breaks. Elias's return was considered big news, and the family wanted to get together to celebrate it. My mother didn't want to come, but she felt that it would still be good for me.

The black Rolls Royce moved up a long drive and my eyes took in the limestone three- story manor, with a bright red front door and windows that were accented with white trim. I could already hear voices laughing and shouting beyond the house, as well as the splashing of water and what sounded to be the smacking of a ball on a tennis court.

My stomach was in knots, having not seen these people since I was twelve; and never once coming to my uncle's home, I didn't know what to expect. All I could really recall of my uncle was his stern detachment and his ever-ready need to quote passages from the Bible. If that was the world I was going to be spending my summer in, then I didn't want any part of it. I knew I was different from them. I knew that I liked guys not girls, and yet I had never been in a situation to act on it, and I was already afraid enough that I would be detected, I didn't need to feel like I would be in a place where not only would it possibly be scoped out, but that I could perhaps be punished for it.

"Here you are…" the old driver said to me, opening the door and letting me out, already attending to my luggage in the trunk. The sun seemed shadowed behind the gargantuan citadel that stood before me, and yet it was all bright in that cool shadowed blue. It seemed that on either side of me the home went on forever, and I came to the realization that I was going to be entering a world that I had never dreamed could ever be for me, it was a world I thought I could only see on television and in the movies.

"Let's go." The driver said to me, walking up the front steps and turning the wrought-iron handle of the front door, pushing it open and allowing the front foyer to envelope me. A half-gasp escaped my lips and my jaw dropped as I took in the immensity of this home. The foyer with its polished hardwood floors, stretching out in one fell swoop as it reached all the way to the large French doors at the back of the house. There was a round oak table covered in amazing flowers, and the walls were painted with delicate Japanese murals. Above me was one of the largest chandeliers I had ever seen and to either side of me were massive sitting rooms, each with their own theme it seemed, expressed through its furniture.

"Wait here." He said and began his walk to the back of the house. I watched him open the French doors and step outside, and within moments I watched the occupants of this home make their way inside and close in the distance between us. My uncle was dressed in white shorts and a white polo with thin mint green stripes, clutching a tennis racket in hand, I was actually afraid that he was going to hit me with it. His short silver hair was thick and his eyes were cold and stern. Patrice followed behind him, wearing a white pleated skirt and powder pink polo, a white sweater tied around her neck, and her dirty blond hair was feathered like Farrah Fawcett. They seemed to be the Lacoste generation, and their K-Swiss tennis shoes looked as if they had just been purchased that morning. Following close behind was Jeffery, who came running in dripping wet, obviously from playing in the pool, the water dripping off of his brown hair and tapping on the floorboards. He was my uncle's son, and so I was guessing that the dark hair had come from him.

"Andrew it's good to see you!" Patrice said to me, one of those cheesy WASP smiles on her face, the kindness so superficial that you could hear its fakeness in the pitch of her words. I was too busy singing "Run to Me" by the Bee Gees to myself to really care, and my uncle stuck out his hand and gave me a firm handshake. He paused and looked at my own lazy, limp-wristed shake and I squirmed.

"Elias get in here!" my uncle yelled out, and I watched as his long shadow first appeared, stretching across the floor, and then his glorious form take shape in front of me and make his way towards me. Elias was tall, lean, with olive skin and long dark hair which grazed his jaw, he was clean shaven and had the exotic dark eyes that one would get if your father had been a handsome Mexican man, which his was, and his lips were so sensuous. His chest had that smooth swimmer's look, and the only hair that could be seen was a thin trail that led from his navel and down his flat stomach and into the area hidden by his tiny black shorts with white racing stripes on either side of the leg. A shell necklace was latched around his throat and fit more like a loose choker than anything else.

He seemed to move in slow motion and I was captivated by him. His beauty that seemed dangerous, forbidden, silent. It was something that I desired to know. It was also something that made me instantly afraid of him.

"Elias, you remember Andrew don't you?" he grinned and threw his towel around his neck, giving his hair a quick dry.

"Oh yeah, how's it go'n man?" he smiled and took my hand into his; it caused me to blush and avert my gaze for just a moment. When I looked up I found him staring at me.

"Um great... it's going great..." my words trailed off and I felt so stupid. How could I have let myself be so obvious in front of everyone, in front of him! I had felt as if I was the biggest freak in the world.

"Well," Patrice began, clapping her hands together. "While I get the lemonade ready, why don't you show Andrew his room... Elias..." she narrowed her eyes to her eldest and he nodded.

"Don't you mean while you have the maid get the lemonade ready?" she gave an annoyed chuckle and grin.

"Whatever." Elias gave a cock of his head, directing me to follow him. I was willing to follow him anywhere.

✦

"SO YOU GLAD YOU CAME OUT HERE?" he asked me, leading me up a grand winding staircase, my eyes focused on his tanned backside and the scattered moles, finally stopping on that taunt ass of his, the thin dark hairs, appearing so soft and tempting me to reach out and pull those shorts down.

"Wha?" he looked over his shoulder, staring at me and grinning, his eyes seeming to pierce right through me.

"I asked you if you were glad to come here." I shrugged.

"Its fine I guess... I mean I didn't really have a say in the matter." He nodded.

"Well, I'll be sure to find ways to... entertain you." I thought I could feel my heart stop, for just a moment, and I think I swallowed hard, in a classic exaggerated television 'gulp.' "This is it." He stopped at a door near the end of the hall on the second floor, pausing for just a moment and causing me to bump into him, my hands gripping his waist. He looked back at me, smiling. I dropped my hands. "Careful it sticks." I nodded and backed away, trying to understand what it was that I was feeling, and was he flirting with me? It was all so confusing.

He stood in the room and watched as I unpacked, and I found myself looking out onto the view of the bay and the San Juan Islands more than I looked at anything else, especially because it would mean having to look at him.

"Do I make you nervous Andrew?" I turned around and saw him lay out on my bed, his shorts stretching with his bent knees, his cock becoming hard and poking out from the left leg.

"Um no. I mean of course not. Why would you?" I turned from him and I heard him chuckle. There was movement on the bed, and then he was on his feet, moving behind me, creeping up on me, reaching his arms out around me, the sun splashing through the bedroom window. I couldn't breathe, not after I felt him press up against me. I felt over dressed. In my white collared shirt and pullover navy blue sweater-vest, the neck with red and white trim, my legs quivering within my tight denim bell-bottoms. I was becoming hot and I was certain that my ears were turning red.

"Look at them down there..." he began, his voice a seductive whisper in my ear. I spotted my uncle and his wife laughing and watching Jeffery splash around in the giant pool. "They would never hear us... they would never know..." he began to slip his hand down my back, slowly, before finally finding his way to the hem of my pants and sticking his finger inside, caressing the crack of my ass. "They would never know that I was fucking you in a way that you will never be fucked again." I closed my eyes and felt the pain of my hard-on against the constriction of my pants. I gasped and spun around, coming face to face with Elias, his eyes taking me in, the scent of his skin, salty and mixed with the aroma of chlorine. I wanted him to do whatever he wanted to me, I wanted him to take me to places I had never been. I wanted it but backed away.

"Um... we should be getting back." He closed his eyes and looked down for just a moment, releasing his grip on my waist.

"Alright..." he looked back up and moved closer to me, I closed my eyes, expecting him to kiss my lips, but to my surprise he moved to my cheek and kissed it lightly. "Lets go!" I watched him make his way to the door, my hands foolishly attempting to conceal my hard-on. "Thank God we're not really related." He smiled and I just nodded dumbly. Where the hell was I? What kind of world had I entered? These questions kept spinning through my head and I was so lost, so confused that I had no idea how to answer them, what was worse, I had no idea how to look any one of them in the eye at dinner.

✦

DINNER BEGAN with an evening prayer, led by my uncle, a prayer that Patrice and Jeffery seemed to take seriously, Elias just gave a quiet yawn and my mind was too busy swimming with the memory of my first one on one encounter with him to really hear anything that my uncle was rambling on about.

I felt as if everyone knew but in their WASP manners felt no need to comment on. I wasn't certain of what these people did or didn't know, the only thing I was aware of was the fact that Elias was staring at me, his leg reaching casually under the table and knocking against my ankle. I did nothing. In fact I figured the best way to play this, to get through the summer was to ignore his games altogether. I acted disinterested with him, hoping that it would send a message his way. I wasn't here to be toyed with, and I wasn't going to be a notch on his belt, and my guess was that he had a lot of those. He picked up a stick of celery and played with it in his mouth, I knew he was imitating a blow job, and though it was making me anxious between my legs I showed no sign. In fact I gave the same kind of yawn that he delivered during the prayer.

"Well I'm done." Elias got up and carried his plate, moving around the table towards me. He bent down and I could feel his breath on my neck. "You're a stone fox..." he said to me in a hushed whisper, meant for no one's ears but my own. I just looked away.

I didn't see him for the rest of the night, and in my bed I found myself staring at the door, silent with bated breath. Part of me hoping that he would sneak in, the other praying that he would come nowhere near me again.

✦

I WOKE UP LATE the next morning, finding the house empty, but hearing "Crazy on You" by Heart coming from the guest house beyond the tennis courts. I became curious, not only was it my favorite song, but also just plain interested in what was going on out there. Were we having a party that I wasn't aware of or was there something else going on? Something much more devious, something concocted by Elias.

I slipped on a pair of tight corduroys over my white briefs and my red polyester polo with white trim around the collar and sleeves. After putting on my sneakers I crept downstairs and out to the back, allowing the music to lead me. I moved along the glistening blue pool and followed a paved pathway, winding around the tennis court and behind a gigantic wall of English ivy and flowers in bloom. The sky was scattered with white puffy clouds and the smell of the bay perfumed the air. It was delicious, and hearing the voice of Ann Wilson and her sister Nancy jamming hard on her guitar, belting out sounds from *Dreamboat Annie*, Heart's first album, was enough to excite me, and give an air of teenage euphoria that only rock and roll can give.

I crept up slowly, seeing the guesthouse, with its French doors wide open, the sounds of people in heavy breath aching to compete against the volume of the record. I said nothing and I approached slowly, seeing two forms begin to take shape. I threw myself against the wall and leaned my head inside, feeling a mild drop in my gut as I saw a young woman leaning against a counter top, her skirt scrunched up and her shirt pulled up over her head while hands gripped her breasts like bicycle handles. It was Elias's hands, and his lips were all over her neck and he was drilling into her, fucking her without the slightest care in the world.

I shook my head and sighed, not expecting to be heard, and I wasn't, not by the brunette chick at least, but Elias cocked his head to the side and gazed at me, his lips curled into a slight grin, and he stayed focused on me, even while he went back to putting his tongue down the girl's throat.

I moved away slowly, and then I simply turned around and gave an embittered chuckle as I walked back to the main house, not even caring about Elias anymore. I could see his game; he was the kind of guy who felt that he was entitled to whoever he wanted. It was ridiculous, and yet I could not deny the fact that I still wanted him. But I knew the score, I knew what was and wasn't, and if we did something I could not spend the rest of my summer knowing that he was out fucking other people. Not that I was needy, on the contrary, I was selfish, probably just as selfish as Elias was.

"Who is it?" I asked, staring at the door to the bedroom, knowing deep down who it could only be.

"It's Elias, can I come in?" I sighed.

"Whatever... it's open!" I was sitting in an Italian style armchair with a gold and black fabric cushion, and my left leg was crossed over my right. I watched him walk in, and told myself over and over again to stay composed, detached. I could not let him know that what I had seen him do had any effect on me whatsoever.

"Hi..." he said this in an almost defeated way.

"So did you have fun giving a tour of the guest house?" Elias nodded, as if expecting it, as if he felt that he deserved it.

"I'm sorry you had to see that..." I shook my head and gave a dismissive wave with my hand.

"Why? It's your thing. This is your life, not mine, and this is what you do... it's none of my concern." The truth was I didn't want to be having this conversation; I didn't want to have to look at him, knowing where he had been, seeing what he had been doing, seeing that he was fucking a girl. I think in the end that's what angered me the most. Not that he was fucking another person, but that that other person had a vagina. It made me want to puke.

"She's just a girl I knew from Mariner..." I looked at him with a questioning gaze. "Mariner High School, my old high school. Most of the kids in this area go there." I nodded. Where he had gone to school didn't mean a damn thing to me, but I was certain that for the people of Bellingham, Washington, what school you called your home must have carried some kind of importance.

"Well whatever, it's groovy, everything's just fine." He came closer to me, his dark hair being tucked cautiously behind his ears.

"You know its okay..." he gripped the arms of the chair and leaned into me, our noses almost grazing, our lips almost touching. "You can let me in, I'm sure you're scared... but I'm not going to hurt you..." I looked away, but he took his fingers to my chin and turned my face back towards him, our eyes staring at one another, I could see the hues of the darkest brown and even grays glittering in the shards of his irises. I could smell him. The scent of Stetson and the salt of flesh. His flesh, flesh I wanted to taste for myself.

He sighed and walked away from me, slamming the door behind him and walking into his room, which was directly across from mine. Before I could judge my own actions, before my common sense could kick in, I was following him to his room, I was turning the knob on his closed bedroom door and I was barging in.

"Andrew?" I said nothing, I simply moved onto his bed, jumping on top of him and shoving my tongue down his throat. His hands were sifting through my hair and mine through his. His mouth was hot and moist, and his tongue was soft against my own. I could feel his cock growing long and stiff, pressing against my hard on, and I wanted it, I wanted it out, I wanted it in my mouth, I wanted it inside of me. I wanted him to fuck me like I will never be fucked again. I wanted him to search through the cavity of my insides. I needed it and I was going to have it.

I pulled my shirt off and he pulled off his, quickly placing his hands on my waist and laying me on my back, his tongue playing with my stiff nipples, moving down my chest, my stomach, he paused to pull off my shoes and unbutton my pants, which he threw off my legs. He grinned before putting his head between my legs, his hot breath on the cotton of my briefs, teasing my erection.

I reached out and undid his khakis, pulling them off of him as well, his own stiff cock eager to get out from the confines of his underwear. I giggled playfully as he slipped off my underwear and trailed his tongue along my shaft, my cock-head twitching at his touch.

I reached out and began tugging on him, jerking him while he sucked my dick, making me feel something I had never felt before. His mouth playing with my sack, enjoying my dick in his mouth. I thought I was going to explode, when he maneuvered me onto my side and put my face in front of his own cock. I gripped the hem of his undies and pulled them off. I had never given a blowjob before, I had only practiced playfully on produce, but I felt confident enough to do it, so I did.

The feeling of a hot dick in my mouth, the semi-circular moving and thrusting of his thighs as I sucked him, tasting the salty taste of precome, his was slightly sweet as well, and it only drove me to keep going. I looked over and saw him working on my own cock, enjoying it, loving it. I knew that I was going to come, and I had a feeling that it was going to be unlike anything I'd felt whenever I jacked off in the past.

I let it out, spilling inside of his mouth and he drank it down, licked it dry and he let go inside of me, it felt hot and sticky, and hit the back of my throat and I had to force it down, but I kept going, though I thought I was going to possibly cough or puke I didn't care. If I just kept doing it, I knew it would get better.

"Come here…" he brought me up to my knees and made his way behind me. He spat on his cock, adding to my own saliva and he laid me back onto it gently. I could feel myself wanting to fight against it, but I would not. I just closed my eyes and forced the muscle to relax, allowing him entrance. We rocked back and forth, at first gently and slowly, then as we slowly rose to our knees, his left hand gripping to my shoulder, slipped beneath my arm and his right hand stroking my dick, I knew I was somewhere between earth and heaven, and with every thrust I felt as if I was going to shoot a load that would go on forever.

He released his grip on my dick and continued to fuck me. I wasn't certain of what was going to happen, but with each thrust I felt myself getting closer and closer, and before I could prepare, before I could ready myself, perhaps lay out a towel, my jism was erupting from my dick and squirting over the bed. I thought he would have stopped, but he didn't. Elias just kept fucking me and I kept coming.

We spent the rest of the summer playing out this strange and dangerous liaison, and if anyone suspected, they never said anything. I was certain that Patrice had a clue, just by the glances she gave Elias and I whenever we went someplace together. But again, she simply bit her lip about it.

At the end of August I went back to Chicago and I knew that I would probably never see Elias again. And in fact I never did. I'm graduating from U.C. Berkeley today and my mother tells me that Elias will be attending, with his fiancé; the whole idea of it makes me laugh. No matter what we'll always share a knowing glance, a shared smile that could be taken as some inside joke, a secret no one will ever know. What I know, and the thing I will always be willing to say but never to share the details aloud, is that years will come and go, the eighties will pass into the nineties and we may even reach the two thousands, but the one year I will never forget is 1979, and its summer will be one that I will recall with a mix of secret joy and secluded angst. I've been with a lot of guys since then; in fact I leave U.C. Berkeley as somewhat of a queer legend. But Elias was right, no one will ever be able to fuck me the way he fucked me.

Sometimes I still watch my bedroom door in the middle of the night, listless with bated breath, part of me hoping that he will come into my room, the other part of me praying that it will never happen again.

ISLAND CALLED PARADISE

JOE FILIPPONE

STANDING ON THE BALCONY of my hotel room, I felt like an insignificant speck in the eyes of the universe. I rested my elbows on the terrace and gazed out along the beach, deserted in the night. I let out a very audible sigh. What a rotten vacation. Josh had hooked up with a new guy every night since we had arrived a week ago. "Straight guys do it, why shouldn't I?" He had told me. He had guys chasing him and I couldn't even get one to look at me.

I could hear the waves crashing against the rocks of the nearby cliffs. The cool breeze flowing off the ocean. The crystallized sandy diamonds glittering underneath the diamonds in the sky.

Why did I let Josh talk me into this? He had said it would do me good: meeting guys, forgetting about my recent breakup with Rick. The only thing this seemed to do was make me feel lonelier. It seemed like every guy who was on this miserable paradise of an island had someone. Everyone but yours truly. Maybe there wasn't anybody out there for me and I was destined to be a bachelor forever.

Stop, I commanded myself, stop feeling so damn sorry for yourself. If you want to meet guys, you're going to have to make an effort. The perfect guy is not just going to fall out of the sky and land in your lap.

A whoosh of air escaped my lungs. My eyes were pulled to the phone. I stared at it, tempted to call the airport and book a seat on the next flight back to Denver.

"What should I do?" I looked up at the stars hoping for an answer but my question fell on deaf ears.

I scanned the beach once more, devoid of life. Everyone had gone to the costume ball that the hotel was throwing. Josh had tried to get me to go saying, "it would be fun," but I was still uncomfortable around the six-foot tall well-muscled gods who looked like they had all stepped out of a workout magazine.

Turning to go into the room, hoping something good was on TV, I noticed something out of the corner of my eye. Coming out of the blackness like a mythological creature rising from the mist was the Adonis of Centocelle. Its marble body turned to flesh, walking along the beach. Tall. Long oil black hair. Shirtless. Body dripping wet from just having taken a midnight swim. Wet pants clinging to his torso like a second skin, revealing every intimate curve in all their glory. God, he was beautiful. My heart started to flutter as I watched him float closer and closer to me. As the silver blue rays of the moon engulfed him, giving me a better look, my heart was ready to explode. Damn, he was really, really hot.

Leaning over the balcony to get a better look, I almost fell onto the ground below. Probably not the ideal first impression. However, my dangerous voyeuristic stunt did allow me to see him walk into the lobby.

No longer having control of my mind or body, I tripped over my feet and succeeded in breaking a green seashell lamp as I scrambled down to the lobby with a quickness that would have made Speedy Gonzales envious. Bursting into the lobby, I stopped and took several deep breaths to get my palpitating heart back to its normal syncopation. Trying to act as if I was casually reading about all the luxuries that the island possessed, I looked around the lobby as nonchalantly as I could, searching for the stranger.

It didn't take me long to locate him in the sparsely populated lobby. He was standing at the front desk engaged in an intercourse of words with the bellhop.

The roller coaster inside me did several loop-de-loops as I looked him over, fully able to appreciate the masterpiece that was in front of me. His long midnight black hair, blacker than I first thought, cascading like a waterfall well past his shoulders, resting cozily in the valley between his well muscled shoulder blades in the middle of his back. His dark olive-skin, proudly displaying his Greek heritage, was still glistening with water from the ocean. Something about picturing him nude alone in the water made my heart try to break out of the claustrophobic cubicle that was my chest.

My cheeks boiled with the hot coals that were pressing into them as my gaze traveled south of his border. His jeans hung obscenely low, ready to fall completely off his hips, and I couldn't help but stare at his tanned butt, peeking out at the world through the top of his Wranglers.

He turned around and I gasped at the sight of his chest and stomach. It looked like they had been hand carved out of the finest marble. He had just enough chest hair to look masculine but his torso didn't look like he was related to a bear.

I choked on my Adam's apple as our eyes locked. I was thunderstruck. The Adonis smiled and walked toward me. I started to panic. This had never happened to me before. I felt a little scared as the kouros got closer and closer. I thought about fleeing, feeling the same way Daphne must have felt when her Apollo first pursued her. What do I do? Do I initiate the conversation or does he?

"Hello," he said to me with a heavy Greek accent that made me melt faster than the Wicked Witch.

"Hi," my voice was as small as my five-feet-six frame. God, he was more beautiful up close.

"I have seen you walking along the beach. I have been wanting to introduce myself. My name is Danny."

"Billy," I said, wishing I had some body spray to attack the sweat that was seeping out from my armpits.

"I have noticed that you spend a lot of time with a guy. Blond hair. Very tall. Like a model. You arrived together."

My face turned the color of fresh red roses at the thought of Danny watching me since my arrival.

"Josh?"

"Josh," Danny repeated the name, "your boyfriend?" I could sense the disappointment dripping off his words.

"Josh?" I said the name of my companion incredulously. "No. No. No. No. Josh is just a friend." I could never think of dating Josh, he was like a brother to me.

"Great," Danny smiled wide and exhaled a long sigh of relief. I could see his dark skin turn a shade of magenta as he asked me, "Do you maybe want to go to the bar and get a drink with me?"

"Sure," I said too quickly and mentally kicked myself. Great, he probably thinks I'm desperate now.

Danny smiled and put his arm around me, taking my breath away, and led me into the bar, my legs shaking like Jell-O the entire time. I couldn't believe this was happening. I was sure that I would wake up any moment and realize that it was all a dream.

"How do you like the island?"

"Very nice," I said, my voice a little shaky, "I've never been to an island before. Josh thought it would be fun before I go off to college."

"I'm going to college also this year. I am hoping to get the degree in business."

"I'm pursuing pysch and soc myself."

"What is this pysch and soc?"

"Oh," I was a little embarrassed, "psychology and sociology."

"Ahh," Danny nodded his head, understanding, "very smart you must be then. Those are hard subjects."

I looked away. The compliment about my brains caught me off guard. However, I felt on top of the world, euphoric that the sun was starting to shine brighter on this trip.

◆

DANNY AND I SAT at the bar drinking strawberry margaritas and talking for hours. It felt magical, as if we were the only people in the world. Actually, we were, much to the disappointment of the bartender who wanted to retire early.

Have you ever met someone and felt an instant connection with them, like you were meant to be with them? I don't know if it was the late hour, the margaritas or actual love but I felt that way with Danny. We talked about everything. Getting to know each other. I did feel a twang of sadness though. I had never known anyone this well. Even after two and a half years with Rick, the only conversation was deciding where to go for a steak or who would pay for the snacks at the movies.

In my short time with Danny, I learned how truly meaningless my relationship with Rick really was. Danny seemed generally interested in what I had to say and was eager to know all about my past: where I grew up, how Josh and I had met, when I had decided to come out, what got me interested in psychology and sociology. It was then I realized that maybe I was better off without Rick. I realized that our relationship had meant more to me than it did to him. His loss, I concluded triumphantly.

That night, I did something I swore I never would. I slept with Danny on the first date. I made a vow to myself that I wouldn't do that. I could never sleep with a guy I had just met. But this time was different. It felt right. Natural.

Danny was the best lover I ever had. While, I didn't have many past lovers, I was hardly what you could call a virgin. Danny was gentle and warm, in his lovemaking. A gracious lover, he was concerned only with bringing me to the highest peak of ecstasy and not worrying at all about his needs. He also knew his way very, very well around the male body, graciously giving every erogenous zone my body possessed ample attention. I felt like the world was moving in slow motion as my body lost itself in Danny's gentle caressing and tender embrace. Hearing him moan out my name, as his body rhythmically thrust into me, was the most erotic experience I had ever had. Plus, he looked damn good without any jeans on.

Afterwards, Danny collapsed on top of me in a sweaty heap. My breathing was shallow and rapid. My stomach rising and falling in rhythm with his. I ran my hands through his hair. This was the best sex I had ever had; the kind of soul fulfilling sex that only exists in myths. I was hoping this would last forever. My Apollo embraced my lips passionately and rolled off me.

"Billy, do you wish me to be going? Do you mind if I spend the night in your bed?"

"Do you want to stay with me?" I asked, smiling at his innocent questions.

"Very much," he brushed the hair from my forehead.

"Me too," I said resting my head against his chest and running my fingers over the hair that made its home there.

He put his arms around me, and soon the rhythmic thump, thump, thumping of his heart had lullabied us both into a magical sleep.

✦

MY EYES OPENED to the warm orange and red waterfall of the early morning light. I breathed in the masculine scent that exuded from my lover's body. A few seconds later, he too stirred and rose.

"Did you find good sleep?" the beardless youth asked as he branded my forehead with his soft lips.

My sigh was one of total fulfillment. "Very much. Did you?"

"Yes. You maybe would be wanting to go down for breakfast with me?"

My kiss was the only answer he needed.

✦

A LITTLE WHILE LATER, we walked into the dining room, arms around each other's waists. We enjoyed a romantic breakfast of scrambled eggs, bacon, hash browns, toast, and orange juice as we made plans to spend the day exploring the island. I was so happy, enjoying the high that was my new drug, causing the dopamine in my body to rise. I never wanted the summer to end.

It was the best day of my life. I never believed that you could fall head over heels for someone you just met. That world only existed in the romance novels I had read and now here I am, in the middle of a real life romance.

Danny and I explored the cliffs on the side of the ocean. Walking into the darkened mouth, with the waves crashing behind us and just the flashlight beam leading the way, I felt like an explorer. We stared amazed at the many different patterns and colors the sea's assaults over hundreds of years had left on the rock walls.

Walking deeper into the cave, we came to a small pool of still denim blue water. The water was so clear, we could see the speckled rocks that littered the bottom.

"Let's go swimming," I said, suddenly adventurous.

"I did not bring my swim suit," Danny said.

"So?" Was my only reply as I stripped and dove into the pool.

Before long, Danny joined me. Our voices echoed off the dark walls as we laughed and splashed each other. Every once in a while, stealing a kiss or two.

✦

LYING ON THE BEACH, basking in the rays of the sun, we were hypnotized by the waves of the ocean, much like the cobra to the snake charmer.

"Nice day," Danny said.

"Mm-hmm," was all I could get out.

Danny put his arm around me and pulled me closer to him. Lying there with him, I never wanted to leave. However, that was not to be our destiny. Soon, the sun had painted its canvas with brilliant shades of orange, red, and gold. Danny and I unwillingly got up and trudged back to the hotel.

"Do you want to spend the day with me tomorrow?" Danny asked, his arms around me as we lay in bed together.

"I was just about to ask you," I said laughing.

It seemed that every day I spent with Danny got better and better. We would wake up in each other's arms, take a long, hot shower together, and then leisurely go down to breakfast. We would talk over breakfast and then spend the rest of the day doing whatever we wanted. We were young, free, in love and in paradise.

✦

AS A RESULT of all the time I spent with Danny, I saw very little of Josh. Finally one night, Josh caught me while I was alone.

"Long time no see," my friend said with a smile.

"You're not the only one who can have a rendezvous."

"A rendezvous? I'm having a different one almost every night."

I laughed.

"So," Josh said, coming in and sitting cross-legged on the bed, "tell me all about this guy. He's hot. For the first time in my life, I'm actually jealous of you."

I held my head with a certain amount of pride. Usually I was the one who was jealous of all the hot guys Josh hooked up with. It felt nice to be in the limelight for once. Josh hungrily gulped down all I had to say about Danny, squealing with delight when I told him about our more intimate moments.

"Oh man, he sounds great. Does he have a brother for me?"

"Yeah," I said, "back in Greece and he's straight."

"I can turn him," Josh said confidently.

I threw a pillow at Josh. He returned the gesture and in no time at all, we were in a full-blown pillow fight, lasting for several minutes. We collapsed in a heap, laughing.

"Shit, we haven't done this since elementary school," Josh said.

"Yeah. Felt good," I said, standing up and brushing back the hair from my forehead.

✦

"YOU ARE AWFUL QUIET TONIGHT, Billy," Danny said rubbing my back as we sat on my bed. "What is wrong?"

"I'm leaving tomorrow. Going back to Denver," the words were like a knife in my throat.

Danny was silent, his rubbing had become less enthusiastic. We both knew this day would come, hoping against hope that it wouldn't; that time would somehow stand still and we would be able to stay on the island forever; never growing older and never leaving each other.

I turned around and embraced Danny tightly. I lost my breath and found tears as Danny returned the embrace. I could feel his shoulders shaking as he wept onto my T-shirt. Soon, we were both holding each other, sobbing. It wasn't the end of the world, but it sure as hell felt like it.

✦

"ARE YOU READY YET?" Josh poked his head in my room.

I had been packing for the last hour but was making very slow progress.

"Almost," escaped from my voice box, barely audible.

"You can't get down, Billy. It was just a summer fuck. You didn't really think it would last forever did you?"

"No," I dully said. Though in my heart I thought it would.

I hadn't seen Danny at all that morning. We had shared a tearful goodbye the night before and I was scared that if I saw him again I would break down. I hated letting people see me cry.

✦

I WALKED TO THE BUS that would take us to the airport and away from the island paradise. Every few seconds, Josh would look back at me and smile encouragingly. I was just stepping onto the bus when a muscular hand gripped my shoulders and turned me around. I found myself staring into the deep, cool, emerald lakes, sparkling in Danny's eye sockets. I suddenly felt ashamed that I had tried to leave without saying goodbye.

"I was hoping to say goodbye before you left."

He gently cupped my face in his hands and kissed me. After we broke the kiss, he handed me a piece of paper with his address, e-mail, and phone number.

"If you are ever in Greece, will you visit me, Billy?"

"Of course," I whispered, my eyes glistening with tiny wet diamonds.

We kissed one last time before I took a seat in the belly of the bus. I looked out the window and watched Danny disappear in the distance until he was just a speck in the eye of the universe.

✦

ON THE PLANE back to Denver, I kept the paper Danny gave me against my heart, unfolding it every so often to stare at his handwriting; as beautiful as him. Josh smirked at me the whole flight home and made me promise to invite him to me and Danny's wedding. I laughed at my friend.

I didn't know if I would see Danny again, feel his soft lips against mine or feel the sensation of him making love to me again but I did know I was better off for having known him. I rested my head against the seat, closed my eyes, let out a small sigh and let the soft tremors of the plane lure me to sleep, where I met Danny in my dreams.

MANNA

GREGORY L. NORRIS

THE MORNING JOEL MET AUSTIN, he felt thirty-five going on a hundred and thirty-five. Another in an unending succession of sweltering dog days baked the dawn into the eighties soon after sunrise. The old air conditioner in his second-story Park Street apartment struggled, making its baleful keen. Probably iced over, Joel thought, thankful that the big jet engine fan on the dresser had distributed the last of its coolness evenly throughout the place. Drawing the mini-blinds might even keep the apartment moderately comfortable for the next several long hours, enough time for the glaze of ice caking the unit's grates to melt. The damn thing was going out with a vengeance, choosing the worst time possible to frost up. It was as if it knew it was headed to the air conditioner graveyard, and wanted to take as many souls as possible with it. Or at least the one responsible for running it to death.

Joel cracked a humorless smile at the idea while showering, his mouth watering for that first heavenly sip of iced coffee, no sugar, plenty of milk and ice. In fairness, he *had* maintained a 'just one more year' policy on the air conditioner since his thirtieth birthday, which felt about a century behind him.

He started sweating again while toweling off. Another day of begging for scraps, of doing his modern-day loaves and fishes shtick, for few if any rewards, and even fewer thanks. He slapped on deodorant. Dressed. Grabbed the tall, perspiring plastic cup of iced coffee. Chugged. The brisk, life-giving brew brought him back to the living and cooled his internal flames. The reprieve was brief, but enough to get him out the door and behind the wheel of the white van, upon whose sides the words "Helping Hands Pantry" had been detailed.

Joel stopped at the first of the three bakeries on his regular route. Four cardboard boxes of day-old bread, frozen and heavy, and probably hard as rocks, even thawed. But you could always make delicious French toast even from yesterday's cinnamon raison-turned-today's granite. Bagels. Donuts. Some cupcakes. The other two stops weren't as generous, but he snagged several bags of spinach pies at the last.

His next hour was spent picking through crates of fruits and vegetables at the bigger of the two grocery stores Joel had gotten to make donations to the pantry. What he collected was the stuff most people wouldn't feed to zoo animals. Carrots, still attached to tops that had gone brown. Crowns of broccoli starting to suffer the same decay. But you could always snip off the bad florets, and Joel always did. Bags of apples, some brown and mushy in spots, most still good enough to distribute. Tomatoes, loose, in a box. Dented canned goods. Milk that had just reached its sell-by date. OJ, too.

Not a lot of these things, not as much as before. People had been a great deal more generous under Clinton the summer Joel had first walked into the dank, aged-smelling cellar beneath the Unitarian Church on Kenoza Avenue in search of a handout. Now that he was running the pantry, Post 911, and with Bush throwing every cent he could lay his fingers on into one war or another, a good percentage of the charity had evaporated. There were days when the back of the van seemed as cavernous as the church's worship hall.

Today wasn't one of those days. Today, the space seemed only half-cavernous.

Joel made it into the parking lot by nine, with half an hour to spare. But as he stepped out of the van's air conditioned interior and into the steamy, neck-deep soup of yet another ninety-plus-degree day, complete with the rotten muggies and a heat index that pushed the numbers into the century mark, it was going to take him half an hour just to get that first crate of picked-through, diseased-looking corn on the cob down to the food tables.

"How did I get this old?" Joel wondered aloud.

The answer was simple, delivered when he unlocked the basement security door and a wave of unpleasant smells—aged wood, mildew, the sweat of countless visitors to the pantry— wafted out, assailing his nostrils.

Life. That's how.

✦

THE ODOR OF SWEAT wasn't unbearable, but on days like today, Joel was glad that the large metal office desk, no doubt a discard from one of the upstairs church offices, and a half wall partition separated him from the steady stream of visitors. Few of the pantry's guests owned cars; most walked to the church from the surrounding neighborhoods. And given the weather, the sourness of stale perspiration quickly turned the basement into a human-smelling swamp.

"Sign in," Joel absently said. "I'll need your Social Security card. You know the routine."

The routine was simple enough. Name, address, and confirmed SS# on a sign-in sheet. Without them, Joel wouldn't be able to procure what crumbs the state government sent them in food aid. From there, it was on to a pass-through window where either Burt or Big Tony, the pantry's muscle, would hand over a bag containing the staples and a single roll of toilet paper. The other Bert— short for *Bertha*—would then lead each guest down the line of food tables, where they could make one fresh vegetable selection, two canned, two breads, and one grab from the bonus table of unclassifiable donations. Cereal and milk if you were a family with kids. No cereal and milk if you were a poor single schlub, living alone without dependants. Bert usually gave the one-and-onlys milk and cereal anyway, and Joel was happy she did.

Nobody got paid to do this; all were volunteers. Burt and Big Tony showed up early each Tuesday and Wednesday to claim the best of the donated food for themselves. Joel didn't have a problem with that small degree of entitlement, any more than he did with Bert doling out extra to the singles; his crew stood on their feet for hours, mostly without complaints. Bert was another matter entirely. She came from money and had been involved with the city's homeless causes from the time of her early twenties—a considerable bunch of decades behind her now. Bert didn't shop at the pantry, but a few times each year, usually around the holidays, she emptied out her freezer and donated all she had at the time to it.

Bert had suggested Joel take over the pantry's responsibilities when the previous guy retired. That, too, now felt like a few thousand years in his past. Between these duties and his part-time job at the library, Joel was seeing more and more silver hair working its way prematurely into his neat, dark athletic cut.

"Lady at Town Hall said I should ask for Burt," a man's deep voice posed on the other side of the half-wall.

"Which one?" Bert cackled in her wonderfully infectious, unique brand of laughter.

"Well, how many are there?" the warm, almost musical baritone cut through the fog of sweat and the fugue of yet another day of hard living.

"Two, at the moment. I'm Bert with an 'e'. He's Burt, with a 'u'."

"I want the vowel that runs this place."

"That would be neither of us. You want our head honcho, Joel."

Joel finished signing in the visitor seated across from the desk and rose, stirring a heavy patch of sour air. His eyes, aimed across the partition, targeted the two bodies standing at the center of the floor, near a support column of ancient red brick.

"And there he is!" Bert chuckled, extending a pudgy hand Joel's way.

Through the dozen or so other people between him and the new arrival, Joel caught a flash of sandy blond hair under a backwards-turned baseball cap, tanned skin showing around a crisp white wife-beater, old Cammies cut off at the knees into shorts, white socks, dirty sneakers.

The man moved through the human obstacle course and into clear view. Joel didn't realize he was staring or that he'd ceased blinking until his eyes began to sting. For a sliver of a second, the sardonic voice in his head wondered if the golden-haired vision was really the Angel of Death, come to relieve him of his mortal suffering. Thirty-five going on a hundred and thirty-five would make him the oldest living human being on the face of the planet, so it was conceivable this was his time to exit the mortal coil.

"I'm Joel," he forced between lips that had gone suddenly, uncomfortably dry.

"Austin," the Angel of Death said, extending a formidable hand.

Joel noticed a trace of dirt beneath his fingernails, the glint of fine golden hairs on the hand's back, and the depth of the tan. Hard earned, from an entire summer spent in the sun. Joel pegged him as being in his late twenties, early thirties, perhaps. They shook, and Joel tried not to wince as Austin's hand clamped down with enough strength to shatter the bones of lesser men.

"First, you'll need to sign in—"

"Naw, I didn't come here for that. I got a truck-load of fresh vegetables, herbs, and corn out in your parking lot. Better than the crap you've got over there." Austin tipped his chin, scruffy with a prickle of golden fuzz, at the food table containing the dregs of the grocery store donation.

"Huh?" Joel stammered as he attempted to break free of the hypnotic pull of the other man's vibrant, pale blue eyes, yet failing. That mouth, with its plump, bee-stung lips, even Austin's ears, sticking out of his golden shag with a charming size that reminded Joel of a monkey's, had conjured his heartbeat out of its stupor and into a gallop. Though Joel was still sweating, a shiver teased the short hairs at the nape of his neck. He fought it, failed at that, too. But as the chill tripped down his spine, Joel managed to wake from the spell he'd fallen victim to. "You're here to donate to the pantry?"

"Yeah, dude. My family owns the Shady Crop Farm, up in Whyndom."

Shady Crop. Joel recognized the name. "The big organic place off Range Road?"

"Best and biggest in the state. We got a bumper this year on everything, so I figured you might be able to use some of it."

"Could we ever!"

Fresh energy coursed through Joel's insides. He rounded the desk and put Big Tony in charge. "I'd sell my soul to get more healthy fresh produce onto the menu!"

"No need to do that. Loan me your body instead," Austin said, a mischievous smirk curling on his face.

At first, Joel didn't get the joke. His mind wandered into different territory.

"Just help me lug in some of the crates," Austin said, as if reading those carnal thoughts. "And you're correct with the healthy and fresh bit. We grow only the finest."

Joel felt the harsh lines around his mouth resist as his lips formed a real smile. Austin shot a look around the place, drinking in the mild squalor and hopelessness, before circling back to Joel. And then, Joel noticed, Austin smiled, too.

✦

JOEL FOLLOWED HIM up the stairs, out of the basement's musty, relative coolness. At the first landing, the oppressive heat surged back and engulfed him. Joel grunted.

"Yeah, ain't this heat a miserable bitch?"

Joel nodded. The cadence of Austin's feet clomping up the staircase had hypnotized him faster than a slowly swinging watch in an old movie. He blinked, swallowed, sucked in a badly needed breath. The air, hot as it was, was also now infused with a clean, masculine smell. Fresh perspiration, a trace of deodorant, moist, male skin…Austin's scent.

Austin pushed open the basement door, and a wall of blinding light poured into the church. By the time the stars burned completely down, Joel found himself standing beside a van much newer and better than the pantry's. It bore a mural of lush green leaves—lettuce, cabbage, and broccoli flowers. In the shade of this painted-on banquet were the words Shady Crop Farm.

Austin unlocked the van's rear doors and tugged. A rich, cool breeze that smelled green, of the earth, poured through the ungodly heat. Joel blinked rapidly to clear his eyes, and could not believe the image that greeted them. Wooden crates of corn, racks of tomatoes, zucchini and summer squash, and bags of fresh herbs lined the interior, all of it kept cool and fresh by the van's internal air conditioning. There was even a plastic milk crate stacked to capacity with amber-filled jars. Honey!

"That's from our own bees," Austin said, again as if picking up on Joel's thoughts. "Good stuff. All organic. Our bees make it from the flowers we grow at the farm."

Joel whistled out a swear. The bounty of produce contained within the van put the pitiful scraps he salvaged weekly from the grocery stores to shame. He couldn't remember ever seeing such colorful, beautiful food, not even in the polished-shiny stacks of produce in the stores, all prettied up for the people who could afford to buy it.

"Why?" Joel gasped.

"Why what?"

Joel forced his gaze to intersect with Austin's dreamy blue eyes. "Why would you do this for us?"

"I already told you. We had extra this year." The other man shifted in place under Joel's scrutiny, turned away, and buried his eyes into the van's interior. "Even if we didn't, it's no big deal."

"It *is* a big deal. Most times, these people have to subsist on crappy, starchy processed foods. This is probably the healthiest they'll ever enjoy."

Austin shrugged, smiled. His focus darted back to Joel. "Well, then, Gramps would be proud of me. He started Shady Crop a billion years ago, and the world's been eating our vegetables since."

Joel was about to question him further when Austin offered the rest.

"Gramps passed away last month, at the healthy age of eighty-eight. So this seems like the right thing to do to honor his memory." Austin reached into the van and grabbed two crates of corn. "So you think the two of us can unload this stuff alone, or should we call in reinforcements?"

Joel felt a genuine smile break out on his mouth for the second time that morning—for the second time, perhaps, in almost a decade. "Let's not kill ourselves in the heat."

They dropped off the first load of crates on the food tables, and this new bounty outshined anything already there to be picked through.

"Okay, people, listen up," Joel said, his voice stilling the crowd. "I need at least six able bodies to help lug in some really great food. Anybody who pitches in gets to take home double."

More than a dozen hands shot up. Joel put them to work, and everyone that day took home double, not merely those who volunteered.

✦

"DID YOU set this place up yourself?"

For not the first time, Joel had felt Austin's stare wandering over his body. Until then, he'd dismissed it as wishful thinking. Now, however, Joel was convinced. He turned to answer and faced the other man directly. Austin's eyes were fixed undeniably upon him.

"Me? No. Just the past five years. There was a guy before me. Probably someone before him. I'm just the next in a long line."

"Yeah, I know how that goes. I've only been running Shady Crop since the spring."

"I'm so glad you are," Joel chuckled. Again, it struck him as funny at how genuine the gesture sounded, how free of sarcasm and droll wit. Smiles and laughter without baggage were such alien sensations. Surely, at one time, his body had known how to perform them, minus the added negatives. But it was easy to relearn the gifts of laughter and smiling while in Austin's presence.

"I've never been up to Shady Crop, but I bet it's beautiful, especially this time of year."

"Yup, it is," Austin said. He stood, arms folded, his eyes never leaving Joel. "There's this lake, out past the corn. My favorite place on the whole damn farm. Great place to go swimming."

"Christ, that sounds good on a day like today," Joel sighed.

"You should come over, take a dip with me."

A jolt of icy-hotness surged through Joel's insides, unleashing alternating beads of fresh sweat on his forehead and goose bumps on his bare arms. "What?"

"What time do you wrap things up here?"

Joel tipped a look at the wall clock. "An hour or so," his mouth betrayed before he could censor it.

"I heard it's supposed to storm later tonight and finally drive this blast furnace out to sea. That leaves us plenty of time to go for a swim. I could use the company, and besides—you said you'd never been up to Shady Crop. This gives you a chance to check out the place that's bringing you fresh supplies."

Unable to say no, Joel agreed.

✦

IT TOOK HIM AN HOUR on top of the one needed to wrap up the morning's responsibilities, and an additional half an hour got wasted changing in and out of the few pairs of shorts and swim trunks Joel owned. There was no decent mirror in the apartment, which he'd again found sweltering upon his return.

Joel cranked the air conditioner and spent the rest of the noon hour trying on options, but hating every combination.

And what for? asked his caustic, inner voice. *It's not like this guy likes you in that way.*

"But I think he does," Joel said out loud.

It's all in your head, Inner Joel countered.

"It doesn't matter. I like him, and he did a big service to the pantry today. Keeping him company at the lake is the least I can do in return."

Another funny thought struck Joel as he settled on a pair of loose-fit navy-colored shorts: he'd been smiling in the mirror the entire time. Smiling, in spite of the merciless heat. In spite of a merciless Inner Joel.

He changed into a pair of clean white socks, laced up his sneakers, and turned off the struggling AC unit on his way out the door. The damn thing would probably freeze up again if left running. Joel only hoped he wouldn't do the same thing before reaching Shady Crop Farm.

The drive to Whyndom, which under normal conditions would have taken less than thirty minutes to accomplish, seemed twice as long. He was already hours late, and navigating through the worst of the afternoon heat. It was as if the asphalt, soft and rippling with heat snakes, was intentionally grasping at the van's wheels with sticky talons; one of those clichéd days where, if you had eggs and didn't mind the grit, you could fry an omelet on the sidewalk.

But it wasn't merely the heat that slowed the ebb and flow of time; it was that nagging inner voice, and it dogged Joel the entire distance to Whyndom.

Normally, he wouldn't have taken the pantry's van on a personal errand, that voice accused. Joel shut it up by telling himself that this was part of establishing good community relations. Hell, he might even procure more donations for the pantry if he arrived in the van. It was also his only means of getting there. Whenever Joel needed to go someplace, he usually begged a ride or went on foot. Whyndom was a good twenty miles north of the city, so with some modicum of guilt, all of it supplied by his inner inquisitor, he took the van.

Joel turned off the exit and entered Whyndom, a bucolic country town mostly composed of battleship-sized modern mansions with tall hedges and a few sprawling farms like Shady Crop that had somehow escaped the ruthless developers. The cool green canopies of shade trees covered the roads. The air was sweeter, cleaner, filled with the smells of meadow flowers, hay, and pine trees, as opposed to the bitter atmosphere of car exhaust, gridlock, and baking pavement behind him in the city.

This was Austin's town. That made it twice as idyllic.

Joel followed Range Road, but was starting to think he'd taken a wrong turn when, unexpectedly, its curve led around a bend and along a stretch of fruit-laden apple trees guarded by a belt of ancient stone wall. The farm appeared ahead of him, straight out of a pastoral painting. The main house, a barn, several outbuildings, and a bungalow-style farm stand sat in a dell across from the orchards, beside what looked like a mile of corn. All of it was surrounded by dense pine forest.

Joel had driven through the familiar world and into some alien landscape, a beautiful, colorful place light years away from his too-small, too-hot, and too-depressing apartment back in the city.

He pulled into the crowded, dusty lot and parked the van in one of the few spots not already occupied by new, expensive-model cars and SUVs. The intoxicating scent of the annuals growing in whiskey barrels that marked the perimeter of the parking lot instantly possessed him. Joel's angry façade cracked further when he spotted a pair of lemon-colored butterflies performing a graceful, lazy tango across the nearest petunias.

The farm stand was open on one side to showcase bins loaded down with corn, the bright orange jewels of tomatoes, and the emerald-green of cucumbers, zucchini, and snap beans. Huge bouquets of flowers tied in string sat in buckets of water around the cash registers, forming yet another garden. There, one golden-haired beauty weighed produce. A second made change. It was as if Joel had discovered some magical, mythological oasis where the heat truly seemed less oppressive, the sun, not so direct.

He approached the register.

"Excuse me, I'm looking for Austin."

The other woman, as well tanned as the man Joel had ventured from the city to meet with, answered. "Are you Joel?"

"Guilty," Joel said. And he started to feel that way just at the mention of his name.

"He's up at the house," the woman said, flashing a warm smile. "I'm his sister, Beth. He's waiting for you."

"Up at the house?"

"It's the one that's not a barn," the first woman said, a smile playing on her lips.

Joel got the joke and waved a hand in her direction. "Gotcha."

He marched up the drive to the grand New Englander. A carpet of marigolds, petunias, and Dusty Miller necklaced the walkway.

How the hell did I get here?

Though he couldn't bring himself to glance at his watch, Joel was aware of its scratched face reflecting the sun, telegraphing that on any other day following duty at the pantry or a shift at the library, he would have been back at the apartment, huddled under the air conditioner, listening to the TV drone on in the background. Televised court shows. Cartoons. A soap opera. Bad afternoon television.

Instead, he was here, gliding along the walkway, high on the scent of flowers, his heart pounding in staggered beats. Pounding so loud, in fact, he could hear its echo bouncing off the distant pines, the house.

It wasn't until the walkway rounded a corner and Joel saw the basketball hoop that he realized the drumming cadence was originating from a ball being dribbled, shot, caught on the rebound, dribbled some more.

Austin stood naked from the waist up and the knees down. His white wife-beater, baseball cap, socks, and sneakers sat in a messy pile on the stone stoop that guarded the house's side entrance. For a second of guilt-free study as Austin raised the basketball, intending to fire it toward the hoop, Joel drank in the other man's magnificence: the bronzed flesh of his chest, glistening with rivulets of sweat; the damp fur of his armpits; Austin's legs, long and strong, dusty with a sheen of golden hairs; even his feet, bare and impressive in size, the second toes longer than the first, like those on classic marble statues. Heavenly distraction.

What little moisture remained in Joel's mouth vanished. He forgot to breathe, until the last one he'd taken boiled in his lungs. Joel gasped, stealing back his breath. Alerted to his presence, Austin glanced over. Some internal register in Joel's addled brain noted the fullness of the smile that blossomed across the other man's plump lips.

"Dude, you found me!"

Austin shot the ball and caught it after it circled the rim, dropped through the hoop.

"Hard place to miss," Joel said through his own smile. "Really beautiful."

"Yeah, beautiful," Austin repeated on the strut over to extend a hand, his eyes scanning Joel up and down. As they shook, Austin pulled him into one of those safe, manly hugs. Close enough, Joel realized, to feel the pulse of the other man's erection swelling against his own.

I'm imagining this, Joel thought. *Maybe I'm really back in my apartment on Park Street, having a heat stroke. This is all some hallucination. Some…*

Joel sucked in a deep breath of the Austin-scented air, held it, then released it, the sigh rolling up from his chest and scattering across Austin's shoulder.

"I'm glad you came," Austin said.

"Me, too."

Their embrace lingered. Eventually, fingers and bodies unlaced. Still so close together, Joel watched Austin's throat knot under the influence of a dry, heavy swallow. Whatever he himself was feeling, Joel realized Austin was experiencing it, too.

Austin gave the ball a final dribble. "You ready to go swimming?"

Shortly after that, Joel found himself trailing the other man through acres of corn. The fragrance of the stalks was sweet; Austin's scent, billowing back into his face, even sweeter.

"So how'd you get involved with the cause?"

"You mean the pantry? I was hungry," Joel answered. "I'm not just the director, I used to be a customer."

Austin stopped in place. "No shit?"

Joel nodded. Austin turned. At some point in their tour of the farm, he'd popped a blade of timothy grass between his teeth. Austin had steadily gnawed it down to within inches of its cone. He spit it out while placing a hand on the center of Joel's chest. At the instant of contact, a cannonade of imaginary fireworks went off through Joel's insides.

"So long as I'm here, you and your people at the pantry will never go hungry again…"

✦

THE CORNFIELD OPENED on a stretch of pine forest dissected by a well-traveled strip of lazy, meandering trail. The fragrance of wildflowers and the white-noise music of summer insects hinted of the lake's closeness before Joel spotted the swimming hole through a break in the trees. A carpet of pine needles separated the path to a thin strip of sandy shoreline. Water lilies lolled on the gentle waves farther out, where the fiery disc of the sun had transformed the surface into an expanse of dappled gold.

"I agree with you. This place is beautiful," Joel remarked. He toed off his sneakers, peeled down his socks, and marveled at the tickle of the soft white sand beneath his feet.

"Not as beautiful as you," Austin said.

And then, as Joel turned toward the sound of the other man's voice, confused by what he thought he'd heard—*hoped* he'd heard—Austin cupped his cheek and crushed their lips together.

The unexpected move made Joel's body go rigid. The shock of Austin's kiss rippled in concentric waves throughout his core, overwhelming him like the surface of the nearby pond when overcome by ripples. Paralyzed, at first he was unable to do anything more than receive Austin's mouth against his own, observing the rough scrape of unshaved lips, the piney sweetness of sweat, the full strength of their erections, crossing swords as they pressed together.

You're not hallucinating this, Inner Joel said. *I was wrong, and you were right. Now do something, dammit, before he thinks you aren't interested!*

Joel unfroze, kissed back, and melted into Austin's embrace.

"Yes," he moaned around a desperate gasp for breath.

The caress of Austin's fingers down his cheek unleashed a fresh shiver. "I've wanted to do that all day," the other man growled.

Joel's eyes met Austin's dreamy blues; in that bottled gaze, he saw their sincerity. "I've wanted you to."

"Good. Now that we got that much clear…"

Saying nothing more, Austin shamelessly stripped out of his Cammies to stand completely naked in the sunlight. Joel was unable to force his gaze lower, though he wanted to. Time again slipped off its tracks. The sound of splashing water shocked him back to the moment, and Joel found himself standing alone on the shore.

"What are you waiting for?" Austin called from ten feet out in the swimming hole. "We're not getting any younger, you know."

Joel shook his head. "That's where you're wrong, my friend."

Smiling widely, he ripped off his T-shirt and stepped out of his shorts and underwear, shedding them like layers of old skin. Naked and hard, Joel walked into the water, happier than he could recall.

The smell of the surrounding countryside, the briskness of the lake, invigorated him. He waded out until the water was up to his knees on his own. Austin's playful tackle baptized him the rest of the way.

"I like you," the other man said once the splashing ceased. "A lot."

Joel leaned closer and pressed his lips to Austin's. He wanted to tell Austin that, for the first time in what felt like ages, he felt cooled, refreshed. *Alive.* That in the past several hours, he'd regressed from a hundred and thirty-five back past thirty-five, all the way to eighteen again.

"I like you, too," he settled for instead, for now.

UNTAMED COWBOY

D.E. LEFEVER

IT WAS A FEW DAYS before the beginning of July, the month generally regarded in Santa Fe as the start of monsoon season. But June 2001 offered no suggestion of a rainy time about to come. The high desert was unusually parched, the air hot, and no hint of humidity. Locals worried about the drought, the forecasts of a destructive fire season and dry wells. Years without much rain brought an infestation of Bark Beetles, killing the Pinons, and leaving acres of brown hillsides.

This June, with no forecast of rain, held the promise of another dry summer. Drew Laub felt guilty. He thrived in the heat and dry days. He could keep the top off his car without watching the afternoon sky. The almost daily dash from the gallery to the parking lot, often getting thoroughly soaked by the time the top was in place, is something Drew would not miss.

Drew finished his lunch at Celebrations, a somewhat funky, quintessential Santa Fe restaurant, located mid-way up Canyon Road and patronized by tourists and locals alike. Seated on the patio at his usual table, he could maintain an eye on the gallery entrance. At this hour on a weekday his sales associate could generally take care of any customers. If she poked her head from the door, Drew knew to cut lunch short and hurry back. But today he hoped it would be one of those times he could relax. He savored the feel of the hot sun on his back and welcomed the quietness of the patio. Only one other table was occupied. A younger man, dressed in cowboy hat and boots, wearing jeans, sat alone nearby, his feet propped on the chair across from him. The few others that lingered at this hour were inside, escaping the sun. Drew looked at his watch; it was well after noontime. Noticing the date, he was glad that Fiesta, the wrapup of summer with the burning of Zozobra, was a good two months away. It was, he reminded himself, barely past the solstice.

Laub's preoccupation with thoughts of summer was dampened only by the realization that he would turn forty in September. He looked much younger than his years with a thick head of dirty blond hair and a swimmer's build that required increasingly longer workouts to retain. With a still youthful face, he had long since forgotten his annoyance at being mistaken for "a high school kid" until the start of his junior year of college.

"Sir, you finished with the pepper?"

His daydreaming interrupted, Drew glanced up at the young cowboy. Beneath the broad brimmed hat he caught a glimpse of steel blue eyes. "Sure." Drew answered. They leaned toward each other as Drew handed him the pepper. Drew's nostrils filled for a moment with a blend of the cowboy's masculine scent and the lingering fragrance of his cologne.

"You just visiting?" Drew asked. "That cowboy outfit says New Mexico, but the drawl sure doesn't."

"Kentucky. Outside Louisville."

"Been here long?"

"Only a couple days. Fixin' to maybe move here."

"What do you do? If you don't mind me asking."

"Looking to start a carriage business . . . like you see in New York . . . Central Park . . . you know . . . for weddings, tourists .. . ." He lifted his hat and ran his fingers through coal black hair, damp with perspiration. Somewhat long in back, it was shiny like wet silk. "Horses . . . ranchin' . . . rodeo ridin' . . . that sort of thing's what I do."

"You?"

Drew pointed across the street. As he did, a figure, with her hand waving, appeared in the gallery doorway. "Sorry. I have to go. Nice talking to you . . . Good luck," Drew said as he abruptly stood to leave. "The gallery is calling."

"Thanks for the pepper." The cowboy said, with a playful grin and a glint in his eyes that made Drew regret the need to get back to work.

Crossing the street, he fought back the urge to turn around, take a final look—wave— say something. Until the cowboy spoke,

Drew was barely aware of his presence. Thinking of summer, he hardly noticed his surroundings. Ordinarily, a good looking man did not escape his eye. It was the somewhat roguish manner of the cowboy's question in a strong, masculine voice that jolted him back to reality. Looking briefly into those steel blue eyes, he wished lunch had lasted longer even though he had finished eating and already been there beyond his usual stay.

Drew wished he had asked the cowboy's name. Was he staying at a hotel? How long would he be in Santa Fe? There was something discomforting about the abrupt end of their conversation – that feeling of being absorbed in a TV program when the power goes off. Once back inside the gallery, Drew quickly forgot the all too brief lunchtime encounter. The main exhibit rooms were busy with browsing tourists, a reminder that in his distraction at Celebrations he had failed to keep an eye to the other side of the street.

✦

A WEEK LATER, seated on the curb along East San Francisco Street, nursing a cup of black coffee, Drew watched the people crisscrossing the Plaza. It was the annual Fourth of July pancake breakfast, an event that always draws a big crowd, especially the locals. Glancing over his shoulder toward St. Francis Cathedral, Drew spotted the cowboy walking in his direction. He was wearing expensive Lucchese ostrich boots and a black, broad-brimmed, cowboy hat, with tight fitting, freshly washed and pressed jeans. His black western style shirt was open at the neck. He stood over six feet, lean and wiry, his rugged good looks the image of a cowboy.

"Don't I know you?" He asked, his steel blue eyes meeting Drew's upward glance. Before Drew could respond, he broke into a grin. "Ok if I pull up some curb beside you?"

"Be my guest." Drew answered. "You borrowed my pepper at lunch the other day. Remember?"

"Wouldn't forget. Name's Jon Sommers." He extended his hand. His grip was strong, his hands rough.

"I'm Andrew Laub. Friends call me Drew."

"You a local?" He asked.

"Sorta, been here about fifteen years. To be a real local means your family has been around at least a couple generations." Drew laughed.

Jon Sommers was friendly, grinned a lot, and fired off comments and questions in rapid succession. Highly animated and energetic, he seemed an enigma, engaging but somehow protective, as though he could converse for hours without anyone knowing much about him. He deflected anything too serious with some comic response or a broad grin and a change of subject.

"Your gallery closed today?" He asked.

"No, my staff's handling things."

"Anything to do around here?"

"Depends. What are you interested in doing?"

"Maybe see something out of Santa Fe. I've spent all my time here looking at the City's rules and regulations or doing paper-work for the bureaucrats at City Hall. Haven't seen anything else. Never expected it would be so difficult . . . I need a business license, criminal background check, business plan . . . lots of requirements . . . makes me think they're not into the idea . . .wanted to know who would clean up after the horses . . . what streets I intend to use . . . hours of operation . . . don't really understand all the stuff they want . . . ."

"Tell me where you want to go . . . I'd be glad to give you directions or make some suggestions of what to see."

"Think I'd like to see the mountains before I go back south."

"I'm headed up to Bandelier National Monument after I finish this coffee." Drew said. "You're welcome to join me if you'd like."

"Sure." Jon answered after a moment of hesitation. "Bandelier National Monument sounds as good as anything. What is it?"

"It's a park. Hundreds of years ago the ancestors of the Pueblo tribes lived there. There are thousands of old dwellings . . . ruins still there in Frijoles Canyon . . . good hiking trails . . . camping, it's a huge wilderness area . . . a nice drive on a day like this."

"Great, let's go . . . whenever you're ready." Jon got to his feet. Drew gulped the remaining coffee and started in the direction of his car, searching his pockets for his keys.

They drove north, past the Santa Fe National Cemetery, onto U.S. 84/285, the Sangre de Cristo Mountains rising dramatically to the east with the valley opening wide ahead. Near the Cities of

Gold Casino in Pojoaque, Laub turned west on NM 502 where commercial development faded quickly into open countryside. Jon seemed more relaxed, his right hand lightly grasping the roll bar. It was the kind of day New Mexicans take for granted, a hot July sun in a brilliant, blue, cloudless sky. With the open top, the sun beat hard against them, the black leather seats absorbing its heat. Jon removed his shirt, revealing hard abdominals, his chest smooth except for a patch of light hair over his breastbone. His arms bore the muscular evidence of physical labor. He was tanned, the color of desert sand, from days spent working shirtless.

Once they reached the higher elevation, panoramic vistas opened for miles to unveil pink mesas and sheer-walled canyons that stretched for miles as the road twisted and turned. Jon's demeanor was less edgy. His speech no longer rushed. Their conversation flowed more easily, absent the attempts at humor to avoid more direct answers. Drew's gaydar gave no reading, but regardless, he liked Jon, especially having discovered a less glib and more reflective man.

"You always lived in Kentucky?" Drew asked.

"No. I'm just from there. I haven't been there in a long time . . . My mother still lives there, though." His tone of voice hinted of sadness.

"I don't want to get personal, so if I'm prying, say so." Drew said. "How long's it been since you've been back?"

'I was almost fourteen when I left. Haven't been back since."

"Tell me to change the subject if you'd like." Drew said. "I don't want you to feel trapped . . . But I'm curious . . . since asking me for the pepper, I've discovered that every question seems to raise another . . . "

"That's ok . . . I ran away when I was in eighth grade . . . been on my own since then. I've never stayed in one place very long . . . don't trust many people all that much. My horses are my friends. I learned a long time ago that I can trust animals."

"I feel honored." Drew said, laughing to ease the tension. "You came along with me today."

"At Celebrations . . . when I asked you for the pepper . . . I knew you were ok. It's in my gut . . . like with my horses. They know me and I know them . . . they know when something's wrong, they know what people to trust. I don't know how, but I know they do. It was something like that when I met you. I'm not good at words, but my gut tells me."

"Why did you run away from home?"

"My step-father soon as beat me as look at me. He did for years. Hit my mom too. She'd never do anything about it. I tried to get her to leave lots of times. I can work hard. I could have taken care of her . . . me and my sisters."

"Didn't you have any family or friends . . . someone who would have looked after you?"

"There was a Priest who was good to me . . . a friend of my mom . . . he looked after me sometimes when I was afraid to go home after school . . . when it got really bad he would let me stay in the church . . . he bought me clothes and a old bike . . . he taught me things . . . then one day he . . ."

Drew interrupted. "You don't need to finish." Jon's expression and hesitancy were answer enough. "Where did you end up?" Drew continued.

"I kept going . . . hitchhiking 'till I got to Texas, a ranch near the Mexican border. The Mexicans . . . they'd tie me on the back of a cow, then swat its backside and send it running. They laughed as I bounced along until the thing stopped. I soon learned to ride on the back of anything. They played jokes and tormented me anyway they could. I made it that far, I knew I could survive."

"Were you there long?"

"I worked on a lot of ranches in Texas . . . fixin' fences . . . runnin' herds . . . I learned to do most anything . . . they saw I worked hard . . . learned some Spanish, even got to supervise the Mexicans . . . but I loved being with the horses . . . I got me enough money to get into rodeo . . . did that for years and saved me a lot of money. Got to where my body took enough of that. I moved to Tennessee, found me a ranch job as a foreman. The owners . . . they liked me. Gave me part of the property where I built a little barn and got me some horses of my own. They made me manager of the place, said someday I could buy it."

"You ever finish school?" Drew asked.

"No. I write down my thoughts in a diary. I don't read or write all that good, but I teach myself what I know."

"How did you end up in Santa Fe?"

"That's enough about me. What about you? Said you've been here fifteen years. Before that? Where?"

"Pretty normal, I guess. I was raised in the Northeast . . . family lived in Marblehead, Massachusetts. I went to college nearby . . . in Boston. Just stayed in the City after I graduated. I worked in retail a couple years, but I hated the long, cold winters."

"How'd you end up here?"

"Right after college my roommate and I drove cross country, stopped in Santa Fe for a couple days before winding up in San Francisco. When my parents were killed in a car accident, I decided to come back here. I found a job at the gallery, then bought it nine years ago with my small inheritance. That's really all there is."

"Married? Girlfriend?" Jon asked.

Drew hesitated. "No . . . I'm gay."

"Thought maybe you might be . . . good looking, nice guy . . . been told nearly everyone here that fits that description is."

Conversation, almost non-stop since leaving Santa Fe, lulled as they explored Bandelier's rock formations and the remnants of a civilization that once thrived in Frijoles Canyon. Tired, they returned to the parking lot and rested on some large boulders at the far end of the lot where only a few cars remained.

"It's getting late." Jon said. "You have plans? I discovered Harry's Roadhouse the other night. I'd like to go there again. We could get some dinner when we get back?"

"Sure." Drew answered.

The sun was getting low on the horizon as they drove out of Bandelier. It had been a long day. Getting acquainted dredged up some unpleasant memories for each. The quiet on the ride back was welcome. The early evening sun raked the desert landscape turning the formations of pale pinks and ochre of the sheer cliffs into an artist's canvass. By the time they reached Santa Fe, the desert had turned a golden brown with the sun a massive fire in the western sky.

Drew dropped Jon at his black, Dodge pick-up truck parked along Washington Street, a couple blocks from the Plaza. With oversized tires, the large model truck was easy to spot. It was polished to a mirror finish, immaculate in appearance, like Jon.

"See you at Harry's." Jon said.

Conversation that night stuck to innocent, light-hearted topics. Following one of Peyton's homemade desserts, they shook hands and went in separate directions. Drew stopped momentarily, watching the black truck pull from the parking lot, its tires grasping the gravel under its weight, as Jon headed toward the night lights of Santa Fe. Drew resisted asking where Jon was staying, or if he had a cell phone, someplace he could be reached.

Frequent trips to Harry's became routine for Drew in the days that followed, anxious to run into Jon. But it was nearly two weeks before Jon reappeared as abruptly as he had disappeared. Early morning, a half hour before gallery opening, Drew looked up to see Jon knocking at the door from the parking lot entrance.

"Thought you got lost." Drew quipped.

"Had to go to Tennessee. Stopped to see if you wanna go to Harry's tonight? Same time? I'm headed to City Hall. Need to review more of those ordinances they're telling me I have to comply with."

"Ok. Sure."

Drew pulled into Harry's at 6:30 sharp. Jon's truck was already there. Its profile stood above the others in the crowded lot. Drew spotted Jon at the counter joking with the waitress. His easy personality made him fit right in at Harry's, a popular gathering spot for locals, with a friendly staff, good food, a casual atmosphere— and priced right. An occasional tourist found the place, directed to its somewhat out of the way location by gallery owners like Drew, long a familiar face there.

"Find what you needed today?" Drew asked.

"No . . . didn't finish, gotta go back tomorrow."

"How was Tennessee? Everything ok back there? You have a good trip?"

"Had to see my lawyer. My barn there . . . I told you about. They never had divided the ranch. I don't have a deed for my part. I put all my money in that place, fixin' up everything. I was gonna buy it. They kept saying one day . . . the way I worked . . . when they were ready to sell . . . they'd be sure it would be set up so I could pay them. Then I find out they're in bankruptcy . . . whole place now's in foreclosure. My lawyer's gonna try to get what's mine."

Jon's unannounced absences and equally surprise returns established the pattern of their relationship. Gone for days, sometimes longer, just as suddenly he'd be there, picking up with Drew like it was the next day. Having survived on his own since age fourteen—no family—no friends, not close enough to anyone who needed, or cared to know where he was, or when he would be back, it was just Jon's way.

By late summer Jon's trips to Tennessee became more frequent, checking on his horses, meeting with his lawyer, and putting finishing touches on his restored carriage. Characteristically unpredictable, as always, he would appear unannounced at the gallery, certain to find Drew there long before and after gallery hours.

Approval of Jon's carriage start-up languished in red tape at City Hall owing, at least in part, to Jon's fierce independence and resistance to a process that made little sense to him. Foreclosure in Tennessee, according to his lawyer, was "complex", and could take an "indeterminate" amount of time to "work things out." Frustrated, Jon took a job in southern New Mexico supervising a major TV cable installation. It was work that had plugged the gaps at other times in his life; climbing poles designated unsafe was no more risk than rodeo, he told Drew.

Friday nights he drove to Santa Fe. It became a routine, one Jon and Drew never discussed or planned. They ate at good restaurants, or shared a beer and a sandwich on the patio of some nondescript café. They relaxed in the mineral springs of Ojo Caliente, drove the high road to Taos, explored Puye Cliffs, and hiked through Carson National Forest. Long summer days, under a big sky, in time outdoors, were Zen-like. Hours were spent streamside in an out of the way glen, discovered on one of their many aimless drives, in Valles Caldera. They shared an old Army blanket spread beside the stream, or sat on boulders overlooking the rippling water, engaged in conversation or watching the Elk through a clearing among the trees.

With summer's end a week away, they celebrated Drew's birthday—dinner and a bottle of expensive wine at Santacafe. There was a quarter moon overhead, the evening still warm enough to fill the outdoor courtyard with late evening diners.

"I envy you." Drew said.

"Why?" Jon asked.

"You're such a free spirit, tied to nothing. You pull anchor and move on whenever you want. You come and go like a migratory bird."

"Funny. I think the same about you." Jon said. "You're anchored where you want to be. I envy that."

"After fifteen years . . . I'm tiring of the gallery. It's a highly competitive business . . . rent keeps going up . . . fine art is a luxury, when people feel the pinch, it's one of the first things they cut."

"If not the gallery, what would you do?" Jon asked.

"I don't know." Drew said. "I've never given it much thought. It was only after I met you that I realized that the gallery is my whole life. I know I made it that way . . . but that's the reality."

"Well, if you really had your choice, what would you want to do?"

"Be a writer, I guess." I was an English major in college. Think there was a time when we all wanted to write the great American novel."

"What happened to that dream?" Jon asked.

"I grew up." Drew said.

"And you?" Drew asked. "If you ever stopped running . . . where or what would you want?"

"That's easy. My dream has never changed." Jon said. "I always wanted my own little ranch . . . some horses . . . "

Next morning, after a shared shower and day old bagel, with thermos mugs of freshly brewed coffee, they left Drew's place before nine, beginning to feel the heat of a waning summer. With Jon behind the wheel, they drove north out of Santa Fe. By early afternoon they were somewhere in Colorado, northwest of Pagosa Springs. The mountain air was cooler with a slight breeze out of the northwest. They drove for miles through expanses of forests and vast open meadowland dotted with patches of trees. A country and western CD playing, they rode in silence, exchanging only occasional glances, or a smile. It was like Jon and his horses—in their gut they knew each other.

Jon pulled to a stop alongside a weathered, homemade "For Sale" sign sticking up in a meadow. He got out of the truck, stopping momentarily with his hands on his hips as he surveyed the field in front of him. Walking through the tall grass, his boots made a swishing sound as it flattened beneath him. He turned, urging Drew to quicken the pace. He stopped on a knoll, beneath some trees.

"We could buy this, Drew."

"Sure." Drew smiled.

"We could . . . " Jon repeated, his eyes locked on Drew's.

"You're serious, aren't you?"

"Yep! I could have my horses . . . put them over there near the stream . . . could build a little house over there . . . you could write . . . it'd be just the two of us."

ABOUT THE CONTRIBUTORS

CURTIS C. COMER lives in St. Louis with his partner, Tim, and their cat Magda and lovebird, Raoul Gomez. His writing has appeared in numerous anthologies, including *Starf*cker*, *Best Gay Love Stories 2004* and *2005*, *Ultimate Gay Erotica 2005, 2006,* and *2007*, *Dorm Porn I* and *II*, *Treasure Trail* and *Fast Balls*.

LEWIS DeSIMONE's novel, *Chemistry*, was published last year by Harrington Park Press. His work has also appeared in *Christopher Street*, the *James White Review*, the *Harrington Gay Men's Fiction Quarterly*, the *Gay & Lesbian Review Worldwide*, the *San Francisco Sentinel*, the *Bay Area Reporter*, the *San Francisco Chronicle*, and the anthologies *Charmed Lives: Gay Spirit in Storytelling* and *Beyond Definition: New Writing from Gay and Lesbian San Francisco*. A native Bostonian, he majored in English at Harvard and earned an M.A. in creative writing at the University of California, Davis.

RYAN FIELD is a thirty-five-year-old freelance writer who lives and works in both Bucks County, PA and Los Angeles, CA with his partner of fifteen years and a red poodle. In the last ten years his fiction has appeared in anthologies and collections, the most recent, *Ultimate Gay Erotica 2007*, by Alyson Books. He also contributes interviews with celebrities and web masters to www.bestgayblogs.com. He's presently working on a novel.

JOE FILIPPONE is currently a student at Red Rocks Community College majoring in theatre and criminal justice. He has been a local Denver area actor of both stage and film for many years. He is also a hip-hop dancer at Motion Underground and Centerstage Starz and Dance. His plays *Mama's Boy* and *Lucille* both received staged readings at Red Rocks Community and his play *After Saturday* also had its world premier there in June of 2006. His play *The*

League of the Super-de-Duper Uber Good Guys was a finalist in The Rocky Mountain Theatre Association's playwriting contest in Billings Montana in 2006. Joe also works for the Crisis Company which trains cops on how to effectively deal with people in crisis situations. Joe loves meeting and talking with new people. You can contact him via www.myspace.com/hiphopjoe or JFilip4675@aol.com.

S.J. FROST currently resides on a small farm in Northwest Ohio. She graduated from the University of Toledo with a BA in English/Creative Writing. Her short story, "No More Mirages," appears in the anthology *Best Gay Romance 2007* published by Cleis Press.

MATTHEW HALDEMAN-TIME loves books so much, he taught himself to read. He also taught himself to write, and has been scribbling fiction for as long as he can remember. In his earliest teen years, he began to write gay erotica, and hasn't come up for air since. While picking up a degree in English literature from the University of Maryland, College Park, he launched a website and developed a strong Internet fan base. Now, at the ripe old age of twenty-eight, he's finally developed the courage to take the plunge into professional writing.

WILLIAM HOLDEN lives in Atlanta with his partner of ten years. He works full time as a librarian specializing in LGBT collections, preservation, and research. He has been writing gay erotica for over six years. He welcomes any comments and can be contacted at wholden2@mac.com.

MARCUS JAMES is proud to be a member of a new generation of erotic writers and finds himself forever entranced by the stories he gets to explore through the framework of erotic fiction. He is the author of *Blackmoore*, and is a contributor to the Alyson anthologies: *Ultimate Undies, Best Gay Love Stories: NYC, Ultimate Gay Erotica: 2007, Dorm Porn: 2*, and *Travelrotica: 2*. An Irish/Latin boy with a lot of "flava" he now resides in San Francisco, though a former resident of El Paso, TX. He is twenty-three years old, and a hopeless romantic. Get it touch with him at: www.myspace.com/marcus_james and check him out at: www.marcusjamesbooks.com

D. E. LeFEVER is a nine-year resident of Santa Fe, New Mexico, recently returned to Southeastern Pennsylvania where he continues the practice of law. He holds an M.A. in American Studies, and his work has appeared in Outrider Press and Alyson Books *Best Gay Love Stories New York City* and Tales of *Travelrotica for Gay Men, Volume 2.*

TOM MENDICINO is making his fourth appearance in the *Best Gay Love Stories* series. He'd like to thank Nick Ifft and Sharon Sorokin, both thoughtful readers.

JEREMY M. MILLER has been writing short stories for two years, and this is his first published work. He is thirty-five years old and lives on the Mississippi Gulf Coast with his partner of ten years.

JOEL A. NICHOLS was born and raised in Vermont. His stories have recently appeared in *Dorm Porn 2* (Alyson), *C is for Co-ed* (Cleis), *Got A Minute* (Cleis), and previously in *Full Body Contact, Just the Sex, Ultimate Undies,* and *Sexiest Soles.* Stories of his are also scheduled for *Travelrotica 2* (Alyson), *Fast Balls* (Alyson), *Distant Horizons* (Haworth), *G is for Games* (Cleis), *Sex by the Book: Gay Men's Tales of Lit and Lust* (Green Candy Press), and others. He won second place in the Brown Foundation Short Fiction Prize 2005 and was a Fulbright Fellow in Berlin. Joel studied German at Wesleyan University and has a Creative Writing M.A. from Temple University. He lives in Philadelphia with his boyfriend, works at an Internet video company and teaches college English. www.joelanichols.com

GREGORY L. NORRIS is a full-time professional writer whose work can be found monthly in a number of national magazines. He is the author of the forthcoming *The Q Guide to Buffy the Vampire Slayer* (Alyson).

STEPHEN OSBORNE has had stories published in several of Alyson's anthologies, including *Hustlers* (edited by Jesse Grant) and *Best Date Ever* (edited by Lawrence Schimel). When he's not writing or slaving away in retail management, he's usually out with Jadzia the Wonder Dog or taking straight boys to drag shows. Hey, someone's gotta do it.

ROB ROSEN is the author of the critically acclaimed novel, *Sparkle: The Queerest Book You'll Ever Love*, and the forthcoming *Divas Las Vegas*, to be published by The Haworth Press. His short stories have appeared in numerous journals, magazines, websites, and anthologies, most notably: *Mentsh: On Being Jewish and Queer* (Alyson, 2004), *I Do/I Don't: Queers on Marriage* (Suspect Thoughts Press, 2004), *Best Gay Love Stories 2006* (Alyson, 2006), *Truckers* (Cleis Press, 2006), *Best Gay Love Stories: New York City* (Alyson, 2006), *Best Gay Romance* (Cleis Press, 2006), *Superqueeroes* (The Haworth Press, 2007), and *The Queer Collection: Prose and Poetry 2007* (Fabulist Flash Publishing, 2007). Please visit him at his website, www.therobrosen.com, or email him at robrosen@therobrosen.com.

J. SARKIS is the author of *Trio Sonata* (Haworth 2002), described by Insightout book club as one of "the best novels of 2002." *Trio Sonata* explores the intertwined lives of a young gay couple and a straight woman.

LAWRENCE SCHIMEL is an award-winning writer and anthologist, who has published over seventy books in a wide variety of genres, including fiction, cooking, gender studies, sports, poetry and more. His short stories, poems, and essays have appeared in over 190 anthologies. He divides his time between New York and Spain.

SIMON SHEPPARD is the author of the short-fiction collections *In Deep* and *Hotter Than Hell*, as well as *Sex Parties 101* and *Kinkorama: Dispatches From the Front Lines of Perversion*. His work has also appeared in over 175 anthologies, including many editions of *The Best American Erotica*, *Best Gay Erotica*, and *Ultimate Gay Erotica*, and he writes the columns "Sex Talk" and "Perv." Find him these days at www.simonsheppard.com.

J.M. SNYDER is a self-published author of gay erotic/romantic fiction. Since 2002 he has released ten books in trade paperback for-mat. He has also begun to explore electronic publication, and have released two e-books through Aspen Mountain Press. His short gay fiction has been published online at Ruthie's Club, Tit-Elation, Sticky Pen, and Amazon Shorts, as well as in anthologies published by Aspen Mountain Press and Cleis Press.

Living on English Bay in Vancouver, BC, **JAY STARRE** writes fiction stories for gay men's magazines including *Men* and *Torso*. Jay has also written gay fiction for over forty anthologies including the Friction series for Alyson, *Travelrotica*, *Ultimate Gay Erotica 2005* and *2006*, *Bear Lust* and *Best Gay Love Stories, New York City*.